THE GREATEST BATTLE OF DZA

From the folds of his robe, Lotus-Born produced the second gold tablet, which glimmered in the morning sun.

The sight caused Black Shen to hiss loudly with desire, so that drops of spittle ran down his long, wispy beard. His yellowish skin turned red with longing, he swept his arm in a semicircle, and the three great crows dove down, to snatch the shining object. A flash of lightning flew from Lotus-Born's free hand, which sent the creatures screaming and smoking back into the sky.

"Does this mean you won't become a servant of *Chos?*" asked Lotus-Born.

"I am *no* servant, especially yours."

"Then let the battle begin."

Other Avon books by
Grania Davis

DR. GRASS
THE GREAT PERPENDICULAR PATH

The Rainbow Annals

GRANIA DAVIS

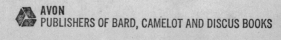
AVON
PUBLISHERS OF BARD, CAMELOT AND DISCUS BOOKS

THE RAINBOW ANNALS is an original publication of Avon
Books. This work has never before appeared in book form.

AVON BOOKS
A division of
The Hearst Corporation
959 Eighth Avenue
New York, New York 10019

Copyright © 1980 by Grania Davis
Published by arrangement with the author
Library of Congress Catalog Card Number: 80-67442
ISBN: 0-380-76224-2

First Avon Printing, October, 1980

AVON TRADEMARK REG. U.S. PAT. OFF. AND IN
OTHER COUNTRIES, MARCA REGISTRADA,
HECHO EN U.S.A.

Printed in the U.S.A.

*For Rinpoche
Sonam and Jamyang,
and the Himachel gang*

Part I

According to Tibetan cosmology, a kalpa *is an exceedingly long, incalculable cycle of time.*

I

A void. Dark, gentle and empty.

Time. Countless eons and *kalpas* of time. Formless time. Time without beginning. Time without end. Timeless time. Time that cannot be counted because there is no one to count.

Energy, swirling through the void like a wind. Churning, formless energy. Boundless energy. Vastly vast, primal energy. Infinite energy filling the void. Swirling and churning through boundless time.

Time. Countless eons and *kalpas* of time.

Energy. Swirling and churning energy.

Energy churning through time. Churning, churning. And gradually, as milk is churned into butter, the energy congeals into matter. The formless becomes formed. The boundless becomes bounded.

Infinity crystallizes, and the universe is formed.

Lumps of congealed matter grow into mighty mountains. Swirls of liquid matter fall as torrents of rain, swell into mighty rivers that rush to restless seas. Fiery matter whirls into great suns and flashes as mighty thunderbolts, then cools from molten lava into rocks and caves. Ethereal matter blows as powerful winds, and floats as mists and fogs and clouds.

The beginning has begun, but time is still uncounted, because there is no one to count.

In the center of the newly formed universe stood a mountain, so tall that its peak was never seen, even by the gods who later inhabited the slopes. The jagged boulders along its sides were formed of precious stones that flashed and gleamed in the light of the fiery new sun.

Around the mountain was a lake, so deep that its bottom was never seen, even by the water spirits that came to swim in its crystal depths.

Around the lake was a circle of lofty golden mountains. Then another lake, and another ring of silver mountains. Another lake, and a ring of copper mountains. Another lake, and a ring of iron mountains. Altogether there were seven rings of lakes and seven rings of mountains.

Beyond the seven rings of mountain and water was the vast outer ocean, *gyatso*. In this ocean were four immense continents, floating like islands, one each to the east, north, south and west. They were formed of earth, and resembled the world as we know it, except that they contained no living beings.

From the core of the central mountain there grew an enormous tree, whose top could never be seen, because it sprouted from the peak of the mountain itself. But its branches hung at all the levels of the mountain, fragrant with flowers and heavy with fruit. Still, there was no one to eat the fruit.

Then a great four-sided thunderbolt, *dorje*, burst upon the sides of the mountain, splintering the boulders of turquoise and jade, and showering the mountainside with sparks. From these sparks sprang the first glimmers of consciousness. They flickered faintly like fireflies, and were almost extinguished in the tireless winds that played across the slopes of the mountain.

Then the fruits of the mighty tree burst open, and began to drip nectar. Sweet as honey and thick as cream. The sparks of glimmering consciousness absorbed the nectar. They derived strength from it and began to take form.

From this union of fire and fluid, yin and yang, the first life was born.

These were the gods and demigods, the *lha*, who lived on the various levels of the mountain, depending on where they were born. They took nourishment from the fruit and nectar of the mighty tree.

The *lha* at the highest level of living beings have no bodies, as we know them. They float about like winds, live off nectar, and have powers that we can't even imagine. Their lives are so long that they cannot be measured.

The *lha* at the next level resemble the shapes of human beings. They are extremely long-lived, though not so long-lived as the bodiless ones above. They live among the fruits and flowers of the mighty tree, and spend their time in the peaks and valleys, riverbanks and caves of their mountainous realm, enjoying pleasures of their own making. They create sonorous musical instruments so that they can while away eons and *kalpas* in song and dance. They test their strength and skill in stupendous games and tournaments, and their passions in prolonged, ecstatic lovemaking. They have tremendous powers to influence the material universe. It is these gods who eventually hear—and occasionally answer—the prayers of mortal beings.

At the third level are the demigods who resemble the forms of animals. They scamper and play according to their shape, one pair flying like birds, another swimming in the river, a third leaping through the branches of the tree with catlike grace. Their lives are long, but less long than those above. None has the desire to kill the other, for the fruit of the tree satisfies all their needs. Instead they frolic and mate with agility and grace. They use their considerable powers for amusement. Sometimes they play tricks in the earthly realm. Often these tricks are benevolent—but sometimes the tricks can destroy lesser mortal beings.

At the lowest level of the central mountain are the spirits and demons who have the shapes that we call monstrous. With great fangs and bulbous eyes, with matted hair and twisted limbs, these beings lurk at the shadowy base of the mountain, among the gnarled roots of the great tree. They don't frolic and play, because they are always hungry. The branches of the tree don't bear much fruit, don't drip much nectar at this bottom level. The demons use their powers to fight and quarrel among themselves for the scant quantities that are available. They are filled with resentment, because they feel that the mighty tree draws all of its nourishment from the huge roots at the base, yet it is the *lha* at the higher levels who enjoy most of the harvest. The demons feel the fruit should be shared by all, and so they are eternally angry. Their lifespans are uncertain, for here they kill one another for food. And woe to the mortal being who encounters one of these creatures, for their hunger and rage are nearly insatiable.

In the lake that surrounds the mountain live the water spirits, who have multiplied and now inhabit all the waters of the universe. Fishlike or serpent-shaped *nagas*, these water spirits swim through a world of crystal and shadow, their ways as unfathomable as the depths of the central ring of water. They live off the debris that drops from the giant tree, and are very long-lived. They use their powers in puzzling ways. No one can ever be sure what a water spirit will do. Sometimes they are generous as a mother, heaping the boats of mortal beings with bountiful gifts of food. Other times they will rage, and send immense tidal waves crashing onto the shores, rending and tearing everything in their path. Those who fall into their realm can never be sure if they'll be lifted up like a child and carried gently and safely to shore—or carried down, gasping and suffocating, to death.

Into the third level, the realm of animal-shaped demi-gods, was born a cheery, inquisitive *lha*, with a body covered in short, thick fur, a powerful tail, long, agile arms and flexible legs. He had clever, dexterous hands, a winsome inquiring expression, short ears, a protruding snout, generously endowed male genitalia, and brightly colored buttocks of lavender and pink. To us, he would resemble some kind of monkey.

This Monkey-God loved swinging freely through the branches of the great tree, picking the choicest and most succulent fruits. When the bright new sun rose in the morning, he and the other troops of monkey-gods would smooth and groom their thick fur, delight themselves with acrobatics, and chatter joyfully while they munched the creamy fruits. They would attract and excite one another, and unite with vigorous pleasure. Then they would doze and dream in the heat of midday, until the cool afternoon breeze revived them. They would race and chase and refresh themselves along the riverbank until the sunset, when they would retire to their favorite cozy cave. There they would snuggle and croon, and perhaps mate again, until they fell asleep in an indistinguishable mass of thick monkey-*lha* fur. The Monkey-God amused himself for many eons and *kalpas* of such days. And of course, the days of the *lha* last much longer than the days of mortal beings.

But after a while, the Monkey-God's mind grew restless. He enjoyed his life of endless pleasure, but he was also an intelligent and curious creature.

What lies below us on the mountain, he wondered, and what lies above?

He decided to investigate. He scampered out of his own delightful glen, down the face of the mountain—for down was the easier way, and he was used to a life of ease. Across the barren slopes, scattered with huge boulders of ruby and sapphire, down into the shadowy realm at the base of the great tree. He somersaulted and cavorted, feeling alert and free. How strange and mysterious it was down here among the gnarled roots! How different from his sunny, leafy glen! How curious, how interesting, what fun!

Then the Monkey-God halted, for there was another creature prowling among the shadows, hunting for bruised, broken fruits. The Monkey-God didn't like the looks of this being, with its protruding beak and bulbous eyes, its taloned claws on numerous limbs, large, shiny black wings, and matted mass of hair. But then, there were many kinds of *lha*, weren't there? Elephant-*lha* and bird-*lha*—perhaps this was some sort of crow-*lha* because of the beak and wings. Well, no matter, better to stop hiding and make friends with the creature, and show him that there was richer harvest higher up the mountain.

With a delicious series of flip-flop leaps, the Monkey-God presented himself to the creature. With horrible snarls, the demon grabbed at the Monkey-God and caught hold of his tail, sank his beak in deep, and bit it right through!

The Monkey-God screamed with pain and surprise. He had never been menaced or injured before, never felt any pain, certainly never been disfigured, felt agony, felt the life fluids gushing from his severed flesh. He grabbed at the stump of his tail to protect and seal it. The demon had eaten his tail, and was rushing towards him, to attack again!

Clutching the agonized remnant of his tail, and whimpering in shock and terror, the Monkey-God ran, faster than he had ever run before, up the slopes of the mountain, over the boulders of ruby and sapphire. He ran and ran, and kept on running, even though the demon had long stopped chasing him, until he reached the safety of his own sunny glen.

There the rich nectar of the fruit quickly healed the stump of his tail, though it would never be long and strong and agile again. Soon the Monkey-God could play again and romp with the rest of the troop. But without his tail,

13

he would never be as deft as the other monkey-*lha*, and having felt pain, there would always be a dark place in the depths of his mind. Nonetheless, he resumed his former life, and didn't stray away for many eons and *kalpas*.

After a while he grew restless again. He had seen the base of the mountain, and it was terrible. What about the heights—would they be worse, or perhaps better? Would the sun be warmer, the fruit sweeter? The nectar had healed his tail; could he find a richer nectar to heal the dark place in his mind?

More cautious this time, the Monkey-God crept up the slopes of the mountain. He would explore, but he would avoid other beings—certainly ones with claws and beaks. As he ascended across velvet green canyons, overhung with fruit-laden boughs of the great tree, he could hear the rushing of water, ringing like crystal over rocks and pebbles of diamond and emerald. Then he heard another sound, so sweet that it made his entire being ache, like the songs of bird-*lha*, but more harmonious and sustained. Irresistibly attracted, the Monkey-God crept toward the source of the music.

In a flowery meadow, he found them, playing on their musical instruments. These were beautiful beings, radiant and glowing, looking somewhat like monkeys, but with flat faces, sparse fur and no tails. Had they also met with the flesh-eating demons? They stood tall and upright. The Monkey-God hid behind an enormous turquoise boulder to listen, but they were immediately aware of his presence. The music stopped.

"Who are you?" they called. "What do you want?"

He stepped from behind the boulder, feeling foolish for interrupting them, "I'm a monkey-*lha*, from below," he said. "I'm looking for rich nectar to heal a dark place in my mind."

"Prayers, prayers," sighed a crystal-voiced one. "Why do they always bother *us* with their prayers? We have no such nectar here," he told the Monkey-God. "Try further up the mountain. Maybe the Perfect Ones can help you."

The radiant beings resumed their music, as though the Monkey-God didn't exist. He felt rather annoyed. Aren't we all *lha* on the mountain, he wondered? Why act so superior? The bird-*lha* also look and sound beautiful, but

14

they don't put on such airs. Well, let's see about these Perfect Ones, further up the mountain.

As the Monkey-God climbed past the level of the radiant, music-making *lha,* the landscape changed dramatically. The lush vegetation grew thin and sparse, then gradually disappeared altogether. The sun grew painfully strong, and the sky was a deep, dark blue, yet the air was very chill. Thick films of ice covered the rivers and streams, and hung in long, frozen shards from the crags of bare garnet and lapis, all glistening and glaring in the intense sunlight. Here the great tree formed no fruit, only nectar dripped like sap from its bare branches. The Monkey-God shivered. His breath steamed in the frigid air. He tasted the nectar. It was rich and sweet, but it didn't affect the dark place in his mind.

Most disturbing of all were the winds that whipped restlessly around this realm like living beings, caressing and buffeting the Monkey-God. It was only after some time that he realized that these winds were the *lha* that inhabit this level of the mountain.

"I'm searching for nectar to heal a dark place in my mind," called the Monkey-God to the winds. "Can you help me?"

His voice bounced off the cliffs and crags of lapis and jade in a resounding series of echoes. A thin wind surrounded him, and whispered directly into his mind.

"You must find the Perfect Ones that hold the Secret of *Chos,*" whispered the wind-*lha.* "The Secret of *Chos* can heal dark places in the mind."

"How exciting, how interesting!" cried the Monkey-God. "Where are these Perfect Ones?"

"They are at the peak of the mountain, but you cannot go there," sang the wind-*lha.* "The air at the peak is too thin to sustain your life. Besides, the Perfect Ones never reveal their secret to any *lha.* We know—we've tried to pry it from them."

"I suppose these Perfect Ones are even haughtier than the music-making *lha* that I met below," cried the Monkey-God in annoyance. "What am I to do?"

The wind wailed and sang through his mind, "You must travel to the farthest continent, the remote southern land, beyond the outer ring of mountains and seas. You must spend eons and *kalpas* in total solitude and silence. Then you will discover the Secret of *Chos,* which will heal the dark place in your mind. Afterward you can meet with the Perfect Ones."

"How mysterious, what fun!" cried the Monkey-God. "Perhaps I should go find this curious secret. Do you think it will restore my tail, too?"

The wind sailed through his mind, "We know nothing about tails." Then the wind grew still.

The Monkey-God tossed his head irritably. "These wind-*lha* pretend to know everything, but they've never even seen a beautiful long tail," the Monkey-God grumbled and rubbed his poor stump. "Well, I'd better go off to that southern continent, and find out about this secret for myself."

The Monkey-God leaped into an enormous somersault, and landed back down the mountain with his own monkey-*lha* troop. Then, because he was a little weary, he rested and played, feasted and frolicked for a few more eons and *kalpas.* But the dark place in his mind wouldn't let him rest too long.

With another great somersault leap, he sailed past the realm of the demons and the first ring of water, and landed in the circle of golden mountains. Another great somersault leap and he reached the ring of silver mountains. A third leap brought him to the ring of copper mountains, and so on, until he reached the outermost ring of barren granite mountains.

One more leap, and he was in the southern continent, called Earth. It was a very lonely and remote place. The Monkey-God sensed that no living being had ever been here before. He was the first. But it was a rather pleasant and attractive land, with lofty, cloud-shrouded peaks, green, fertile valleys, vast forests, high, grassy plateaus, rushing rivers and tossing seas. Although the ground itself was made of soil, rather than precious gems, everything glowed with bright colors. Green vegetation, blue waters and sky, gray rocks, white beaches and clouds, pink sunsets, and multicolored deserts, and flowers, and fruits. Altogether a very agreeable place to spend a few eons and *kalpas.*

The Monkey-God spent some time exploring, looking for a place to set up his camp. He tasted the various fruits. They weren't so rich and life-prolonging as the fruit of the central tree, but they were tasty, nourishing and varied. Finally the Monkey-God wandered into a high, hidden valley, surrounded by the tallest mountain peaks. There was a great crystal river of melted ice, broad and deep, racing down the center of the valley floor. The fruit trees and their harvest were abundant. The carpet of grass was deep and green, turning to gold when the fat grain heads ripened. The cloudless sky was the color of deep turquoise. The tall, rocky, snow-capped mountains were honeycombed with caves, and gave the valley some protection from the many fierce storms which whip through the highlands of the southern continent called Earth. The days were mild and very sunny, though the nights were always cold, because the valley lay on a high mountain plateau. The place felt homey and comfortable to the Monkey-God, who was weary from so much travel.

Here in this high valley, called Dza, he decided to stop and make his camp. Here he would wait for the necessary number of eons and *kalpas,* until he could learn this fascinating Secret of *Chos,* which would heal his mind and restore his tail.

On the central mountain, among the demons who dwell in the shadowy roots at the base, a young demoness was quarreling with some others over a piece of ripe fruit which she had found.

"Want, *want,* mine, *mine!"*

"Gimme that, *gimme!"*

"No, *mine!"*

The demoness was small for her kind, and weak. She was no match for the gang of large, burly, warted creatures who leaped at her from the shadows, before she had a chance to take even one bite of the fruit. Such a lovely, ripe fruit. So juicy, sweet and good. If only she could get one bite.

"Mine, *mine!"* she screamed at them, popping the fruit between her tusked jaws.

At the sight of the fruit in her mouth, her attackers went beserk. They leaped on her and pried her jaws apart. The fruit, now bruised and damaged, fell to the ground. With a tremendous blow, one of the warted creatures knocked her out of the way. The gang fell upon the fruit, fighting and quarreling among themselves.

"Gimme, *gimme,* want, *want!*"

The blow to the demoness was so powerful that it sent her flying through the air with a great deal of momentum. She flew away with such force that she got caught in a powerful current of wind that carried her right off the central mountain, beyond the first ring of water, and the ring of golden mountains, beyond the second ring of water, and the ring of silver mountains. In fact, the wind was so strong that it carried her all the way to the seventh ring of granite mountains. Here the current died out, and she landed with a resounding thud.

The demoness looked around and started to cry. She was bruised and battered from her beating and fall. She was scared witless by this barren, isolated place, and worst of all, she was hungry—so hungry. Saliva dribbled past her tusks at the thought of that lost piece of fruit. Tears ran out of her great, bulbous eyes. The demoness sat by herself in the ring of granite mountains and sobbed and wailed.

How to get back to the central mountain? How to get back to the luscious fruit? The demoness began to race around and around the ring of granite mountains, growing more and more frantic as she realized that she was truly lost. There was no way back except through many rings of water, and she knew that the water spirits would never allow a demoness to survive in their realm. There was no way back. No way to get off this barren ring of granite, where nothing lived, nothing grew, nothing for a poor, lost demoness to do but run around the ring, slowly starving to death over many eons and *kalpas.* The cries of the demoness turned into screams of pure terror and despair.

Her cries and screams were so loud that they reached the Monkey-God, who was enjoying the peace and solitude of the Valley of Dza. He rubbed his ears, not quite certain. Was there really a sound, or was he imagining things? Perhaps it was the Perfect Ones, trying to tell him the secret, at last! But no, this didn't have the sound of any perfect secrets. In fact, it was a horrible sound, truly dreadful, making the dark spot in his mind feel worse. Yes, distinctly worse.

Making his head ache, in fact. A terrible, grating sound, growing louder, then softer, but constant and shrill, intense and sickening. The Monkey-God got up from his soft seat of grasses and leaves and began to pace back and forth, irritably. The wind-*lha* had said he needed total solitude *and* silence. What was this dreadful, disturbing sound? It seemed to be coming from the north, from the ring of granite mountains. Best to go and find out.

With a jump, the Monkey-God reached the icy northern tip of the continent, and scanned the ring of granite mountains. The noise was louder now, and even more unpleasant. It seemed to be coming from some creature that was racing around and around the granite ring. Strange. Nobody could live in those mountains, because there was nothing to eat. How odd!

The Monkey-God jumped up to the top of a small hill to get a better look at the strange creature. He peered and strained his eyes. Ugh, it was some sort of demon! Not so ugly as the one he had met before. This one had the tusks and bulging eyes and matted hair that distinguish its kind, but its body seemed rather small, soft and frail, with little round breasts and narrow, fragile-looking bones.

Still, even a small demon can have very sharp teeth, and the Monkey-God didn't want to lose any more limbs out of curiosity. He patted his stump consolingly. But what was the creature doing there, and why wouldn't it be quiet? He had to have silence, or his whole quest was hopeless. Those cries were so loud and shrill that his entire head was throbbing. Time to find out what's going on—from a safe distance, of course.

"Hey, little demon," he called from across the waterway that separated them, "why are you making so much noise?"

The demoness stopped running, and her eyes bulged wider than usual. There was a friendly-looking, furry *lha* across the channel of water, another living being here to help her!

"Please, *please*," she cried, "help me, *help* me! Feed me, help me, feed me, help me, gimme, *me,* gimme, want, *want!*"

The demoness looked so pathetic that the Monkey-God couldn't help feeling sorry for her. He wouldn't go near her, that was sure, but at least he could toss the poor creature some fruit. He began to gather fruit from the nearest trees, and tossed them across the waterway.

"Yes, *yes!*" shrieked the demoness. "Want, *want!*"

Actually it was fun, throwing the fruit and watching her scamper around, trying to catch it. The Monkey-God had been alone for quite some time now, and it felt good, like a game. He aimed the fruit at her open jaws, now stained and dripping with juice. Sometimes he would throw a perfect shot and the fruit would land right in her mouth. They would both laugh, *lha* and demon laughter breaking the silence of this uninhabited land. Sometimes the fruit would fly high, and she had to leap for it, catching it in her small claws, and licking the pulp off her sticky fingers. The Monkey-God amused himself, throwing armloads of fruit for the demoness, all the long *lha* day, until he could see that her belly was growing quite round, and she wasn't running for the fruit so wildly as before. In fact, she was just nibbling at it now, and staring across the water at him, with great, bulging eyes. Staring.

The sun was starting to set, and the air was growing chill, when she dropped the piece of fruit in her hand and started to cry again. That annoying, piercing cry that made the Monkey-God's head ache.

"Lonely," she cried. "Cold, lonely. *Lonely,* cold!"

"Well, you can't come with me," he said firmly. "I'm going to sleep in my cave. You won't starve, so go to sleep. I'll bring more good fruit tomorrow."

"Yes, *yes,* come with you. So lonely, come with *you!*"

"Not with those sharp teeth," said the Monkey-God. "I've learned about your kind." With a stern toss of his head, he somersaulted back to his soft, moss-lined cave in the high Valley of Dza.

But the demoness was inconsolable. Frightened again, now that she was alone in the deepening dusk, she sat by the shore and howled. Howled as the sun set, howled as the moon rose into the sky, howled so that the Monkey-God couldn't get any sleep at all.

Angry, he jumped back to his side of the channel. "Hey there, you be quiet, or you won't get any fruit tomorrow."

This made the demoness more frightened, and she howled louder. "Lonely, scared," she cried, "scared, *lonely!*"

"You can't come with me, because you'll bite with those sharp teeth."

"No, not bite, never bite *you.* Too full to bite." The

demoness pointed to her full, round belly. "No room to bite."

"But what about tomorrow, when you're hungry again?"

"Bite fruit, not *you!*"

"If I take you to my cave, will you be quiet, and promise not to bite?"

"Very quiet, *so* quiet! Lonely and scared makes loud cry. Never, never bite you!"

"Very well," sighed the Monkey-God. She really did look awfully small and helpless, and if she didn't quiet down, he'd never get any sleep. He'd take her to the cave tonight, give her another good feed in the morning, then return her to the central mountain, and resume his peaceful, quiet life, searching for the Secret of *Chos* in the Valley of Dza.

He leaped across the channel, picked her up in his arms, and carried her in one jump to his hidden valley. The moss in the cave was soft and warm, and she snuggled up to him gratefully, burying her face in his fur. She really was quite a small and delicate creature. Absently, he stroked her body with his thick furred hand, and waited for sleep to fall upon them.

But instead of sleepiness, he felt a strange and intense heat. Odd. The Monkey-God was very familiar with desire, but demon and *lha* were never supposed to mate. Still, had demon and *lha* ever snuggled this close before? He tried to ignore the sensation; this wasn't supposed to be! He'd give her more fruit, and take her home tomorrow, back to her own fierce kind. He tried to sleep, but the hot, sensual feelings grew stronger.

The demoness was making little mewing and purring sounds, and rubbing her body against his. Can demon mate with *lha?* The demoness climbed into his lap. "Want, *want*," she whispered.

"No," said the Monkey-God, trying to push her away. But somehow the push became an embrace. The demoness wrapped her legs around him, and pulled his throbbing body inside her own.

Yes, demon can mate with *lha*, quite joyously. The Secret of *Chos* forgotten, the Monkey-God became lost in an embrace that lasted for many eons and *kalpas*. Many offspring resulted from this passionate union. But because

21

they could not eat the fruit of the great tree, they were born as mortals. The Monkey-God and the demoness were also deprived of the life-sustaining fruit of the central tree, and they also entered the cycle of mortal existence.

Thus the Valley of Dza was populated.

II

Many eons and *kalpas* have passed. Dza is now a kingdom, bustling with people and animals. The deep, willow-lined crystal river of melted ice still rushes down the center of the valley. The banks and grasses on the valley floor are still a velvet green, and carpeted with flowers during the spring, turning to gold in summer. The many old fruit trees still give abundant harvest of sweet apricots and mulberries from their ancient, gnarled branches. The high, eternal snow peaks, honeycombed with caves, still tower around the valley, and give it some protection from the fierce winter storms. The cloudless sky is still the color of dark turquoise. The days are mild, and the sun is extremely strong and bright. But the nights are very cold, even in the middle of summer. Because the altitude of Dza is high —very high.

The people of the valley have a short, sturdy, muscular build, straight black hair, and skin that is a deep, ruddy tan. They aren't pretty people, but they are very striking in appearance, with their narrow, slitted eyes and their extremely prominent cheekbones. They are relaxed and friendly folk, who enjoy a good joke. In fact, they laugh a great deal, as an antidote to their rigorous environment.

Despite its beauty, Dza is a harsh homeland. Although the mountains offer some protection, the extremely high altitude creates a severe, unstable climate. The winters are long, cold and storm-ridden. Even in the middle of summer, a sudden hailstorm can mean the loss of the entire barley crop. Nonetheless, the people joke freely, in a language that outsiders might identify as a dialect of east-central Tibet. However, few outsiders ever visit Dza, for it is guarded by *la,* nearly impassable mountain passes.

The peasant farmers of Dza live in small huts, built from stones collected from the rocky soil. The mortar is a

23

kind of abode, made of mud, dung and straw, and dried by the sun. Rock and mud walls keep people warm and dry in the winter. Building with wood is unheard of in Dza, for trees are scarce, and they are living things, inhabited by tree-*lha*. The peasants busily tend their fields of barley, and their fruit orchards during the short growing season of Dza.

At harvest time, there is a great market festival, with picnics and games, music and dancing, on the banks of the river. The peasants bring their barley and sun-dried fruits, to trade with the herdspeople who live outside the valley, in the high, silent plateaus.

Beyond the first wall of mountains that protect Dza there are great, flat, barren grasslands. The altitude of these plateaus is even higher than Dza, and water is very scarce. They are above the timberline, and no tree ever grows.

However, the yaks and woolly goats and sheep thrive on the deep tough grasses of the highlands. The herdspeople live rough, nomadic lives, following the grazing pattern of their flocks. They have no permanent dwellings. Their homes are thick, hairy yak leather, made into tents. Their clothes are woven from the fleece of sheep, or fleece-lined leather, cut into rough chuba robes. Their food is the milk, butter, cheese and meat of the yak, goat and sheep. Their companions are the large, fierce shepherding watchdogs. Their entire lives are bound up with their animals. They follow the beasts as they eat, and in turn, eat the beasts and their by-products.

At harvest time, the leaders of the nomadic herdspeople put on their best chuba robes, and wipe off the thick butter which protects their faces from the intense winds and sun of the unprotected plateaus. With skins and bladders brimming with milk, cheese, curds and dried meat, they enter the Valley of Dza and set up their tents along the riverbank, eager to trade for grain, fruit and news. The farmers and herders greet each other warmly, as old friends. They laugh and joke, bargain and haggle, gossip and drink barley beer and buttered tea far into the night. For herders and farmers are all people of Dza, speaking the same language, and owing allegiance to the same king.

It is said that long ago, Dza had no king. Then a *lha* came from the great central mountain to rule over the people. There was a cord of rainbow light connecting his

24

head to the heavenly mountain realm. But the cord was accidentally cut and the king of Dza became a mortal man.

The king has his fortress on a high hillock near the only real entrance to the valley. This mountain pass, the *la,* is open perhaps a quarter of the year, when the summer sun melts the glaciers that block it. It is the duty and the privilege of the king to guard the pass from any outsiders, though few ever attempt to visit Dza. However, there are bandit gangs, and outlaws, even in these remote highlands, and the people need protection from packs that wander on horseback, terrorizing peaceful mountain kingdoms.

The large landholders form the aristocracy of Dza, and among them, it is the bravest and most charismatic who takes the title of king. Sometimes there is a contest or duel among various contenders to the throne, but generally the people agree on the strongest leader in the kingdom.

This man, his family, wives, sons, daughters, servants, retainers, and *shen,* the family sorcerers, live in the mighty stone fortress that overlooks the pass. When the king dies, one of his sons, grandsons or brothers will usually have enough influence to retain control of the kingdom. The lineage will last for a few generations, until it finally peters out with some weakling or idiot. Then the nobility must select another strong king to guard the pass and live in the fortress with its many rooms and stories, its stone walls, watchtowers, and battlements.

The people of Dza respect and admire their king for his strength. They are always willing to join his militia when bandit gangs threaten—in fact, they enjoy the excitement. But they also regard the king as one of themselves. He's a man of Dza, to whom they extend their tongues in the traditional gesture of respect. But he also enjoys a good, bawdy joke if they meet him strolling by the river.

The *shen* are different. Although they are men and women of Dza, their ways are not those of other folks. These sorcerers have tasted otherworldly powers. They can communicate with ghosts, demons, waterspirits and *lha.* They can heal and make prophecy, and read omens on the dice. They have great power for good—and evil. They are respected and feared. No one would ever try to joke with a *shen.*

*　　*　　*

Into the royal family of Dza, one bright afternoon in early autumn, an infant was born. His mother didn't labor too long, for he was small, and her womb was healthy and experienced. She was in her own small stone room, near the main courtyard of the fortress, drinking hot buttered tea, when her time came. Like many of the women of Dza, she delivered herself expertly and efficiently, without any help or complaints. In Dza, a midwife or *shen* is called only if there is a problem of poor health, or bad omens. In this case there were no such complications. Soon the infant lay washed and red-faced on a fur robe, squalling for his first meal.

"Such a hungry little monkey," crooned his mother, who was one of many princesses of the royal household. In fact, looking down at the new one, she saw that he was rather monkeylike—nothing worrisome, all new babies look funny. But this one was hairier than most, with a soft black down visible on his forehead and long, flexible limbs.

"So," she said, picking him up and holding him close to give suck, "I think your name should be Monkey. You will be known as the Monkey-Prince of the Kingdom of Dza."

The baby looked up at her with a curious, inquisitive expression on his face.

"You're a smart little monkey, aren't you?" said his mother. "Are you busy remembering all your past lives? Were you a wicked fellow in your last lifetime, or were you just a carefree little animal, playing in the forests? We'll never know, because we all forget the past so soon. Though it marks us forever."

The baby cut her musings short by peeing down her arm. "Oh, what a bad boy!" she cried, "already playing tricks on his poor mother, while she's still bleeding and sweating from your birth."

The princess turned the baby over to clean his backside. Then she noticed a birthmark that hadn't been visible before. At the base of his spine was a small, round welt, almost like a scar.

"There, you see," she laughed, "you really *are* a monkey. That's where your tail should be!"

The princess held the baby close, to feed and caress him, and the newly born Monkey-Prince looked up at her with curious, intelligent eyes.

*　　*　　*

The Monkey-God, now embodied as a young prince of Dza, had an enjoyable childhood in the great stone fortress. He loved to test his long, agile arms and legs by climbing over the rough stone walls, and shinnying up the gnarled old trees to pick the sweetest, ripest fruits. None of his companions in the royal household was as dexterous and lithe as the young Monkey-Prince, though some were built with more muscle and strength. When it came to climbing, jumping and somersaulting, the Monkey-Prince outdid all the children in Dza Valley.

Everyone agreed that his name had been well chosen, for this child had the sinewy grace of a little monkey—and also the mischievous curiosity. Many times he was caught, climbing to reach some forbidden treat, and only the sharp whack of a stick on his little backside could keep him quiet.

The Monkey-Prince had no memories of anything in the past, yet his childhood was not entirely carefree. He was always aware of a dim, troubling sensation, as though a cloud was creating a shadow or dark place, somewhere deep in his mind. He could not find any reason for this unpleasant feeling, and neither could his mother when he sometimes complained.

One day, as he was nearing adolescence, his mother found him sitting in a dark niche in the courtyard, crying.

"What's the matter, little monkey?" she called. "Did someone catch you stealing mo-mo dumplings, and whack your behind?"

"My head is bothering me again, Mother. When I look inside, most of me feels light and free, and clear. But one place feels heavy, dark and painful, like the sky during a hailstorm."

"This has gone on too long," said his mother. "I think it's time to consult with the court *shen.*"

"I don't like those people, they frighten me with their glary, stary eyes! Still, it might be fun to try some of their weird potions. I always like to taste something new and strange."

"I know," said his mother, "that's why you're always in trouble. Speaking of trouble, there's a half skin of ripe yak butter missing from our rooms."

The Monkey-Prince quickly hid his greasy fingers in the folds of his chuba robe, and smiled innocently. "I think

27

you're right, Mother," he said. "I think it's time to consult the *shen* about the dark spot in my mind."

"And then we'll consult with the stick about that butter," grumbled his mother.

The *shen* lived in a compound of their own, within the walls of the fortress. They spent their time conducting sacrifices to the ancestral family spirits of the king, and propitiating the *lha* that control the weather and the crops, with offerings of food, scented smoke and the blood of animals. These were their ordinary duties, but at times they were called upon for extraordinary displays of occult power. When an evil force had taken control of someone's mind, they were obliged to enter the dangerous twilight world of the trance state, and battle with malicious creatures from the nether realms. When danger threatened the kingdom, they flew through the air on their drums to rouse and warn the people.

All of this required intense energy, courage and concentration, which drained the normal human feelings from the *shen* and left them as creatures who belonged neither to this world or the next. The *shen* weren't physically strong and powerful. In fact, they were usually marked by a childhood of illness, deformity, or weakness which required long periods of solitude and rest. It was during these intervals of fever and isolation that they made contact with the spirits that gave them their power—and separated them from ordinary folk.

The Monkey-Prince was reminded of this as he and his mother entered the compound of the *shen*. These small, weak, twisted sorcerers did not see or speak as people did. Their eyes stared far beyond our world. Their lips mumbled constant incantations. Their spindly, deformed limbs twitched and grasped convulsively, overcome by forces too strong for a human body to bear.

Just then, the entire *shen* compound was in a state of almost hysterical excitement. The night before, the King had a vivid dream of a jeweled box, containing a gold tablet covered with strange inscriptions. It flew through the air, into the central courtyard of the fortress. Vivid dreams weren't so rare, but when the king arose, there was the jeweled box! Right there, containing the golden tablet and strange inscriptions, just like in the dream. The *shen* were all puzzling and jabbering over the inscriptions, which no one could understand.

"How exciting!" cried the young Monkey-Prince, running over to look at the magical objects, which were glowing with a strange light. "What could they mean?"

A pockmarked, shriveled old *shen* pushed him away. "Stand back," ordered the *shen*. "Such things aren't for the eyes of naughty boys like you. They contain a special, extraordinary *secret*."

Secret? *Secret*. Somewhere the Monkey-Prince had heard about this secret! The word triggered a response, right in the dark place in his mind.

"Wait," he called to the old *shen*, "I have a feeling about this. I came to consult with you about a dark place in my head, but I have a feeling that this secret can help me. I want to learn more about this secret."

No one, not his mother nor the *shen* nor anyone else in the royal fortress, had ever heard the Monkey-Prince speak in such a serious tone of voice.

"So, stay and study with us, if you'd like," said the old *shen*, "but be warned that we have special ways of trapping young thieves who steal our mo-mo dumplings, and our punishments are far more severe than your mother's stick."

To everyone's surprise, the Monkey-Prince didn't lose interest in the strange tablet. Instead, he moved his few belongings into the sorcerers' compound, and sat with his healthy, agile young limbs among the twisted and deformed *shen*, puzzling over the inscriptions. But no dream, no vision appeared to help them decipher the meaning. Even a heavy trance of juniper berries and other herbs yielded no results.

"It must wait for its own time," said the old *shen*. "The tablet will reveal the meaning when it is ready. In the meantime, let's look into the mind of our restless young prince here, and see what's troubling him."

All of the ritual implements of silver, feathers, turquoise and bone for an exorcism were arranged in the courtyard of the sorcerers' compound, and a time was selected when a full moon would rise over the wall. The pockmarked old *shen* went into a light trance to determine the nature of the problem. He found that there was some connection with the demon realm. A stronger potion would be needed to give the sorcerers enough strength to combat the negative forces which were clouding the young prince's mind.

"We need something strong and effective," said the old *shen*, "for the dark spot is extremely deep and dense. We must use serpent venom to destroy the darkness!"

The other *shen* shuddered convulsively. They had assumed that a minor rain cloud was irritating the mind of the cheery young prince. Now the old *shen* was prescribing the most powerful of their potions. They would be drained and weakened for months after a serpent-venom exorcism. Yet they couldn't let such darkness remain in the boy's mind. It might grow and consume him. The *shen* would exhaust their own feeble bodies to combat the evil.

The pockmarked old *shen*, working by the light of the full moon, began to pass small mounds of barley paste mixed with rare and precious serpent venom to the sorcerers, who sat in a circle, beating their drums and chanting. The last and largest mound of paste was given to the Monkey-Prince, who ate it with willing curiosity.

The beating of the drums became mingled with the beating of his heart, which was pounding loudly and painfully in his chest. Oh, so painfully in his chest, sick and painful, with severe cramps radiating through his entire body. Such sick and painful feelings he had never felt before! He wanted to vomit, to cry, to run away, to die, right there— anything to put a stop to the sick agony that was running through him. But he did nothing. He just sat pale and sweating in the cold, clear night, inside a circle of pale and sweating sorcerers, who were also feeling the sick pain of the venom, but who knew how to transcend it by chanting and beating on their drums.

Gradually, one by one, the spirits of the sorcerers left their sickened, painful bodies and entered the mind of the gasping, gagging Monkey-Prince. He could feel them inside, rummaging around his head like his mother in the kitchen. He could feel them poking and prodding at the dark place in his mind. Trying to rouse it with shrill cries and challenges, trying to dislodge it with their ritual implements of human bone, trying to waken it with their beating drums. Pound, pound, pound. But the dark place remained dense, immobile, intact. Nothing that the *shen* could do had any effect on that lump of blackness.

Gradually, as the bright sun rose, the effects of the

venom wore off. The *shen*, trembling and pale, as if they had just suffered a severe illness, had to admit to the Monkey-Prince that his problem was beyond their powers. Perhaps it would reveal itself in time. Perhaps the strange inscriptions and the dark place would yield to the *shen* simultaneously, in the future—when they were ready. Perhaps there were more powerful *shen* outside the fortress walls, who could penetrate the blackness. Perhaps the reclusive *shen* who inhabit the caves in the mountains . . . perhaps Black Shen, the most powerful of them all, if he could be found . . . perhaps . . . perhaps . . . but right now, the problem was beyond the understanding of the court *shen* of Dza.

Feeling unhappy and ill, the Monkey-Prince gathered up his few belongings and left the compound of the *shen*. Once outside, he realized that he could never resume his games and tricks with the other boys. He said goodbye to his mother, to the king, and to all his friends, and left the fortress, to search for other, more powerful *shen* who could help him.

For ten years he journeyed among the honeycomb of caves that dot the snow-covered mountains surrounding the valley of Dza. During this time, he turned from boy to man. He lived off wild fruit and nettle tea. His chuba robe grew ragged. He looked more like a beggar than a prince, with tangled hair, and face bronzed by the harsh weather of the mountain slopes. He sought out the recluses who inhabit the mountain caves.

Each of the *shen* had something new and interesting to teach him. During all of this time, the Monkey-Prince never lacked for wonders to excite his boundless curiosity. One old recluse taught him the secret of spells and incantations. Another showed him the power of the heartbeat drum. From another he learned how to compound herbs into salves and potions, and how to make powerful medicines from grains of sand and roasted barley. He learned the blood sacrifices to placate the local *lha* and spirits.

He spent three long years with a very powerful *shen* who lived in a solitary gnarled tree on a barren mountain slope. From this ancient, birdlike recluse he learned how to reduce his body to the size of a flea, and how to merge himself into the rocks.

This *shen* tried to teach him how to fly through the air

on a drum, but the Monkey-Prince wasn't skilled enough. He became stuck in the air, spinning wildly around and around. No matter how hard he tried to say the proper spells, he couldn't get that drum to land. The *shen* and his most powerful disciples had to stand on the twisted branches of the tree, beating their own drums, blowing long horns, stirring up winds with powerful incantations, until the wayward drum and the frightened Monkey-Prince were safely brought to earth. They decided that the agile young prince had better learn the hundred-length stride for rapid movement—and leave flying drums to those who were truly born to be *shen*.

But no matter how much the Monkey-Prince learned during this decade of search, none of the *shen*, even the most powerful, could dislodge the dark place in his mind.

"Perhaps when it is ready," they said, "perhaps it will hatch like an egg. Perhaps when the court *shen* decipher the secret inscriptions on the golden tablet. Perhaps if you could find Black Shen, and persuade him to help you ... perhaps ... perhaps ..."

Until the Monkey-Prince grew tired of wonders and tricks, and decided to seek Black Shen himself.

The name of Black Shen was always mentioned with a slight shudder of awe and fear by the other sorcerers. For it was well known that many eons and *kalpas* ago, he'd gained his extraordinary and formidable powers by entering into an alliance with the most evil beings of the nether realm. These spirits had given him the strength to become more powerful than any *shen*, but in return he had given up all human warmth and feeling. This was known by the other *shen*, but where Black Shen could be found, or how the Monkey-Prince should approach him, nobody knew.

"He lives up," the sorcerers said, pointing to the vast, snowy peaks. "He lives up there, somewhere in the west. He will only help you if you can appeal to his greed, which is endless. But watch out, because he's full of nasty tricks. Maybe you should wait. Perhaps the court *shen* will decipher the inscriptions. Perhaps we should try another exorcism ... perhaps ... perhaps ..."

But the Monkey-Prince was tired of waiting. In the tenth summer of his search, when he was twenty-two years old, he left the caves and trees of the reclusive *shen,* and began heading up the rocky western slope of the mountain range. He paused only to gather wild berries, and to search out the small turquoises and other gemstones which are scattered in rough shards throughout these vast mountains. He tied these small stones carefully into a clean, white scarf, as an offering to Black Shen's boundless greed. The Monkey-Prince traveled for months without seeing any other persons, though birds and animals were numerous. As he climbed higher, the vegetation grew extremely sparse, until there was only colored lichen, and the air grew chilly, with great gusts of wind.

Somehow that seemed familiar—a high, barren, windy mountain. But before he had time to think about it, he reached a shallow crevice that seemed to have volcanic activity. The ground was scorched, blackened, and hot to the touch. The air was filled with gritty, poisonous clouds of a strong, sulfurous odor. Nothing lived or grew here, except weird fleshy, heat-loving algae, and lichen. Never before had the Monkey-Prince felt so isolated as at this place where no wind stirred the heavy, reeking fumes, and the sun couldn't penetrate the thick layer of gloom. Suddenly, a flock of immense crows came flying overhead, wheeling around the Monkey-Prince, and crying a shrill, mocking dirge.

The Monkey-Prince looked up and realized that these were no ordinary crows. Instead of feathers, the creatures had plumage of sharp, thin knives. Their beaks were shaped like swords, and their claws were shiny with venom. The Monkey-Prince had reached the realm of Black Shen. The great birds were flying overhead, preparing to dive and attack the intruder.

"Wait!" called the Monkey-Prince. "I have a gift for Black Shen."

The crows uttered a cry of a different note, and waited for a response with their heads cocked to one side. The answering cry came from behind a hillock, up the slope. The great birds flew slowly in that direction, with the Monkey-Prince following behind. The hillock was the beginning of a large series of well-hidden, roomy and comfortable caves. Glimpsing inside, the Monkey-Prince saw that the caves were sumptuously furnished with hangings and furs, rich carpets and cushions, and gold, jewels and ivory wrought into goblets, icons and decorations of every kind. The Monkey-Prince wasn't invited inside to enjoy these comforts. The great birds led him to the entrance of the main cave, surrounded by a garland of human skulls, which framed the figure of Black Shen himself.

The sorcerer had a sallow, yellowish complexion and a long, thin, wispy beard. He wore a black brocade chuba robe and apron, ornamented with beads of human bone. He had a large-rimmed black hat, banded with the skulls of infants. His arms and neck were wreathed with jewels and bangles of every kind. In his right hand, he held a thigh-bone trumpet, which he used to direct the actions of the great crows. In his left hand he held a jewel-encrusted goblet, filled with blood, which he sipped with great relish.

Near the entrance to the cave was a large bed of burning coals. A ragged, dejected-looking little slave girl was turning an enormous spit over these coals, filled with meat for Black Shen's supper. With a little gulp of nausea, the Monkey-Prince recognized these gobbets of roasting flesh as the inner organs of human beings.

Black Shen called to him, his lips coated with warm blood, which dripped into his wispy beard, "Hey, what filthy beggar dares to disturb the peace of my cave? I smelled your stink all day, as you approached. Lucky I already have my supper!" Black Shen laughed loudly at his own humor.

The Monkey-Prince extended his tongue in the traditional Dza greeting and said, "I am the Monkey-Prince of the Kingdom of Dza. I'm sorry to disturb you, but I'm troubled by a dark place inside my mind. None of the other *shen* can cure it, and they all say that you have the power. So I thought maybe you'd give it a try, if you wouldn't mind, sir. I mean, it really bothers me and, well, I brought you a little gift . . ." The Monkey-Prince lamely handed over the small collection of rough jewels, wrapped in the customary white scarf.

Black Shen took the package, looked at it with a sneer, and tucked it inside his rich chuba robe. "You expect me to perform miracles for a bag of filthy pebbles? Listen, Gopher-Prince, or whatever your name is, that dark space is no ordinary disturbance. It was placed in your mind by demons, many eons and *kalpas* ago. No ordinary power will remove it."

34

"That's right! The court *shen* said it was demon-caused —how did you know? And how could it be so long ago? I'm only twenty-two years old."

Black Shen smiled, his teeth coated with dark blood. "Demons placed it there, and only demons can remove it. And only *I* have influence with the demon realm. But I don't use my powers for a sack of gravel. I demand a stiffer fee."

"I could help you," said the Monkey-Prince. "I don't have any more jewels or gold, but I could be your servant for a while. I know some good tricks." The Monkey-Prince performed a few of the feats that he had learned from the other *shen*. He reduced himself to the size of a flea and merged with a tiny stone, then made the stone spin around. He resumed his own size and made Black Shen's goblet levitate without spilling a drop of blood. He muttered a spell and caused a thick cloud of mist to arise, which obscured everyone's vision.

"Stop, enough!" bellowed Black Shen. "No more of your trained-dog tricks. You think I need the help of *you*, who can't even fly a drum?"

"Well, I mean, you said . . . I don't know. What price do you want to cure me?"

"Something special," smiled Black Shen. "Something that you would be especially skilled at getting for me. Something that was *supposed* to be mine, but accidentally got lost."

"What is it?"

"It's those blasted *Chos* inscriptions."

"*Chos* inscriptions? That name sounds very familiar—what is it?"

"You know, those wretched inscriptions on the golden tablet. The ones that your court *shen* are all fussing about, the idiots—they're trying to read them, but they'll never succeed. Those inscriptions were supposed to be *mine*. They landed in your silly fortress by accident. Your king will never be able to understand them, or use them. Only *I* know the Secret of *Chos*. I want you to go home, to Dza, to visit your family. They'll all be glad to see you. Wash your face, and comb that matted hair, and I'll give you a clean chuba robe. Your mother will kiss you and feed you mo-mo dumplings. All the princesses will sigh over your handsome face. The king will greet you warmly.

35

You'll have a good time, fill your chopsticks and belly, and get drunk on barley beer. Then you'll take those inscriptions and bring them back to *me!*"

"How odd," said the Monkey-Prince. "I knew that tablet had something to do with my problem."

"Of course—it's *my* tablet, and *I* can cure your head."

"But I can't do what you ask, because I'm not a thief," said the Monkey-Prince.

"It's not thievery, because they're *my* inscriptions. But if it'll make you feel better, I've got another gold tablet in the cave, with some gibberish on it. It's not the same writing, but it's good, solid gold, and no one can read either one down there in Dza. It won't make any difference, and you won't have to worry about thieving."

"Good, solid gold, just like the other one?"

"I said so, didn't I? Don't pester me, chipmunk, my patience is short."

"I have to think about it."

"Don't think too hard, weasel, it makes your head ache."

The Monkey-Prince grimaced, because that was true. If only he could get rid of this problem once and for all. If Black Shen could read those *Chos* inscriptions, he could probably cure him, and would it really make any difference in Dza? They hadn't deciphered the things in ten years. And it *would* be nice to see his mother, and taste her juicy dumplings again.

"That's right," murmured Black Shen, "that's good thinking, little rat. So, I've got to go away now. Some people in the north have been using my name disrespectfully. I want to send them a little hailstorm to teach them better manners."

"But a hailstorm will destroy the barley crop right now!" protested the Monkey-Prince. "They'll starve this winter."

"Starvation is a good teacher of respect," sneered Black Shen. "Anyway, you rest here tonight. The slave girl will give you supper and a clean chuba robe. Tomorrow my crows will fly you down to Dza for a little family visit. I really *want* those inscriptions!"

"Just one thing," grimaced the Monkey-Prince. "Do you have anything to eat but those organs?—I mean, I've never been fond of liver."

"Yes, yes, there's plenty to eat. But stay away from my possessions—*all* of my possessions!" Black Shen rose up in the air on his great drum, whirling through the sky with his black robes flying, and followed in a V formation by his flock of screaming crows.

"I told you I'm not a thief," the Monkey-Prince called after him. He sat down, confused, by the entrance to the cave. He really didn't know what was the right thing to do. To steal from Dza was unthinkable. But he wanted so badly to be rid of this darkness. Would the tablet be missed, if something of equal value was substituted? But why did Black Shen want those inscriptions so badly? The Monkey-Prince certainly didn't want to enhance that terrible power. With a sigh, he put his head in his hands.

The slave girl, who had been busy with the spit, got up and came over to him. "Is there anything you want?" she asked.

Something in the tone of her voice made him look up, startled. She was looking down at him, smiling. She was a small girl, with light, fragile bones and small round breasts visible under her ragged chuba robe. That wasn't particularly unusual. There are lots of small girls in the regions around Dza. But her face *was* unusual. Her hair was long and thick, and her eyes had a peculiar protruding bulge which made them far wider than ordinary slit-eyed folk. Her smile was also very wide, revealing pointy little teeth. Her expression was very friendly.

Strange, she looked familiar—very familiar, as though he had known this girl somewhere in the past—the far-distant past. The Monkey-Prince felt another wave of confusion, then a wave of pure, searing lust for this little creature.

"Is there anything you *want?*" she repeated.

III

The demoness, now embodied as the slave girl of Black
Shen, stood looking down at the confused and ragged
youth. Strange feelings rose up inside her. They began
when he first arrived. At her first glimpse of him, she was
startled. She thought he might be one of her brothers, or
some old friend from her girlhood village, someone come
to rescue her, to take her from this terrible life, this fright-
ful place. But no, scanning his face carefully, she knew
he wasn't from the little hamlet of barley farmers where
she was born into this life—the only one that she remembered.

Yet he looked familiar. More than familiar. He had a
special quality that made her want to reach out and touch
him. She wanted to throw her arms around him and laugh
with joy at his arrival, to weep into his neck as she poured
out her misery. Why did she feel this way? Certainly
Black Shen never evoked such feelings—that monster
who used and abused her at his whim. She had never felt
such a total response to anyone, ever before in her short,
unhappy life.

"Is there anything you want?" she asked him. Without
even thinking or willing it, her hand reached out and
brushed against his thick tangle of black hair.

He reached out, caught her hand, and looked up at
her. "What's your name?" he asked her.

"Drolma. *He* almost never uses my real name," she said
bitterly.

"Yeah, I noticed that. How do you come to be here?"

Tears began to well out of her large, protruding eyes.
"My family was poor," she wept, "very poor. We were
barley farmers in the southern part of Dza Valley. When
I was a little girl, about seven, a tremendous hailstorm
wiped out all of our crops. Black Shen came to our village

39

on his drum, with his yellow skin and screaming crows. We were all *so* frightened. He went to the village headman, and told him that *I* was responsible for the storm, that I was a demon-child, because I have such big eyes—and demons have big eyes, you know. But I'm *not* a demon. I don't know why my eyes are big. Some people have big noses, ears, breasts or bellies, and no one says they're demons. But *he* convinced them that the storm was my doing. He told them they'd never have a good crop again, unless they sold me to him. The monster, *he* made that storm, I know it! He gave them enough grain to last through the winter—if they were very careful. Then he took me away on his drum. Oh, I didn't want to go, I was so scared! I screamed and screamed, and held onto my mother's legs. She was crying too. She loved me, but she had other children, and she couldn't let the whole village starve to save me. He took me here. That was ten years ago, and I've been frightened and lonely, ever since. He does whatever he wants to me—and his wants aren't wholesome. No, he has evil, nasty desires. I don't know why he picked me. I'm not a demon, I'm *not!*"

Drolma fell down to her knees in a fit of hysterical weeping, and buried her face in the Monkey-Prince's lap. He ran his hands over her long, silky black hair, trying to comfort her, yet feeling shaky with physical desire.

I'm not very wholesome myself, he thought, lusting after this helpless, pathetic girl. Yet somehow his hands moved of their own will, stroking her hair, her back, gently touching and exploring her face, neck and arms, reaching inside her chuba to feel the heat of her delicate body and breasts.

She didn't resist his caresses. She looked up at him with her great eyes, and moved her body closer to him. Feeling as if his entire body would explode with desire, he pulled her against him, pulling aside both of their ragged chuba robes with feverish haste. Still she didn't resist him. Her own urgency seemed to match his own.

"I *want* you," she cried, as she climbed astride his lap and pressed her body against him. "I don't even know who you are, I only know that I want you!"

With a groan that shook his whole being, the Monkey-Prince thrust himself inside her, and exploded. She continued to move against him until a convulsive shudder passed through her body. They wrapped their arms closely around each other, and sat very still, their breath still heavy and jagged.

"Who are you?" she whispered, "why have you come here?"

"Just as I told Black Shen, I'm the Monkey-Prince of Dza. I came here seeking help. Nothing more."

"No, you came here to take me away from that devil. Some *lha* sent you here to rescue me. Maybe you don't even know it, but it's true. We must escape quickly, before *he* returns. He'll know what we've done, he always knows. If he catches us, he'll destroy us."

The Monkey-Prince looked around him in dismay. The whole thing had been so sudden, so intense, that he hadn't given any thought to the consequences. Yes, of course Black Shen would know. The sorcerer had said not to touch any of his possessions, and his rage at being disobeyed would be as intense as the Monkey-Prince's own passion. No more thoughts about whether to pay Black Shen's price. Now he must think about how to save his life. *Their* lives, for certainly he wouldn't abandon the large-eyed girl who was curled so trustingly in his lap. Perhaps the *lha* had sent him to free her. Who could know about such things? Why else did he experience such a tremendous surge of feeling? He had seen and desired other girls before, but never, *never* like that. Even now he could feel his passion rising again, almost as powerfully as the first time. He began to rub and caress her body with his hands.

No, he wouldn't leave her to face Black Shen's rage alone. She was special, precious. She would stay by his side, as his wife, for the rest of their lives. Obviously it was intended to be so. His hands and his lips caressed her small, warm breasts. So round, like perfect, ripe fruit. And in time these fruit would spout sweet nectar. Fruit . . . nectar . . . so strange, so familiar. None of his searchings had ever brought him anything like this. But *how* would they escape Black Shen, he who knew and saw everything? How could the Monkey-Prince, with his puny tricks, combat such power?

Their thoughts and embraces were interrupted by a loud, shrill cry above them. One of Black Shen's great black crows, with the knife-sharp feathers, was circling and wheeling overhead. Looking, watching, spying. How long had he been there before he cried out to announce his presence, with a sinister, mocking note? The couple looked up at the beast, who looked down at them with glinting eyes. Then, with a final warning note, the great black bird wheeled around and flew swiftly to the north, to inform his master.

The Monkey-Prince and Drolma separated with regretful haste, and wrapped their thin chubas tightly around their frail bodies. Suddenly it felt cold and dark here in this desolate place. The sun had fallen behind the snowy peaks and night was settling in. The great bed of coals had nearly died out from lack of attention, leaving no source of light or warmth. There was nothing to sustain them now, but the pure wonder of finding each other, the spontaneous joy, the taste and scent of their coupling. Only that remained, and the gathering cold and dark, and a feeling of pure dread as the shape of the great, whirling drum came rushing toward them from the north.

Black Shen's drum landed with an angry thud, in front of the main cave. "So, little rabbit," he said, "you like a wet, hairy burrow to crawl into, eh? Except that she's *mine!*" The sorcerer's lips were twisted into a snarl, and his entire body quivered with rage.

The Monkey-Prince and Drolma stood with their arms unthinkingly around each other, terrified and saying nothing. Their closeness further enraged Black Shen. With a flick of his finger, he caused a jolt of lightning to flash between them, separating the pair. Drolma cried out, her arm red and singed.

Seeing her hurt, the Monkey-Prince felt a great wave of anger. There's no hope that I'll survive this, he decided, so let me die honorably. Let me hear one cry of pain from those blood-soaked lips, before I hear no more.

Mustering all of his power and courage, the Monkey-Prince levitated the sorcerer's thick, heavy gold and jeweled goblet, just as he had done earlier that day. But this time he sent the dense metal vessel smashing against Black Shen's sallow brow.

The sorcerer roared out with surprise and pain. There was a small nick above his left eye that poured a thick trickle of dark blood. The great crows began wheeling
42

and darting overhead, screaming restlessly, for they relished the scent and flavor of blood, and it confused them to see it coming from the flesh of their master.

"Rabid dog!" bellowed Black Shen. "You would have died in any case. But now you'll die most painfully—roasting slowly in your own juices, and the juices of your beloved, while I ready my chopsticks for a late supper." With an elaborate hand gesture, Black Shen caused a bonfire to appear, a few lengths away from the entrance to the cave.

The Monkey-Prince felt a knot of fear in his stomach. He was ready to die—indeed, he had no choice—but the agony of fire burning his flesh made him sweat and tremble. His leg had been burned as a small boy, and he had never forgotten the excruciating sensation. Fire always terrified him.

Black Shen, sensing his thoughts, smirked.

Quickly, the Monkey-Prince decided that if he and Drolma must feel the agony of fire, Black Shen would feel it, too. With a quick surge of power, he sent a burning stick whirling through the air, whipping across Black Shen's face. To the Monkey-Prince's dismay, the sorcerer only laughed out loud.

"Puny jackal," he snorted. "Fire doesn't harm me. Fire is my friend, my plaything. Look!" Black Shen sealed himself in a relaxed, comfortable posture in the center of the bonfire.

Drolma began to weep softly, at the hopelessness of their situation. She thought her deliverance had come. But this lad who thrilled her body and heart with such intensity was obviously no match for *him*. Her liberator would be the one she always feared and expected—Shinje, the lord of death.

Black Shen sneered at them from his seat in the center of the fire. "Your little trick didn't work, dung beetle, but I appreciate its intention. You favor flying firebrands, eh? Then here, enjoy some flying firebrands!" Black Shen sent a flurry of flaming twigs and branches swirling through the air around them. The Monkey-Prince and Drolma ducked down, protecting their faces with their arms, while Black Shen rocked back and forth with laughter, and the great black crows screamed triumphantly from above.

"But enough of these games," said Black Shen. "It's

getting late. I've had a long day, and my appetite is growing. Maggot-nipples was so busy yowling like a cat in heat that she let my supper grow cold. These slave girls are very unreliable. Now I'll have to cook my own meal."

With another hand gesture, Black Shen caused a rope-like substance to wrap itself around the frightened couple, binding them tightly. "Sweet, very sweet," he said. "Now you're together again. You can rot for a thousand *kalpas*. Go ahead, embrace each other. Work up a little *heat!*"

With another wave of his hand, the sorcerer directed the fire away from himself, and pointed it in a rapidly moving stream toward the bound pair. The Monkey-Prince and Drolma watched, horrified, as the flames wove and darted toward them, like venomous snakes. But instead of leaping on the pair, and devouring them at once, the fire formed a flickering circle around the couple. The flames didn't touch them, not quite, but they could feel the intensity of the heat. The sweat poured off their faces in sticky streams. Their hair began to curl and scorch. Their lungs inhaled the dry, smoky heat and they began to cough violently. They could feel the beginning of blisters on their flesh.

"Yes, a little heat for the young lovers," sneered Black Shen. "Meat should cook slowly, or it won't become tender. Keep an eye on the kitchen," he called up to his circling crows. "I want to rest in my cave. I'll come back later to add salt for flavor."

The Monkey-Prince was barely aware of Black Shen's taunts, or his departure into the cave. He was much too involved in the agony of his own body. And he was much too busy trying to remember and form the words of a spell, through his cracked, blistering lips. A spell. What was the spell that the old tree *shen* had taught him, for making rain? What were the words, the mental images, the special prayers and intonations? Oh, if only he had listened more carefully to those kindly teachers! Tears ran down the Monkey-Prince's face and mingled with his sweat, as he longed to be back down the cool mountain slopes; longed to remember some trick that would free him from this hell. Cool, cool mountain slopes . . .

With extraordinary effort and concentration, he managed to summon a small, puffy cloud that briefly obscured the starry sky, and piddled a few drops that hissed in the scorching, burning flames. But that wasn't good enough. Not nearly good enough! Cool mountain slopes . . .

Then suddenly, with a strange and perfect clarity, he remembered the spell that would allow him to blend into the gray rocks of the mountain, itself. Would that work? Yes, it would probably allow him to escape from this ring of torture, but what about Drolma? Could he carry her along? If he merged into the cool, gray rocks, she would be left behind to roast! He *must* summon enough power to perform the spell for both of them.

He wrapped both arms and legs tightly around the body of the girl. Her head was lolling to one side, and she didn't move or speak. She was already unconscious—perhaps already dead! But no, he could feel her chest moving as it labored to draw sustenance from the smoky inferno. Could he take her with him into the heart and soul of the mountain, and once hidden, could they escape Black Shen's searching eyes and crows? Could he revive her and bring her back to herself? No matter. *Something* had to be done—soon. The Monkey-Prince felt himself on the verge of losing consciousness. Clutching the girl, as though she were part of himself, he quickly repeated the words and images, the prayers and intonations of the spell.

Suddenly the heat was gone, replaced by a soothing, chilly damp. Dark gray. Now all of the world was a dark gray. Dark, damp gray, solid gray—yet permeable. The Monkey-Prince was dimly aware of his own body cells mingling with the crystals of cool gray rock. There were no longer arms, legs, genitals, faces. No more blisters or scorching heat. Just a vastly vast expanse of cool, permeable gray. The Monkey-Prince allowed his mind and the loose conglomeration of his cells to float aimlessly through the cool gray. Was Drolma with him? There was no way to know. He couldn't even be certain that his own body parts were intact. Body no longer had any meaning. There was only gray. Cool, soothing gray. The Monkey-Prince floated without thought in the gray.

Had he actually managed to merge with the mountain? Or was this the land of Shinje, lord of death? The Monkey-Prince couldn't know. Did he float alone, or did Drolma float with him? His body had no boundaries, so he couldn't tell if another body was with him. How much time had passed, how long had he been floating? Timeless time, time

45

without time. The Monkey-Prince floated timelessly through the cool gray.

Then he became aware of a light in one direction, very remote and pale, yet distinctly lighter than the surrounding gray. He propelled his mind and the loose collection of his cells in the direction of the light. It grew stronger as he approached, then almost blinding.

With a sudden bump, the Monkey-Prince and all his cells formed again as his own familiar body, as it landed on the rough floor of a shallow cave. He was still alive! He had passed through the entire body of the mountain! *They* had passed through the mountain, for his arms and legs were still clutching the unconscious body of Drolma in an unshakable grip. He and Drolma were still alive— they had eluded Black Shen and passed through the entire body of the mountain!

But where were they? The Monkey-Prince looked out of the opening of the shallow cave. The bright sun blinded him for a while, and filled his eyes with tears (or was that relief and joy that filled his eyes?). Finally his sight cleared, and the Monkey-Prince looked out onto the great, high treeless plateau that stretches endlessly beyond the mountains that surround Dza.

Drolma's body shuddered, and she began to cough. Her eyes opened, and her coughs turned to wracking sobs.

"Don't cry," said the Monkey-Prince. "You don't have to cry anymore. We've escaped. We're free!"

But there were years of pent-up tears that had to flow before Drolma recovered and grew calm. The Monkey-Prince sat with her all the while, hugging her and stroking her hair. Finally she grew still.

"What happened?" she asked. "Where are we—are we dead? I don't understand."

"We passed through the mountain. I remembered the spell. We're on the other side of the mountain range. Look out there—you'll see the flat grasslands stretching as far as you can see."

Drolma rose stiffly and stood at the mouth of the cave. The sun was just sinking with a dull, red glow.

"It's beautiful!" she said, laughing for the first time since they had met. "I always wanted to see the land of the herdspeople. Is this where they live?"

"I guess so. I've never been here before, so I'm not really sure."

"What'll we do now?"

"We'll sleep in this cave. Tomorrow we'll try to find some food. Then we'll cross the *la* pass to Dza. I'll take you to the fortress, to my mother, the princess. She'll be so happy to see us! She'll cook mo-mo dumplings, filled with juice. Her dumplings are the best in Dza! Oh, I'm *so* hungry, I wish I had some now. You'll become my wife. You'll be a princess! Would you like that? When the next caravan comes from the east, I'll buy you blue brocade for a new chuba robe."

Drolma's face was bright and her eyes were shining. "You've never tasted *my* mo-mo dumplings. They're as juicy as your mother's. I'll make mo-mo every day. We'll make them together. Men are better at shaping the dough. But are the *la* passes to Dza still open?"

"I don't know. I hope so."

It was growing dark now, and quite cold. In these high plateaus, the temperature drops below freezing at night, even in the middle of summer, and now autumn was well advanced. They huddled together in the most sheltered part of the cave, enjoying the warmth of each other's body. They embraced and chatted bravely, mostly about their favorite foods. They were *so* ravenous. Finally hunger dulled into weariness and they fell into a deep, exhausted sleep.

When they awoke, the sun had risen high, but the light wasn't bright, because the sky was unusually overcast with thick, gray clouds. They looked out in dismay. A storm was coming. Perhaps just a quick light rain of late summer—or perhaps the first big storm of the winter season, which would close the passes to Dza. It didn't look good. Lightning flickered around the distant peaks, and there was a dim rumble of thunder.

"Come on," said the Monkey-Prince, "let's try to find something to eat, and get back here before the storm breaks. Maybe we can gather some dry grass and make a little fire with my flints, to keep warm."

Apprehensively, they stepped out into the gray, glowering day. A chill wind whipped through their thin, ragged chuba robes. It wasn't only fear of cold and hunger, of rain and snow that worried them. What they most feared was hail. At these altitudes, there are no layers of warm air to reduce the size of hailstorms. Here they can be the size of a man's fist—and far more dangerous.

Yet they couldn't stay in the cave any longer. They were both growing weak and faint from lack of food and water. They wrapped their arms around each other and began to move across the endless plateau, searching. Searching for something to eat, something to drink. Perhaps some edible roots, or grasses that still held heads of grain, this late in the season. Perhaps a stream with clear water to quench their thirst. Perhaps some small rabbit or rodent that could be killed and eaten. Perhaps . . .

The storm struck them with a blast of lightning so close that they could smell the scent of its fiery ozone trail, so close that the flash and the deafening clap of thunder were simultaneous. Then it was all around them, lightning crashing and exploding in every direction, blazing through the sky with brilliant, jagged trails. They crouched down from fear, and from the instinctive knowledge that they shouldn't be the tallest standing objects. Then the clouds burst open in a drenching, freezing rain that soaked through their thin chuba robes in seconds.

But it was rain—only rain. Not hail. Only rain.

They crouched down, trying to elude the deafening explosions of lightning, the freezing, pouring deluge. They could see each other's worried face, illuminated at intervals, as the lightning danced its jagged dance directly above them.

Then gradually, slowly, the lightning began to move off to the south, to grow distant, with several heartbeats between flash and crash. The rain became a thin, partially frozen slush. Now the lightning was far away, playing at the tips of the southern peaks. The thunder resumed its low, distant growl. The wind softened, and the sky poured a light, frozen confection. The first snowfall of autumn. Now the passes of Dza would be closed until next summer.

The clouded sun had reached the peak of its arc, and was beginning the descent. The temperature was dropping rapidly. They were soaked, cold and miserable.

"We've got to find some shelter," she said. "We'll freeze to death out here when night comes."

"I know."

"Should we get back to the cave?"

48

"There's no fire there, no food or water. Let's search a little longer. We still have some daylight. The cave isn't far."

They headed farther out onto the plateau.

"Look!" cried Drolma.

Far off, in the northern distance, they saw some strange black shapes. A group of large, black mysterious objects stood unmoving on the horizon. Was it huge rocks? Huts? Or perhaps the crows of Black Shen, waiting to pounce, like owls on mice? They moved closer, peering and trying to identify these strange objects. Would there be help, or danger? Or were they merely neutral features on the landscape?

Their ears solved the mystery before their eyes. They both began to laugh with relief, when they recognized the unmistakable bellowing of a herd of distant yaks.

Yaks. Beautiful great yaks. Yaks mean food. Yaks mean warm furs. Yaks mean that people are very nearby. Hand in hand, the Monkey-Prince and Drolma began to race through the tall grasses, toward the herd of yaks.

They reached the great, ungainly beasts just before the sun set. There was still enough light to see these strange creatures, who look like the result of a quarrel between demon and *lha*. Great, fleshy bodies, with thick tufts of black fur and large, fatty humps on their necks to store extra food reserves. Slim, almost delicate hooves, a tail shaped for whisking flies, sharp horns, and large, mild, friendly eyes. Ungainly, unlovely creatures, yet one of the few that can survive in these highlands.

The herdsmen had left the dogs to tend the animals, while they went off to seek shelter from the storm, and to spend the night in their leather tents, a short distance away. They were inside now, sipping their buttered tea, warm milk and barley porridge, making offerings to the local *lha*, and curling up with their wives and children between thick, louse-filled furs.

The Monkey-Prince and Drolma had no need to disturb the herdsmen, yet. It was almost dark, and they were too weary to go any farther. They saw what they wanted, right here. Among the herd were several *dri*, female yaks whose udders were thickly engorged with milk. The dogs were pacified with kind words, and the yaks glanced down at them with friendly, curious eyes, as Drolma and the

Monkey-Prince knelt down and drank their fill of sweet, warm milk from the crusty teats of the yaks.

Their hunger satisfied, they stood up and pressed their chilled bodies against the great creatures, burrowing into the thick, vermin-ridden fur to warm and dry themselves. The animals formed into a softly lowing circle, as the darkness fell, an instinctive formation to protect one another from wild beasts and the icy winds that howl across the plateau at night.

Inside the circle of crooning yaks, Drolma and the Monkey-Prince curled up and slept soundly, comforted and satisfied by warm yak milk and warm yak fur.

Shortly before dawn, the herdsmen galloped up on their swift little ponies, to begin the morning milking. They found the pair sleeping soundly, surrounded by a ring of softly lowing yaks.

IV

The Monkey-Prince and Drolma were taken a short distance to the tent village of the herdspeople, a small scrap of humanity huddled on the vast, featureless landscape. The watchdogs barked suspiciously and the people surrounded the couple and exclaimed in their own rough dialect. It seemed truly wondrous to them that anyone could survive such a cold night in the open, wearing only the thinnest chuba robe. Wondrous, and perhaps a little magical. These people weren't used to any strangers in their village, and this pair seemed particularly strange.

"Note the girl," they muttered among themselves. "See her large, staring eyes. Note the long and delicate limbs of the lad. I think they're not quite human. I think they're demon or *lha*, but which?"

"I'll ask the spirits," said the rustic, toothless old *shen* of this herding clan. He gummed some juniper berries and muttered a singing chant, then fell back upon the ground, comatose.

After a while, he said in an indistinct mumble, "They're not quite human, nor quite demon or *lha*. But they are kindly, harmless, helpless. They need *our* help. Some evil pursues them. They must escape, hide, or they'll be devoured. We must hide them, shelter them. We owe them a great debt, as we owe our own parents and ancestors, from eons and *kalpas* ago. We must repay this debt, and act as *their* parents now. We must protect them, take them into our clan. They must become one of our own. Protect them, shelter them as our own . . . our own . . ." The voice of the old *shen* trailed off into a resounding snore.

"The *shen* has consulted with the spirits," said the *gowa*, the village headman, holding the elaborately carved and feathered staff which symbolized his rank, "the youth and his bride will become part of the tribe of Har. The lad will be adopted as one of my own sons. We'll give them herds to care for. I'll furnish a place for them in my own tent, with a cooking pot and fur sleeping rugs and warm chuba robes. They'll travel with us to the winter grazing grounds and learn our ways."

The people all nodded gravely at the words of the village *shen* and headman. The Monkey-Prince and Drolma were led inside the headman's rectangular, sloping roofed tent, to be fed and warmly dressed.

The inside of the yak-hair tent was smoky and close, with the strong odor of roughly cured hides, and the urine of many babies who had slept in these hides. Near the single entrance of the tent was the firepit, which held several large cooking pots that steamed with more appetizing odors. All around the walls of the tent were the thick sleeping hides, and wooden chests and sheep and yak-skin bags. These contained the personal belongings of the family, and butter, cheese, tea, dried meat and fruit, and *tsampa*, the barley-flour staple. Because this was the tent of the headman, some of the bags of food had grown quite black and rotten, to indicate that this was a very wealthy family, with ample reserves of unused food. A low, long table for eating and craftwork was in the center of the tent.

From the rafters hung the saddles and swords of the family, and the tall, cylindrical butter churns, nicely worked with metal. In one corner of the tent was a little shrine with butter lamps flickering, and offerings placed for the local *lha* and spirits, and a silver-worked chest that held the family jewels and other valuables.

The morning milking was now finished, and the entire family gathered for breakfast, before the animals were taken to more distant pasture for the day. The family of the headman was large, with numerous sons and daughters-in-law, in wool or sheepskin chuba robes, which were gathered around the waist with colorful woven belts. On these belts the people hung their small knives, in decorative sheaths, their flints and their chopsticks, in metal-worked cases. In addition to the loose, belted, high-necked chuba, the women wore colorful blouses with long, flowing sleeves, and gaily striped aprons. The headman's wife and wealthy daughters-in-law wore rings, necklaces, and long earrings and head ornaments of silver, turquoise, coral and amber. Everyone's feet were tucked snugly into thick felt boots, worked with embroidery.

Grubby children darted around, looking for mischief, and small babies amused themselves on the little piles of yak-dung ashes, which help to keep them clean. There were many ragged old folks, grannies and grandpas, old aunts and uncles, widows and elderly retainers who had become permanent fixtures in the family group.

The Monkey-Prince and Drolma were used to large, bustling families, and settled back comfortably on a sheepskin rug near the table to sip their rich buttered tea, and *thukpa*, a soupy stew made of barley flour, mixed with dried meat and cheese. After breakfast, the men of the village sang their yodeling tribal songs, as they got ready to take the herds to the clan grazing lands. The women settled down to tend their babies and cookpots, the young calves and lambs, and to busy themselves with the endless task of spinning and weaving wool and felt for chuba robes, boots and blankets.

Drolma was outfitted with a long, patched but warm chuba, belt, blouse, apron and boots. The headman's wife shyly gave her a small silver ring, with a tiny turquoise. The Monkey-Prince was given a thick sheepskin chuba, baggy trousers, boots, and a warm, fur-lined, embroidered cap. Sleeping rugs of wool and hides were unrolled for them. They spent the day contentedly helping with the camp chores, and making friends with these rough, high-cheeked people, the swarms of dirty, curious children that followed them about, and the large mastiffs whose acceptance is essential for any camp member.

At dusk, the men tethered the animals for the night, and came back with buckets brimming with milk or water, for a supper of thick *thukpa* soup. They reported that the snow which had fallen during the night now formed a thin cover over the grasslands. Everybody slept soundly in the headman's tent, or outside under thick furs. When they awoke, they discovered that more snow had fallen, silently during the night. Now the grasslands were covered with a thick layer of white. The constant winds which sweep across these plateaus always leave enough patches of grass free from snow so that the animals can graze. Nonetheless, it was clear that winter was settling in quickly, and it was time to move to the winter campground.

Although the clan moves monthly during the summer, to find better pasture within their traditional territory, the move from summer to winter camp is always a big event in the annual cycle of nomad life. Numerous prayers must be chanted, and offerings provided to the *lha* and spirits of both locations, to appease them for creating a disturbance, and to ensure a safe journey. The old, toothless clan *shen* worked hard during this time, twitching convulsively in his shabby chuba, while he recited the chants and invocations.

Everyone worked hard, singing the seasonal songs as they packed the tents and all the belongings, and tied them onto the yaks. Just before the caravan moved off, a final fire was kindled with flints, on the firepit of the headman, and a bit of *tsampa* flour was offered to the fire *lha*. Everybody waited anxiously to see if the flour would cause the fire to smoke. If smoke rises, then the sacrifices have been accepted and the next camp will have good fortune. But no smoke means that the *lha* are angry, and there will be bad luck.

Everybody grinned happily as the thin column of smoke began to rise. But then a sudden puff of wind caused the plume of smoke to blow away.

"Good fortune, followed by some evil," muttered the old *shen*.

The winter camp was located in a sheltered, wooded canyon in the foothills. As the Har tribal caravan traveled, they met other nomadic family groups, moving from their own traditional summer pastures to their hereditary winter sites. Each meeting meant a stop for buttered tea and gossip.

The journey lasted many days. The first job, upon arriving, was to unpack the tents and all the belongings. The second job was to build a large wall of yak dung, collected during the move, all around the camp, to act as a windbreak, and to provide a source of dried fuel.

Winter in this forested canyon, with its large old trees, rushing stream, and windswept, grassy upper slopes for grazing, was beautiful, but cold. The storms howled and the temperature dropped. The stream soon froze to an opaque surface. Icicles hung thickly from the frosted trees. The days were short, and the nights long and black. The people wore their thickest furs, and covered their faces with a layer of butter, when they left the tent to tend the animals, to prevent their high-cheeked faces from freezing. Frostbite was a constant danger. Those who were foolish enough to leave their boots on overnight would find their feet numb and swollen and the flesh ready to rot by morning. Some of the older animals were butchered and their flesh frozen in storage chests, to provide food for the people, and to reduce the need for fodder.

Despite the hardships of winter, the Monkey-Prince and Drolma were content. Warm chuba robes, hot *thukpa* soups, and buttered tea and strong barley beer kept their bodies warm and plump. The stories, songs and tasks of winter kept them busy. They kept each other happy in their thick, fur bed. The other members of the clan and the headman's family soon ceased to regard them as outsiders. They became part of the Har clan.

The Monkey-Prince was grateful for their kindness, and felt very peaceful living among them. Yet he was still troubled by the dark spot in his mind. And he still intended to cross the pass into Dza, next summer when the glaciers receded.

For Drolma, it was the happiest time in her life. She loved playing with the babies and children, and helping the other women with the cooking, spinning and chores. She loved the Monkey-Prince, and she loved these friendly, generous folk. She was quite content, and hoped to spend the rest of her life among the Har people. As the winter progressed, she grew even more cheerful, for her little belly under her thick chuba robe was growing as round and bulging as her eyes.

Shortly before she was due to give birth, she found a large, spiral seashell, lying glowing and pearly in the snow. She brought it to the headman, whom she now called father-in-law. He looked at Drolma in surprise, and summoned the clan *shen*.

"A marvelous omen!" they exclaimed. "Your baby will be a man-child, and very great."

The people all gathered around to see the wondrous object, which shone with translucent glimmers of rainbow light. For in these highlands, so far from the sea, a seashell is as precious as any jewel. After she found the shell, the people began to treat her with special tenderness and care.

Spring was just beginning. The earliest wild magnolias were starting to put forth their buds in the forest, and the first tender shoots of wildflowers and grasses were appearing in the slushy, melting snow of the upper slopes. The day felt special. A sleety rain had been falling, alternating with periods of bright sunshine, so that in midday, a brilliant rainbow was seen arching across the sky, spanning both sides of the canyon.

"Another sign," mumbled the old *shen.*

On this day, Drolma's belly, which was now round and firm as an egg, began the rhythmic contractions of birth. Because this was her first time, the headman's wife acted as midwife.

It wasn't easy. Drolma's body was small, and her hips narrow. The baby was large, and her womb wasn't experienced. Sweat poured off her face, even though the day was cold, and she whimpered and clutched at her belly as the contractions became agonizing cramps. The headman's wife comforted her with crooning songs, while the Monkey-Prince sat brooding and worried, outside the tent.

Just as the full moon rose over the trees, the baby was born, a large and vigorous boy whose exceptional beauty was apparent to everyone, even in the first moments of his life. Drolma relaxed and smiled, and brushed her wet, tangled hair away from her forehead. The headman's wife cleaned the infant in warmed water, wrapped him in felt, and gave him to his mother to suck. The Monkey-Prince was called in to see his new son, and stood looking down at mother and child with shy pleasure.

"My visit to Black Shen brought me great treasures," he said.

At the mention of that name, Drolma's face clouded over. Then she smiled again, at the wonder of this tiny baby who was so beautiful, and so clever, knowing how to suck the very first time, without anyone teaching him.

That night, both the clan *shen* and the headman dreamed that the infant sat with a wheel of golden light around his head.

"The infant is special," said the *shen.* "He'll be a great king or warrior or *shen,* when he is grown. We must celebrate his arrival. We must give thanks that he has chosen to be born into the Har clan. His name will be Tashi, which means good fortune."

A celebration, yes, a party. The people in the regions of Dza are always glad to have reason for a feast, a celebration, especially when the world is frozen and cold.

"Bring out the strongest barley liquor," cried the men. "A beautiful baby has been born into the Har clan. He'll be a great warrior or king! Bring out the last of the dried apricots, the one's we've been saving all winter. Make dough for mo-mo dumplings. We'll stuff ourselves tonight!"

"But what meat will we put into the mo-mo dumplings?" asked the women. "Frozen yak meat is dry and strong-flavored. It doesn't make good, juicy dumplings."

"A deer," said the headman. "We'll hunt a fat deer and use the meat to stuff our dumplings, and use the bones for rich marrow *thukpa* soup."

"Let the father of the child hunt the deer," said the old *shen*. "Let him show his gratitude to the spirits and *lha* for such a fine new son, with an offering of deer meat."

"Yes, yes," cried the people. "We'll drink barley liquor and eat dried apricots, and the baby's father will hunt a deer to stuff our mo-mo dumplings!"

Drolma sat outside the entrance of the tent, on a thick fur rug, holding her baby, Tashi, snug and warm against her body. The sunshine was bright, and the sky was a deep blue, but the air was still cold enough that fur rugs were hanging from the branches of trees to freeze the lice and vermin that annoy the people. Everyone's breath steamed frostily in the air, as they prepared for the feast. Dung and firewood were collected, and a large, cheery bonfire was kindled in the clearing outside the headman's tent. Skins of the strongest barley beer and precious stores of dried fruit and other delicacies were taken out of their hiding places in the deepest part of the storage chests. The old *shen* recited the proper prayers and incantations. The Har people, growing tipsy, began their haunting mountain songs and yodels, and their wild, leaping nomad dances.

The Monkey-Prince and a group of his best friends fortified themselves with barley liquor, and armed themselves with bows and arrows to hunt fresh deer meat for the feast. The Monkey-Prince and Drolma embraced warmly before he set off.

"Please don't be gone long," she whispered. "I worry when you're away."

"Look," said the people, laughing amiably, "the baby

57

is barely dry from the womb, and those two are kissing and hugging, eager to make another one. Have a little patience, you two!"

Teasing and joking, the people sent the Monkey-Prince and his friends off to hunt, while Drolma sat in the bright sunshine, feeling weak but happy, enjoying the songs and dances in honor of her beautiful new baby.

But even nomads grow tired, and finally the people had danced and leaped, sang and yodeled until their legs and throats were exhausted. They had been drinking barley beer all afternoon, and everyone was rather drunk.

"Let's go inside the tents and rest for a while," they said. "Who knows what beautiful babies might be conceived on this festive day? Let's nap and revive ourselves, then we'll make the mo-mo dough, so it'll be ready when the hunters return. I'm so hungry, my chopsticks are jumping out of my belt. I can taste them already, fresh deer-meat mo-mo, juicy, hot and sweet!"

The people went inside to relax and slow their spinning, drunken heads. Drolma and the baby stayed outside to wait for the hunters. She was slightly tipsy herself, and she dreamily watched the sun drop among the large trees of the canyon.

Suddenly a large, dark shadow appeared overhead, then another and another. Drolma snapped out of her half-doze with a start. She was afraid to look up.

Then came a loud, mocking cry, pitched somewhere between a laugh and a scream. The sound was unmistakable. Like a moth drawn to its doom in a campfire, Drolma's eyes were drawn toward the sky. She already knew what was up there. It couldn't be anything else. Yet maybe, just maybe her ears and eyes were wrong. But no, it was what she feared. Overhead, darting and wheeling in a V formation, and screaming in triumph, were three of Black Shen's enormous crows, circling with their knife-sharp wings.

"No!" she cried, terrified, clutching Tashi closer to her breast. Her breath came in short, panicked gasps. She felt dizzy, drained, ready to faint. She wanted to grab her baby and run inside the tent. She wanted to scream long and loud to awaken the people.

But she could do nothing. She sat there, pale and trembling, frozen with horror, as Black Shen's whirling drum landed in the snow in front of her, with a dull crunch.

"You're very ungrateful," sneered Black Shen, "not to invite me to your fine party. Old friends should always be included in celebrations. The rowdy singing, and drunken, uncouth laughter, was so loud that I heard it all the way in my cave across the mountain. I came right over to share your joy. I've been looking for you, wondering where you went off to, without saying goodbye."

Drolma shrank back, holding her baby so tightly that it began to cry.

"I'm sorry I didn't bring a gift. I should contribute something to the feast. I heard that a very fine treat is planned. Mo-mo made of fresh deer meat. But deer are *so* scarce at this time of year. The hunters might not be successful. Wouldn't that be sad? These elegant friends of yours would be *so* disappointed. What should we do?"

Drolma snapped out of her state of frozen terror, screamed long and loud, and scrambled to her feet.

Before she could move off the fur rug, Black Shen muttered a few words, and snapped his fingers with a loud crack that sent Drolma's head spinning into total blackness. When she recovered, she was still standing. Black Shen stood with his arms crossed over his black brocade-and-bone chuba, laughing loudly. "Ha! Fresh deer meat for the feast."

Drolma looked around in confusion. Where was Tashi? The infant was no longer in her arms! There was something warm pressed against her leg. She must have dropped him in her swoon. She looked down, and nearly swooned again. Pressed against her leg was the trembling, frightened body of a little fawn.

Drolma stared at the little animal, and at her own leg in horror. It was no longer her slim, booted leg, no longer her body. Now her leg, her body were covered in short, tan fur. She had been transformed into a plump doe!

Black Shen roared with laughter, until his sallow face turned red. Then he leaped back onto his drum, to rejoin the crows that were circling and screaming overhead. They flew out of sight, beyond the trees, leaving the two terrified animals, the doe and her fawn, standing alone on the fur rug.

The screams and laughter awakened the people inside the tent, but they were groggy, and assumed it was the hunters returning and joking with Drolma. Who else could it be in this remote place? Gradually, however, the sounds made them curious, and they came out blinking, in the bright afternoon light.

"Look," cried the headman, pointing at the doe and fawn. "Our supper has come to us! Is this another omen?"

Drolma stared imploringly at the people with her large, doe eyes. Didn't they realize what had happened?

"Where's Drolma?" asked the headman's wife.

"Probably gone to the bushes to pass dung," said her husband. "Quick, get my bow and arrows, before these two *lha*-sent creatures escape!"

Hearing this, Drolma panicked. They *didn't* understand! They would shoot her and her beautiful baby. With a quick leap, she sprang off the fur rug. Making sure that the fawn was following close behind, she sprang gracefully away, into the forest, running and leaping with her heart pounding in her chest. She wanted to scream, to cry out to the people. But deer don't scream or cry. They only run. Run. Run for their lives. Drolma ran for her life with her baby following close behind.

Soon they were in the shadowy depths of the forest. Here the ground was covered thickly with snow. The air was still, and very cold, and the sunlight was dim and pale through the thick pine branches. They were alone in the forest, amid the large trunks of ancient trees. Occasionally a bird cried, a branch creaked, or a small animal moved in the underbrush. Otherwise, it was cold and silent in the forest, and terribly lonely.

Drolma stopped to rest, and to nuzzle her poor little baby. Her whole body was quivering with shock, but the tiny creature didn't seem worried that he was transformed from infant to fawn. He only knew that his mother was nearby, with her teats warm and full of milk. For the little fawn, all was well. He nuzzled up under his mother's body, and began to suck, while the large-eyed doe stood panting and frightened.

The Monkey-Prince found them standing there, a doe and her nursing fawn, deep in the forest. He stood behind a tree watching them for a while, feeling uncertain what to do. They seemed so peaceful, so vulnerable, standing like that. How could he shoot them? Should he destroy animal mother and child, in order to celebrate human mother and child?

Yet how could he go back to the camp emptyhanded? They had found no game all afternoon, no deer, rabbits, marmots. Nothing. The forest was strangely quiet today. Doubtless the animals were in sheltered places, waiting for spring to come. Yet these two stood so still among the trees. It would be so easy to kill them.

But he didn't *want* to kill them! He'd never been a hunter. He was always content to live off fruit and milk and *tsampa* flour. No. That was a lie. He was grateful to accept plentiful bowls of yak-meat stew from the Har people. He'd eaten their food all winter. They never asked for any payment. They fed him and Drolma generously, and this was the first time they had ever asked him to provide some food. How could he disappoint them? They were all waiting back at the camp, drinking and singing and preparing the mo-mo dough. They were eager for fresh mo-mo. The dumplings would make Drolma smile, make her strong again. The *shen* said he must make offerings of thanks for the baby. He shouldn't fret like a woman. These were only animals, this doe and her baby fawn.

With great reluctance, he raised his bow and arrow and stepped noisily into the clearing, hoping the animals would hear him and run.

But they didn't run. The doe looked up at him with large, sad eyes and stared and stared. Why was she staring like that? Why didn't she run? "Run before I shoot you! *Run!*"

The group of Har tribesmen, the Monkey-Prince's hunting companions, came tromping behind him, through the woods. "Eh, did you get anything yet?" they called. "The people won't be happy with old, dried meat tonight."

Run, you creatures, run before the others come! The Monkey-Prince stared at the doe, who stared so strangely back at him.

But the others were already there. They saw the animals, though they were too far away to shoot.

"Shoot them, you idiot," they called. "Shoot them before they run away!"

With a feeling of doom rising inside him, the Monkey-Prince notched the arrow, pulled the bow, closed his

61

eyes tightly, and shot. The arrow sank deeply into the flank of the doe, piercing vital organs. Still staring at him, she sank down, blood gushing from her wound.

The little one will die of hunger, the Monkey-Prince realized, so he put another arrow into his bow, and shot the fawn through the heart. The tiny creature collapsed and died instantly.

"Good shot!" cried the men, behind him.

The doe was lying on the ground now, bloody and gasping, her limbs twitching convulsively. Yet still she stared at him with her great, bulging eyes. Staring, *staring* with large eyes, until she also died.

With a feeling of dread, the Monkey-Prince walked over to the bloody carcasses. The meat must be butchered and taken back to the camp. But as soon as he touched the bodies, they instantly resumed their human shapes.

Drolma and her beautiful baby lay dead in the snow, deep in the forest. The shaft of the Monkey-Prince's arrow was bedded deeply in Drolma's left hip. The head of the other arrow had pierced the baby's heart. The Monkey-Prince had shot them—his wife and his beautiful son, here in the dim forest. Their blood stained the snow. They didn't breathe anymore. She didn't stare anymore. They were both dead. Dead. *Dead.*

With a long, loud cry of grief, the Monkey-Prince ran off into the forest, to seek his own death.

V

Running, running through the forest of tall pines and wild magnolia trees, just coming into bloom. Running and sobbing, overwhelmed with the misery of what he had done. Running, running away from his frightened companions, the terrible corpses, hoping to become a corpse himself. Running, running, looking for a tiger, a snow lion to maul him, a cliff from which he could leap. Running, running away from the horror, but the horror wouldn't let him escape.

The Monkey-Prince ran sobbing through the forest. He didn't find any wild animals or cliffs to end his misery. Instead he came upon a very odd camp. Actually, he heard it before he saw it. There was the weird sound of deep chanting, in a strange, unintelligible tongue—*"Om ah hum vajra guru padma siddhi hum, Om ah hum vajra guru padma siddhi hum,"* over and over again, accompanied by the sound of many small hand-drums, and a clear bell.

There was also the curious sound of gushing water—strange at this time of year when all the creeks and rivers were still frozen. A camp of forest *shen,* the Monkey-Prince decided. Good. They could prepare a potion to end his wretched life. Gasping for breath, with tears still streaming down his face, the Monkey-Prince stumbled into the camp.

He stopped short, for even in his misery, he could see that this was no ordinary encampment of forest recluses. These were very strange beings, indeed. In the center of a clearing, ringed by early-blooming magnolias, in front of a small, bright fire, sat a man in crosslegged position. He was of ordinary size, but his appearance was quite extraordinary. He had the face of a foreigner, not a man of Dza. The look of the Hind people, who live across the sky-high mountains far to the south. His face was a deep brown, with round eyes, and a long, narrow, curved nose. He had none of the flat, broad-cheeked, slant-eyed features of Dza people. Hind foreigners are a rare sight in Dza, but more rare was the subtle glow that emanated from the skin of this man, and from his richly, embroidered brocade and fur robes, worn in the style of Hind. In his two heavily jeweled and glowing hands, the man held a small bone and silver hand drum, and a heavy brass bell, with *dorje* thunderbolt designs.

Next to the man sat the most beautiful woman the Monkey-Prince had ever seen. Even in his sorrow, he was astonished by her beauty, and the kind look of wisdom that shone from her face. She had the features of a woman of Dza, and wore a magnificent brocade-and-fur chuba and headdress of turquoise, in the style of Dza nobilty. She radiated the same soft glow as the man. In one jeweled hand she held a small, three-sided *phurbu* dagger, worked with precious stones and a thunderbolt design. In the other hand she held a bone-and-silver cup.

The pair sat in front of a colorful striped tent, whose posts were hung with flags and banners. At their feet lay a large winged tiger, looking sleek and placid as a peasant's housecat.

Around the pair sat an astonishing circle of large forest demons, with hairy bodies and claws, with fangs and tusks and bulging eyes, holding bone hand drums, and chanting those strange words. Then came a circle of *shen*, in rough fur chubas, also holding hand drums, and reciting the peculiar chant, *"Om ah hum vajra guru padma siddhi hum. Om ah hum vajra guru padma siddhi hum."*

The Monkey-Prince stood at the edge of the clearing, his head whirling with shock, and stared at this bizarre assembly—the foreign man and his beautiful woman, all aglow. The circle of demons and *shen*, sitting docilely chanting and worshiping the pair. Just beyond the tent, he saw the source of the rushing water. It was a large out-cropping of rock. From the center gushed a curious free-flowing fountain of very clear water. The horses of the group were tethered near this rock, in order to drink. The Monkey-Prince stood and stared.

The glowing foreigner became aware of his presence. He stood up and bowed in the foreign manner of greeting. At first the Monkey-Prince shrank back, frightened. But a man seeking death can laugh at fear, so the Monkey-Prince extended his tongue in the traditional greeting of Dza. The chanting and drumming stopped.

"Welcome, Monkey-Prince of Dza," said the foreigner.

"You know me?"

"Yes, your story is known throughout the forest, and throughout Dza."

"Good, then perhaps you know the latest episode, and will kindly lend me the woman's *phurbu* dagger, so I can end this dreary tale forever."

"It never ends forever," murmured the stranger. "Your tale will continue in the next embodiment. But now I have something better to offer you than the dagger."

"What is it? My needs are very limited now. I seek only death."

"Before you die, perhaps you wish to hear the Secret of *Chos,* which I have brought over the sky-high mountains to Dza."

The Monkey-Prince laughed grimly. "Secrets! I no longer have any interest in secrets. A man in his last moments of life has no use for headache potions!"

"I think you'll be glad to hear the secret," said the glowing stranger, "but I have something else to offer you of more immediate value."

"Offer me the dagger."

"Better than the dagger, I offer you revenge."

"Revenge?"

"Yes, revenge against Black Shen, who is both our enemy and the enemy of *Chos.* That monster who transformed your poor wife and child into a doe and fawn, to create this terrible tragedy that streaks your face with tears."

The Monkey-Prince's face twisted with rage and pain at this news, and tears sprang to his eyes again. Then he recovered himself and said softly, "I accept your offer of revenge, stranger, and after we have destroyed Black Shen, I'll take the loan of your dagger."

"After we've destroyed Black Shen," said the foreigner, "you can use his dagger."

"Who are you?" asked the Monkey-Prince.

"Come," said the stranger, "sit by the campfire, warm and refresh yourself with hot food and buttered tea. You must be strong if we are to battle Black Shen. While you eat, I'll tell you my story."

Shakily, the Monkey-Prince sank down beside the glowing man.

"My name is Lotus-Born," he began. "I come from Urgyan, a land far to the west. My name comes from my birth. I wasn't born from a woman, like ordinary men, but from the center of a large flower—a water lotus, which resembles the wild magnolias of this forest. One day a great lotus, in the center of a clear lake, burst into bloom, and there I was, seated in the center, a handsome little boy. The people took me directly to the king of that land, who was childless, and he adopted me as his son and heir. Yet as I grew to manhood, I realized that I wasn't meant to be a prince, but a seeker after knowledge and wisdom."

"Me too," said the Monkey-Prince.

"Yes, we have much in common," said Lotus-Born. "I left the kingdom of my birth, and journeyed to the vast, hot, teeming land of Hind, which lies south of your sky-high mountains. Many great kingdoms lie beyond Dza, you know. In Hind there are wise men and scholars, powerful magicians and *shen*—which the Hind people call *siddhis.* I traveled along their humid, sluggish river, Holy Mother Ganga, seeking out the wisest of the wise, the most scholarly of the scholars, the most powerful of the magicians and *siddhis,* and I learned something from each of them."

"So did I!" said the Monkey-Prince, startled to hear his own tale echoed by this glowing man. "Were you also troubled by something dark in your mind?"

"No, my reasons were different than yours. For me, the search was the essence of my being. I lived only to seek knowledge. In time, I, Lotus-Born, became famous as a wise man and scholar, a doctor and astrologer, a powerful magician and *siddhi,* a great *shen* in your language—perhaps the greatest of the white *shen.* I traveled to many realms and world-systems, to gain further knowledge. When my own beloved teacher, my *guru,* was ready to cast off his aged and feeble body, he called me to his bedside. He gave me two golden tablets, containing the Secret of *Chos,* the highest secret of the Perfect Ones, who dwell at the peak of the mountain, which is in the center of our universe—but I think you've forgotten that place. In addition to the tablets themselves, my teacher taught me how to read the inscriptions, explained their sublime meaning and showed me how to use their hidden powers."

"So you can actually understand that tablet?" asked the Monkey-Prince, incredulous.

"Understand, explain, and use," said Lotus-Born. "But remember, there were two identical tablets. Black Shen wanted to increase his terrible power and he had enough strength to fly one of the tablets through the night, to Dza. But my power was strong enough to land it in the fortress of your king, rather than at the door of Black Shen's cave. He was furious! Your court *shen* and I were powerful enough to keep the tablet in the fortress, though your king couldn't understand the inscriptions. No one in Dza could understand them, not even Black Shen, for all his boasting. Now five generations of kings have reigned in Dza, since that tablet landed."

"Five generations! But I've been gone only about twelve years."

"Hah, you think so? Remember the time you spent passing through the mountain. Human bodies don't move quickly through mountains. Believe me, much time has passed. Your mother died of contented old age, years ago. Her body provided a feast for your cleansing vultures."

Tears sprang into the Monkey-Prince's eyes once again.

"Five kings have ruled since you left Dza valley. The king who reigns now is a wise and good man. He has two intelligent wives, one from a mountain kingdom in the south, and another from the great empire in the east. Both were born in places where *Chos* is known and flourishing. They gave your king some simple images, and teachings in the ways of *Chos,* and this has ripened his curiosity. He sent messengers far and wide, to invite wise men to Dza to explain the inscriptions, and to give him teachings. Despite the extreme hardships of the journey, several very wise men have answered the invitation, eager to be of service to your king, and to spread the doctrine of *Chos.* Each of those profound teachers was turned back, before he could even cross the *la* passes into the valley of Dza."

"Turned back by the glaciers?" asked the Monkey-Prince.

"No, not by glaciers—they have enough power to cross

the rivers of ice. They were turned back by Black Shen, whose greed is greater than any mountain. He still craves that tablet. He thinks it will increase his power, but he can never use it, in a million eons and *kalpas*."

"Why not?"

"Because the secret of *Chos* is the secret of compassion for all beings. There is tremendous power in this, but Black Shen could never understand it.

"Eventually, I, Lotus-Born, was invited to Dza. Your king's messenger pleaded with me, saying that only I had the strength to combat Black Shen, and the skill to instruct your king in *Chos*. I wasn't eager to leave the warm, mango-laden banks of holy Ganga, but that night I dreamed that all the trees of Hind bent toward your land of snows. I couldn't refuse the plea. I traveled to your frigid, barren mountains with the aid of my winged tiger. I have fought all the way, for the allies of Black Shen are numerous. As you see, I made many conquests. Many of the demons and *shen* who formerly served Black Shen have become my followers, and are learning the way of compassion." The glowing stranger swept his hand in a circle to indicate the demons and *shen* who sat at his feet.

"I accomplished much in Dza Valley. I instructed your king in the secret meaning of the tablet. I gave the skills of reading and writing to the court. I caused water to flow over dry, parched areas of the kingdom, so that grain and fruit can be cultivated, for that is one of my skills—you can see the water gushing from that solid rock. Best of all, here in Dza, I met my female counterpart, Yeshe. The only woman, among the many I have known, whose mind and energy matches my own." The radiant woman smiled adoringly at Lotus-Born.

"She was part of your king's own harem, chosen for her extraordinary beauty—yet too beautiful for him to ever touch, too fine, too perfect to spoil. I recognized her at once as my female half, and requested her as a gift from your king. He agreed readily, and so did she—quite readily, for she also longed for her male half. When I am gone from Dza, she will continue the teachings of *Chos*. In the meantime, Black Shen and his forces are still strong. I spread the doctrine of compassion, while he spreads the doctrine of hatred. The two cannot coexist. If *Chos* is to take root and flourish in Dza, Black Shen and his allies must accept and learn the way of compassion, or be destroyed. I need *you* as my ally."

"Why?" asked the Monkey-Prince.

"Because you have more power than you realize, and because your sorrow and need for revenge will give you special strength. Any great feeling, even hatred, misery, rage, any demon or *shen,* can be transformed into the service of compassion. That is part of the secret. The sorrow which you now feel can be transmuted into great peace. That is also part of the secret. But now I've told you my story, and I already know yours. I've not regretted coming to Dza, no not at all."

Lotus-Born laughed heartily and patted the glowing woman's leg. "Come, we've talked enough. Eat your supper while it's hot. We must sleep well tonight. I chose this isolated spot for the battle, so we don't frighten the people in the valley. We meet Black Shen here, tomorrow at dawn."

The scream of Black Shen's crows and the thud of his landing drum wakened the camp, well before the sun was up. Lotus-Born yawned, rubbed his eyes, and climbed slowly out of his sleeping rug, pulling his warm robe around his smooth, well-muscled body. "You're too early," he called to the sorcerer, whose bone ornaments and sallow skin gleamed with eerie phosphorescence in the predawn darkness.

"This isn't a day for hibernating," called Black Shen. "You challenged me to a morning duel, so let the duel begin!"

"I challenged you to a duel when the sun rose," said Lotus-Born, yawning noisily. "I don't like to be dragged from my bed."

"The sun will rise soon enough," sneered Black Shen.

"Not so soon," replied Lotus-Born. In his hand was the triangular *phurbu* dagger which the glowing woman, Yeshe, had held the day before. With a mighty thrust, Lotus-Born sank the dagger into the frozen soil. "There," he said. "That'll hold the sun for a while, until I take my morning tea."

Black Shen uttered a low snarl, and retreated into the shadows of the forest.

"That's one of his tricks," said Lotus-Born to the Monkey-Prince, "trying to take us by surprise. But the battle can't begin until the sun rises, and the sun won't rise until I'm ready."

With growing astonishment, the Monkey-Prince realized that the beginning rays of light, low in the eastern sky, didn't rise any higher, didn't become any brighter. Lotus-Born's dagger had halted the sunrise! Smiling at the Monkey-Prince's obvious amazement, Lotus-Born enjoyed a leisurely breakfast, and performed his morning yoga exercises and chants.

"Now let the sun rise," he commanded, removing the dagger from the ground. All at once, the world was flooded with light.

"You'll pay double for that," threatened Black Shen, returning to the clearing. "Your death will last as long as that wretched sunrise. But who do I see in your camp? The little Gopher-Prince. I thought his family was all chopped into soup meat, yesterday. Was his skull too tough?"

"The Monkey-Prince of Dza is my ally," said Lotus-Born.

Black Shen exploded with mirth, while the Monkey-Prince stared at him with loathing.

"Enough idle talk," called Lotus-Born, loudly. "It's time for you to renew yourself, Black Shen, time for you to accept the ways of *Chos* and the doctrine of compassion for all beings."

From the folds of his robe, Lotus-Born produced the second gold tablet, which glimmered in the morning sun.

The sight caused Black Shen to hiss loudly with desire, so that drops of spittle ran down his long, wispy beard. His yellowish skin turned red with longing, he swept his arm in a semicircle, and the three great crows dove down, to snatch the shining object. A flash of lightning flew from Lotus-Born's free hand, which sent the creatures screaming and smoking back into the sky.

"Does this mean you won't become a servant of *Chos?*" asked Lotus-Born.

"I am *no* servant, especially yours."

"Then let the battle begin."

To the Monkey-Prince's great surprise, instead of one Lotus-Born, standing and glowing, there were suddenly many Lotus-Borns in the clearing, tens, hundreds, multi-

70

tudes, an entire army of Lotus-Borns, standing and radiating light.

Black Shen snarled and moved his hand in an elaborate gesture. Through the sky, from the west, flew an enormous demon, carrying two rocks the size of small mountains, which he dropped onto the crowd of Lotus-Borns. But as the immense objects fell, Yeshe clapped her hands, and the rocks crumbled into a cloud of dusty snow.

In a rage, Black Shen summoned a multitude of tiny female spirits, who showered flames from between their legs, onto the army of Lotus-Borns. Each Lotus-Born gushed a spout of water from his mouth, which quenched the flames into a puff of steam.

From the north flew an immense white yak, blowing whirlwinds and blizzards from his nostrils. In unison, the Lotus-Borns cried a mighty spell, and the winds died down.

A venomous snake with a thousand heads slithered through the forest. Lotus-Born set loose a mongoose with two thousand heads, which devoured the monster.

From the south flew an army of ogres carrying weapons of every kind. They battled in hand-to-hand combat with the Lotus-Borns. One by one, the demons were subdued, and their weapons were taken.

Black Shen watched the battle with intense concentration, while the Monkey-Prince watched Black Shen. Magic tricks are very exciting, he thought impatiently, but they won't give me my revenge.

The glowing woman, Yeshe, was busy herding the defeated ogres, spirits, demons, and the great white yak into the edge of the clearing. With an anguished cry, the Monkey-Prince snatched the triangular *phurbu* dagger from her belt and rushed through the battling hordes, toward Black Shen. Ogres attacked him on all sides, but he fought them off wildly, with the desperate, reckless strength of one who doesn't care if he lives or dies. Single-mindedly he moved toward Black Shen, who was watching the battle intently, jumping up and down with frustrated rage, as he saw his creatures fall, one by one.

Then the sorcerer caught sight of the Monkey-Prince approaching. The two faced one another. The Monkey-Prince raised the dagger and lunged toward his enemy. With a short laugh and a casual gesture, Black Shen sent his own knife straight and deep into the heart of the

71

Monkey-Prince. Blood gushed from the wound, but the Monkey-Prince didn't fall. With his last strength, he continued his forward rush. Black Shen's eyes widened with surprise and fear as the Monkey-Prince, spouting blood, raised the dagger, and plunged it into the vulnerable spot between the sorcerer's eyes.

Black Shen fell, thrashing wildly, then screamed the cry of a crow, so loud that it split the ground through the center of the clearing into a deep chasm. He gave one last convulsive lurch. Then Black Shen lay still on the ground, with the dagger protruding through a stream of dark blood in the center of his brow.

The crows went berserk, diving and swooping and tearing themselves to bits on the branches of trees. The battling ogres dropped their weapons and stared in wonder. The Monkey-Prince stood still for a moment, a fountain of blood, then he fell.

Suddenly the clearing was very quiet.

All of the demons, ogres and spirits stood in the clearing and watched, respectfully, as the multitudes of Lotus-Borns were absorbed back into one. He and Yeshe knelt down beside the body of the Monkey-Prince. The blood had stopped flowing, and lay in a sticky, congealed puddle on the snowy ground.

Together, the glowing couple began to trace an elaborate design on the bare chest of the Monkey-Prince, using the sticky blood. In low, deep voices, the pair began a rhythmic chanting of the potent syllable *HRI*.

The Monkey-Prince recovered consciousness with a loud sob. "I'm already dead, why do you bring me back?" he cried.

"Your tale has ended in this embodiment," said Lotus-Born, "but stay with us a little while longer, to help me complete mine."

The Monkey-Prince raised himself up weakly, on one elbow. "You gave me the revenge that you promised," he said, "and your powers are greater than any I have ever seen, for I am dead, yet I remain alive and feel no pain. I will do whatever you ask."

"Then look," said Lotus-Born, pointing to the sky.

There was a sound of low, approaching thunder, and the sky grew dark. But it was no storm. It was the sound

72

and shadow of multitudes of whirling drums, thousands of beating wings, as all of the *shen*, all of the spirits and demons of Dza arrived to join the great assembly that was gathered in the forest.

From every corner of Dza they came, flying on their whirling drums, from the valley itself, from the great snow mountains, the forests and vast, barren plateaus. They landed in the snow with soft crunching sounds. From every rock and tree, river and *la* mountain pass, glacier and canyon came the spirits and demons that give life to natural places. They all sat in a great semicircle at the feet of Lotus-Born.

The Monkey-Prince recognized his old friends among them, the ancient court *shen*, mountain *shen*, tree *shen*, and the old *shen* of the Har tribe. They wept with pleasure to see him again, and with sorrow to see the pallor of death upon his young face.

Lotus-Born, his glow increased tenfold, held up the shining golden tablet. "All is illusion, a magic show created by mind," he said. "That is the secret of *Chos*. Form is emptiness, emptiness is form. There is no suffering, cause of suffering or cessation of suffering. There is only mind. Thus taught the great *śramana*, long ago. The secret of *Chos* is that there is no secret. The wisdom of *Chos* is that there is no wisdom, only mind. The mind of Black Shen can create a world of hatred and fear. The minds of the followers of *Chos* can create a world of compassion for all beings. All of you who are assembled here will become the protectors of *Chos*, now and in the future. You will wear the sacred cords around your necks, and become the guardians of *Chos* in the kingdom of Dza."

Lotus-Born began to pull long, glistening red cords, tied in elaborate knots, from within the solid-gold tablet. Yeshe took a cord and tied it around the neck of each *shen*, demon or spirit. It took many cords to circle the neck of the great white yak, who now lay calm and docile, near the center of the clearing. As the cords were tied, the hand drums of the *shen* began to sound, and the entire assembly began the low, droning chant, *"Om ah hum vajra guru padma siddhi hum."*

When all the cords had been distributed, Lotus-Born stood with his hand resting on the head of the great white yak. "Now you are the protectors of compassion. Fly! Fly with me to the valley of Dza. There we will build a mighty temple. In one day, we'll complete the thick stone walls, the golden-tiled roofs, the mighty columns, the gardens and courtyards. The interior will be hung with magnificent silk banners and paintings. There will be a jeweled altar, with butter lamps always burning, to hold the golden tablet that reveals the secret of *Chos*. Together we will build this temple, forever we will protect it, and spread the doctrine of *Chos*. Compassion will be the ruler of Dza, and all will prosper and flourish. Fly! Fly to the base of the king's fortress. I will join you there soon."

With a great whir and flutter, the whirling drums, carrying all of the *shen* of Dza, with their robes flying, rose up into the air, and headed over the mountain, toward the valley. With a beating and flapping of wings, all of the demons and spirits and ogres joined them. With a mighty leap, the great white yak crossed the entire mountain range.

Now the clearing was almost empty. There remained only the glowing couple, Yeshe and Lotus-Born, framed by the early-blooming magnolias, the dying Monkey-Prince, lying weakly in the blood-stained snow, and the body of Black Shen. With a sweeping gesture of his hand, Lotus-Born rolled Black Shen's body into the deep chasm in the earth, created by the sorcerer's own death cry. Now only the three of them remained in the very quiet clearing in the forest, as the sun began its descent into the flowering trees.

"The temple of *Chos* will be built in Dza," said Lotus-Born. "It will house the golden tablet, but it won't house *this* tablet. The other tablet, which is now in the fortress of your king, will be enshrined in the great temple."

"And you'll keep this tablet for yourself?" asked the Monkey-Prince in a weak, soft voice.

"No, I have no more need for the tablets—my work here is almost done. This tablet will be hidden, until it is needed in the future, to defend *Chos*. Only you and Yeshe will know where the tablet can be found."

"But I'm dying," said the Monkey-Prince, who felt sleepy and confused. "Why trust me with the hiding place?"

"Dying men can be well trusted with secrets," said Lotus-Born. "You'll carry it with you, through death and out the other side."

"I don't understand."

"You don't need to understand. Look, I'm placing the tablet in the cleft of this big rock fountain, deep, deep down, where the water gushes out. Do you see? Don't let your mind lapse yet. Look and remember!"

"Yes, I see," said the Monkey-Prince, in a hollow, distant tone. "The golden tablet is deep in the cleft of that rock, where the water gushes out. I see. I'll remember."

"Now I have one final thing to tell you," said Lotus-Born. "I told the others that all the world is illusion, created by mind. But for you, there is a deeper, more hidden meaning. For eons and *kalpas,* you have been plagued by a dark spot in your mind. But I tell you this, Monkey-Prince, it cannot be. Because *mind itself is part of the illusion.* That is the highest secret of *Chos,* the secret of the Perfect Ones."

"How can that be?" asked the Monkey-Prince, very confused. "If all the world is created by mind, and mind itself doesn't exist, then what is there?"

"Something new for you to think about," smiled Lotus-Born, gently. "Now I can't hold you to life any longer. It's time for you to be gone, gone, *gone.*"

The Monkey-Prince fell back, exhausted, on the snow, his eyes closed and his head spinning. "Yes," he whispered.

"If you ever need me in the future, you can call to me at sunrise or sunset, remember that. Now you must pay attention one last time," commanded Lotus-Born in a loud voice.

With great effort, the Monkey-Prince opened his eyes and tried to focus on the luminous figure.

"HRI!" shouted Lotus-Born, with a voice like thunder.

In a tremendous rush, the Monkey-Prince felt his life-force and consciousness exploding up through his body, and out the top of his head, in an infinite burst of light.

Now the Monkey-Prince was in the realm of Shinje, lord of death.

Dissolving, dissolving. Earth sinking into water. Water into fire. Fire into air. Air into ether. Ether sinking into air. Air into fire. Fire into water. Water into earth. Earth sinking into water. Water into fire . . .

Blackness. No thought. Non-being.

Then gradually, like a body rising to the surface after

a dive in a deep pool, consciousness resumed. But how, and where? The Monkey-Prince looked around, confused. Yes, he was still in the clearing. There was the great chasm caused by Black Shen's death cry. There were the newly flowering magnolias. There was the magical rock fountain, where the tablet was hidden. But no one else was there. Where was Lotus-Born? Where was Yeshe. Where was he? Was he alive, dead? He didn't understand.

Perhaps he hadn't really died, after all; perhaps he had merely swooned, while the others went to build the great temple in Dza. Well, he'd remedy that error, soon enough, when he could get a knife. A knife . . . he had been badly wounded by Black Shen. Why did he feel no pain, nothing at all? Was he lying on the ground, delirious? He couldn't be sure.

If only he could visit the camp of the dear Har tribespeople, one more time, before the welcome release of death came, at last. If only he could see the face of his beloved Drolma, once again, at peace, at rest.

Instantly, without warning, the clearing in the forest was gone, in a whirl of multicolored light that made the Monkey-Prince blink. He opened his eyes again, and suddenly, there was the Har camp! All of the people were clustered in the trampled snow, outside the headman's tent. He could hear the sound of wailing, and realized that they were mourning the death of Drolma, and the baby. He quickly elbowed his way through the crowd—strange that no one seemed to notice his arrival or presence—the husband, father and murderer. Strange.

Even stranger was what he saw on the ground. There were Lotus-Born and Yeshe, seated glowing in the center of the crowd, chanting in low, deep voices, "Oh nobly born Monkey-Prince, Drolma and Infant Tashi, use this occasion of your death wisely, to realize the Secret of *Chos.*"

The chants were addressed to three corpses that lay on fur rugs, on the snowy ground. The Monkey-Prince looked down at the body of his infant son, Tashi, with the great, gaping wound in his heart, and tears sprang to his eyes. But the other two corpses were weird, like nothing he had ever seen before. Stretched out on one fur rug lay a large, dead male ape, covered with fur, with purple snout and buttocks, and only a stump where his tail should be. On the other fur rug lay the grotesque body of a small, female demoness, with round breasts, sharp fangs, and eyes that bulged beneath closed lids.

What was this—a mock funeral, a joke? Where was Drolma's body? Why were they addressing this ape by *his* name? The Monkey-Prince rushed over and shook Lotus-Born roughly by the shoulder.

"Stop it," he cried, "stop calling these two monsters by *our* names! Where is Drolma's body? What is happening to *me?*"

But Lotus-Born completely ignored the cries and the rough shaking, and peacefully continued his chant.

"Make him stop," screamed the Monkey-Prince hysterically to the headman and the gathered Har tribespeople. "This is terrible! Where is Drolma's body? Make him stop this evil chant!"

The Monkey-Prince ran around the crowd, shaking people and shouting into their faces, to attract attention. But the people looked right through him, as if he didn't exist. They gazed mournfully at the corpses, and listened to the low chant.

Startled, the Monkey-Prince realized that he *didn't* exist. He was dead, a corpse, a ghost. The people couldn't see him, because he was no longer there! The monstrous shapes on the ground were part of some horrible vision.

Terrified, the Monkey-Prince raced away, into a blinding swirl of multicolored lights. Scurrying, confused, through a blazing arc of fiery blue light, that roared with a sound louder than thunder. Running toward a comforting disc of cloudy white light that sang sweet music—almost plunging into the misty white. Then suddenly, quite clearly, he could hear Lotus-Born's voice, "Be not fond of the dull white light . . ."

Racing away, confused again, toward a torrent of glistening white light, like the foam of a waterfall—but unsure if this was the light in Lotus-Born's warning, or the *other* one, and feeling uncertain and angry. Then drawn toward a billow of gray smoke, thinking to sit and rest his eyes. But inside the smoke, he saw a world of people and other creatures, tortured and in agony. Their bodies were tied to flaming stakes, dipped in boiling butter, tormented by fiendish devils, trapped by razor-sharp shards of ice, gnawed by beasts—yet the bodies writhed and begged for mercy, and did not die. Horrified, the Monkey-Prince raced away from this smoky hell realm.

Toward a bright-yellow beam of light, like a ray of intense sunshine, too strong, too dazzling. Nearby, another ray of dull-bluish light, like a cloudy summer day. The Monkey-Prince ran toward the misty light, hoping to rest himself. Instead, he found himself back at the Har camp. Lotus-Born and Yeshe still sat there, chanting to the three terrible corpses, "Be not fond of the bluish-yellow light. It is your own ego, wishing to return. Be strong and abandon it . . ."

The Monkey-Prince took one last lingering look and raced away again, toward a halo of blazing red light, guarded by two immense peacocks. But as he approached, the red light grew too powerful, and he shied away, toward an arc with a dull-red glow. As he peered through the second arc, he saw strange creatures, human in shape, but with great, huge bellies, and tiny little mouths, the size of pinholes. They wept and sobbed for food and drink to fill their cavernous, swollen bellies, but although nourishment was available, they couldn't pass it through their minuscule mouths.

The Monkey-Prince was repelled, and scurried away from these frustrated creatures, toward a light of shimmering, glistening green. Once again, he shied away from the area of green which was too intensely bright, and sought out the dull green of a shadowy forest. But the forest was filled with battling armies, that hacked at each other with bloody axes and knives. Frightened, the Monkey-Prince ran again.

Now all the lights whirled around him, in a blinding rainbow of white, blue, yellow, red and green. He could see *lha* and demons, dancing like flames in the rainbow lights. In the center of the glittering swirl was an area of calm, dull blue. The Monkey-Prince plunged toward it, but found animals snarling and devouring one another. Once again, he retreated and could find no rest.

Now demons were emerging from the blinding rainbow, haloed by multicolored flames, and holding skull cups of blood. Each had numerous animal-shaped heads, and many blotchy arms and legs. Swaying and stomping, the immense demons danced with their terrifying mates, whose multiple heads were shaped like wolves, vultures, scorpions and pigs, and were covered with mats of writhing serpents. Their ornaments were human skulls, and battle axes wreathed with intestines. Their many mouths uttered loud, fearsome crackling sounds and growls. Their hands grasped and clawed. The huge demons danced toward him, filling the horizon in every direction. The Monkey-Prince stared, frozen for a moment, then raced away.

Suddenly, the intense lights and visions disappeared. The Monkey-Prince found himself in a vast expanse of twilight gray, with enormous winds that buffeted him about, and loud crashing sounds. The wind blew him to a great red cliff, overlooking a pounding sea. A freezing rain poured down upon him, then the wind blew him again. It carried him to a tiny, peaceful temple. The Monkey-Prince crawled inside, to rest and calm himself. He felt so cold, so tired, frightened and miserable—so terribly and totally alone. Then the wind blew again.

To the court of Shinje, lord of death. The great, black bull-headed one sat on his mighty throne, counting out pebbles of white and black, to decide the fate of souls. The wind blew again.

There was darkness, and a mighty hailstorm, and the shouts of something chasing him through the black night. The wind blew again.

To a clear, glassy lake. The Monkey-Prince looked down, and saw no reflection. The wind blew again.

To a landscape of glittering, golden temples, that blinded his eyes . . . to an immense forest filled with revolving circles of fire . . . to a landscape of misty rock caverns . . . to a treeless, desolate plain . . . to a gloomy village, where the sound of wailing could be heard . . . to a clear lake, with mating swans . . . to a flowery meadow with mating horses . . . to a tree-lined shore with mating cattle . . . to a city filled with large, handsome houses.

Here the wind stopped. The Monkey-Prince wandered through the deserted streets of the city, in crisp, clear daylight, wondering who inhabited these fine houses. He looked inside one mansion, and saw it was a doghouse, filled with mating, yelping dogs. He looked inside another, and saw it was a henhouse, with a great, proud rooster rapidly mounting each of the hens. Another was the nest of insects, with an immense, bulbous queen depositing eggs, which her buzzing servants would tend. Another house was a stable, with the smell of hay and dung, and the grunts of mating horses, cattle, pigs and yaks. Another dwelling held a collection of wild animals. Mating tigers growled and heaved. Mating songbirds added straws to their nests. Mating rabbits uttered tiny squeals of pleasure.

Then he saw two deer, a doe and stag, nuzzling at one another, in preliminary play. The Monkey-Prince thought of Drolma, and felt drawn to the doe; he wanted to run inside that house and embrace her.

Then he heard Lotus-Born's voice in his mind, "Be not drawn to the animal realms . . ."

He reluctantly moved away from the doe, and peered inside the next house. There he saw two people, locked in embrace. The man was an indistinct blur. But he could see the features of the woman with startling clarity. She was an ordinary and worn peasant matron of Dza, with thick, knotted hair, narrow slitted eyes, flat nose and high, flat cheekbones mottled with a light sprinkling of pockmarks. Her earlobes were extremely elongated by heavy rings of turquoise and gold. Her breasts and belly were flaccid and drooping, from bearing many children. She grunted and sweated, as the man heaved on top of her.

The Monkey-Prince felt a sudden burst of powerful sexual longing for this woman. He moved forward to get a closer look.

Suddenly, from the wet organs, between her straining thighs, came a beam of clear red light, which played across the Monkey-Prince's lips and throat, with a resonant musical tone that sang *AH*. The Monkey-Prince felt the light piercing his throat, and felt his own vocal powers grow strong and sonorous, as he briefly lost all thought and merged his own voice and being in a pure chord, with the musical red light, *"Aaaaaah."* His voice grew more and more powerful. He could sing with the tone and clarity of a *lha! "Aaaaaaaah."*

The singing light faded, and the Monkey-Prince moved next to the bed, where the couple thrusted and writhed. He wanted this woman. Wanted to hold and fondle her. He could feel his own organ straining and swollen with passion.

He wanted to push this other, shadowy man away, and thrust himself inside her. Thrust, thrust, deep inside . . . then suddenly, without warning, his own semen burst from his body, and spurted out in a great white arc, onto the woman.

At that moment, the Monkey-Prince's being collapsed in, upon himself, and dissolved into nothingness. And his essence entered the womb of the woman who lay upon the bed.

Part II

According to Tibetan history, the king asked Lotus-Born to bow down, but Lotus-Born shot a great bolt of lightning from his fingertips, and the king knelt down in awe. Thus Chos came to rule in Tibet.

VI

Nearly a year had passed since Lotus-Born built the great temple in Dza, and departed to his own land of Hind.

In the small farming village of Tser, on the treeless western slopes of Dza valley, there had been celebrations because the worst hardships of winter were finally past, and it was time to greet the new, Wood-Monkey year. In Dza, each year is named for an animal, and one of the five elements.

The new year isn't the only recent arrival. A new son has been born in a large farming family of Tser. This family had many offspring (perhaps *too* many), so there was no extraordinary rejoicing, yet the warm-hearted parents were always glad to welcome one more into the bustling household.

While her mother and sisters-in-law prepared mo-mo dough for the new year, the new mother sat holding the baby inside the large stone farmhouse, near the oven. She was a somewhat worn matron of Dza, with thick knotted hair, narrow slitted eyes, flat nose and high, flat cheekbones mottled with a light sprinkling of pockmarks. Her earlobes were extremely elongated by heavy rings of turquoise and gold. Her breasts and belly, under her wool chuba robe, were flaccid and drooping from bearing many children.

One of the sisters looked down at the baby. "I think he resembles my second son; don't you?"

The new mother shrugged. "I don't know, maybe a little, but your boy is plump. Look at this new one—his arms and legs are so long and thin, he looks just like a little monkey."

"A monkey!" cried the sister. "What luck, we can name him after the new year. Wood-Monkey. How does that suit him?"

Just then, the baby puckered up his little face and began to cry. This baby's cry was unusual. It wasn't the disagreeable squall of most babies. Instead, it had a sonorous, almost melodious tone—more of a song than a cry.

All of the women in the big, warm kitchen smiled, as the baby crooned a long *aaaaah,* of protest.

"I don't think he likes that name," said the shriveled old mother-in-law, a big grin highlighting her toothless, sunken face. "With that fine voice, he wants to be known as a singer of epic tales and great songs. We should call him Monkey-Song."

The baby stopped fussing, and managed to focus his eyes on his wizened grandmother. "You see, he likes *that* name," said the old woman, smugly. "Let him be Monkey-Song from now on."

Monkey-Song was a happy, agile child who enjoyed racing with his cousins up the hillsides, to chase the family's small flock of goats. His long, slender limbs were always covered with a proud layer of boyish grime, and his clothes were ragged hand-me-downs from cousins and brothers who had romped through the brambles. His long legs were full of tricks, and his long arms were full of mischief.

Everyone in Tser liked Monkey-Song, because of his grace and friendliness, and because of his beautiful voice. Even as a toddler, he could hold a note with perfect pitch. He was always in demand, when the family sat around the oven in the winter, reciting tales of kings and warriors, demons and *shen.*

"He sounds like a golden bell," said his father.

His rich, clear voice didn't keep him apart from the bustling life of a farm household. The stone house was large, by Dza standards, with small, dirt-floored rooms, warmed by metal braziers, leading from the big, central kitchen. Large wooden cupboards held the family's clothes and other possessions. Outside the kitchen was a big courtyard, heaped with straw, where the family's goats and pigs were kept at night, guarded by large mastiffs. In the courtyard was also the household shrine, tended by the women of the family, who burned scented juniper wood and tsampa flour, to placate the local *lha* and demons.

The house was clustered near the handful of others that

made up the village of Tser. Around the village, and up the slopes, was common grazing land, for the cattle. The farmland was worked in strips, by the men of the individual households. The local nobleman plowed the first furrow, in the spring. Each family held hereditary leaseholds on strips of land, owned by the big estate of the local nobility.

Families could buy and sell this land, so that some became rich through fortune or guile, while others lost their land and became poor hired hands. But all of the households were related through blood or marriage, and helped each other in times of great need. Everyone pitched in for the planting or harvest.

After the harvest, the uncles, fathers and brothers took part of the crop into the center of Dza Valley, for the great trading festival on the willow-lined riverbank. They would exchange barley, dried fruit and news for meat, hides and gossip.

Monkey-Song played with his cousins, brothers and sisters, using stones and sticks as toys. They herded the flocks, and collected dung and nightsoil for fuel and manure. They helped dig irrigation ditches in spring, picked wild berries in summer and chopped straw during the harvest.

Yet Monkey-Song was vaguely aware that he was different from the other children. It wasn't just his voice, or his unusually long, thin arms and legs, or his ability to dream up tricks and mischief. What made Monkey-Song different were strange feelings, deep inside him. Things bothered him. He felt sad when the men hunted on the hillsides for deer. He often couldn't swallow deer meat, though his appetite was usually ravenous.

His head bothered him, too. There was an aching, cloudy spot, deep inside his mind, that bothered him even in the midst of romping and play. He also felt lonely. This was very odd, because his life was full of family and chums. Yet he always felt that someone very important and dear was missing. He never mentioned these feelings to anyone, not to his closest cousins and friends. He knew they wouldn't understand—he, himself was confused! They would only ask silly questions, or jeer.

So Monkey-Song smiled and joked, romped and scampered, played tricks and hid, and sang and sang through his boyhood. Everyone in the village loved this good-natured (if somewhat naughty) and talented boy.

As Monkey-Song grew and changed, so did Dza. The brilliant sunlight, dark-blue sky and clear air still reflected the gemlike colors of the soaring, treeless mountains, capped with ancient glaciers, and the grassy slopes and orchards of the fertile river valleys. However, the valley was growing more crowded, and the men came home from the harvest festival with fabulous tales of the Great Temple.

After Lotus-Born subdued all the demons and *shen* of Dza, and taught them the ways of *Chos,* things changed dramatically. The Great Temple rose with magical speed, and everyone who saw it was filled with awe. The men of the family said it was a marvelous place, quite unlike any of the rough stone buildings of Dza.

Mighty pillars supported rooftops plated with shimmering gold. Four huge gates faced the four directions, and banners and prayer flags flew in the breezes. The high walls were covered with murals and silk banners that told the legends and tales of Dza and *Chos.* The doorways and roof-beams were of colorful carved and painted wood, and the windows were covered with pure, translucent silk. There was a magnificent altar, worked with gold and precious stones, which held the golden tablet. The rumor, throughout the valley, was that most of the gold and jewels had come from the cave of Black Shen himself. This gave the temple an even greater feeling of power and mystery.

Now that there were no more obstacles, the king could invite great scholars and teachers from the hot southern land of Hind. These wise men and women crossed the sky-high mountains during summer, when the glaciers that block the *la* passes had receded. The king housed them comfortably in the temple, and many chose to remain and teach, rather than face the arduous journey back to Hind. Thus their numbers gradually increased.

The king spent much of his time with the teachers, engrossed in *Chos,* and in the magical new power of the written word. He encouraged the nobility to learn the doctrine of *Chos,* and the marvelous skills of reading and writing. Many *shen* flocked to the temple, to learn the power of the Secret. Often they stayed on, to become disciples and servants of *Chos.*

Gradually, this began to affect all of Dza. Hunting, games and feasts were still the favorite entertainments, but new pastimes also became popular. The scholars of Hind invited the people to meetings at the temple, where they taught the doctrine, and demonstrated their mental agility through lengthy debates, on fine points of the inscriptions. Much of this was beyond the understanding of the people, yet a visit to the temple always filled them with wonder. Some of the nobles and *shen* also learned the techniques of debate, and were able to join in discussions with the wise ones.

Priests who were skilled in ritual began the performance of elaborate ceremonies and *pujas*. The doctrine was chanted constantly, in deep, sonorous tones. Great musical instruments were made of bone and brass, large, thundering drums, tremendous horns with throaty, eerie tones that could be heard for miles in the clear air of the valley.

On special days, the wise ones of the temple dressed in crimson robes and walked in slow processions through the valley, chanting deeply with the pounding drums and great horns. These processions were suppose to pacify the *lha* and demons, to attract the people to the temple, and to find a mysterious person who had been promised by Lotus-Born, before he left Dza.

When the people mourned his departure, Lotus-Born told them not to weep, because someone special would soon appear to take his place as abbot of the Great Temple. So far this wonderful person had never been found, and eventually many people forgot both the prophecy and the dynamic *Chos* of Lotus-Born. The processions became a ritualized form of entertainment for the people.

Yes, Dza was changing, less wild than before, more ordered and formal. The royal household and nobility were strengthened by contact with foreigners, and the new ability to read and write. And especially by the Great Temple. Here was proof of the power of *Chos* that no one could dispute. The temple became a central focal point of the kingdom, in a way quite different from the independent, reclusive old *shen*. Now people hesitated to joke with a king who possessed the mysterious power of the written word, and who controlled the mighty temple.

* * *

One bright day, in early autumn, when Monkey-Song was eleven years old, the people of Tser had a chance to see all this for themselves. A runner came from the King's fortress, with dirty rivulets of sweat streaking his sun-burned face. He gratefully accepted a bowl of *thukpa* soup at Monkey-Song's house, while all the local people clustered around. The runner drank his soup and wiped his face. He had run for two days, he said, to tell the people in the western part of the valley that a great procession from the temple would soon arrive. The village should make preparations to receive and feed the wise ones.

The mothers and aunts looked around the cluttered kitchen in dismay. There was always enough food for guests, but it was simple and coarse, surely not suited for wise ones! Where would they sleep? They must be used to soft carpets, not hard pallets and rough wool blankets.

Monkey-Song wasn't worried about guest accommodations. He danced around the kitchen when he heard the news. "How exciting," he cried. "I've always dreamed of seeing the Great Temple, and hearing the wonderful music!"

"You'll hear the music," said the runner, "but you won't see the temple. It's far away, in the center of the valley. They don't carry it with them, you know."

"Maybe they'll take me back with them, to see the temple. I'll sing for them, and they'll take me along."

"Maybe you'll go without supper tonight," said his grandmother, "as punishment for such boastful talk."

Monkey-Song fell silent, for Granny usually carried out her threats. But his face glowed, and his body wriggled with excitement.

The entire village scrubbed and tidied, cooked and prepared soft straw mats. Nothing happened.

"That man was probably a liar," grumbled Granny. "A vagabond beggar, tricking us for a bowl of soup."

On the third day, they heard news from the village below Tser that the procession had arrived! The wise ones would spend the night in the next hamlet. Tomorrow, they would be at Tser in time for the midday meal. The preparations became a frantic bustle, as additional cookfires were lit in the courtyard, to steam the mo-mo and boil the soups and great pots of buttered tea.

The big cupboards were ransacked for the very best clothes. Monkey-Song received a new set of hand-me-downs, which increased his excitement. He scurried wildly around the sprawling stone farmhouse, watching the preparations, bumping into people and knocking things down, stealing fresh mo-mo from the pots, and earning an abundant harvest of whacks and slaps.

"The boy won't calm down," complained his mother. "You'd think the wise ones were coming just to see *him!*"

"It's the music that excites him so," said his father. "Don't worry, he'll behave."

"They're coming to take me to the temple," the boy whispered to his closest cousins. "You'll see."

"Make him stop saying that," complained the cousins to Granny. "He'll bring demons by talking so proud."

No one slept well that night, and Monkey-Song didn't sleep at all. He was up well before dawn, shivering in his new chuba robe, waiting for the procession to arrive. He wouldn't come inside when the family ate their breakfast, shortly after sunrise.

"Come and eat," ordered his mother. "They won't be here for hours yet. You'll be so weak by midday that you won't even enjoy the music."

"I want to wait here, Mother," he said. "I don't want to miss them. They're coming to fetch me, and take me with them, Mother."

"Why do you say such crazy things?" asked his mother, annoyed. "The wise ones have no use for a ragged lad like *you*. They're all foreigners, nobles and *shen*. Even if you're clever, a peasant boy doesn't belong in the Great Temple."

"I know, Mother, but please let me wait here, I don't want to miss the music."

His father brought him out a bowl of soup and curds.

Actually, Monkey-Song didn't know *why* he was talking like that. It *was* crazy. His strangeness was starting to show! The wise ones didn't care about *him*, he knew that. They'd never take him to the temple. Yet he wanted it so badly that it almost seemed real. It was because of those feelings that bothered him all the time. He was sure that the wise ones had some secret that could help him. He felt certain that once he heard the beautiful temple music, it would resonate inside him, and clear the awful, cloudy feelings inside his mind. He wouldn't feel that strange loneliness any more. He was sure of it!

They could hear the music in the distance, long before they could see anything. When the procession finally arrived, it was magnificent beyond anyone's expectations. The people, all dressed in their best clothes, stood lining the narrow, muddy rut that was the main street of Tser, and watched in silent awe. The wise ones were so numerous, more than anyone had the skill to count. Many of the foreigners had shaved heads, and their bald pates gleamed in the bright sun. Their chuba robes were of brilliant crimson, like flowers—or blood. Most impressive of all was the shining image of the great gold tablet. The leader of the procession held a smaller replica of the sacred original, up high, for all to see. The sun caught the golden inscriptions, with glistening fire.

When Monkey-Song saw it, he jumped up and down, pointing, and cried, "Look, look, the Secret, *the Secret!*"

The leader looked at him, in surprise, before his granny hushed him up.

The wise ones were chanting to the beat of the great drum. Now the music of the mighty horns began. No one in the village had ever heard anything like these eerie, wailing tones, which sent chills up the people's spines. It wasn't a melody, it was an echo of the vast natural beauty of Dza—drumbeats like thunder, great horns like mighty mountains, and high-pitched horns whose voices soared to the dark-blue sky.

As the horns sang, Monkey Song added his own voice as a harmonious chord, in a long, drawn-out *aaaaaaaah*.

Once again, his granny tried to hush him, but the boy was so intent on his song, with flushed face and gleaming eyes, that his father gestured to leave the lad alone. The leader of the procession looked at Monkey-Song, puzzled, and signaled for the music and chanting to stop. The wise ones fell silent, and the only sound that could be heard was the crackle of cookfires and Monkey-Song's bell-like *aaaaaaaaah*.

When the boy realized that everyone was staring at him, he stopped singing and looked around, ashamed and frightened. They'll really whack me now, for interrupting the procession, he thought. I'd better get away.

92

He scampered past his granny and ran through the gate of the courtyard, where he stumbled over a heap of straw and landed flat on his belly—right into one of the cooking fires!

"Aaaaah!" he cried, in pain and fear.

The people of the village and the wise ones all gasped in horror and surged toward the gate, to pull the boy from the fire. Falling into a fire was no minor or rare accident in Dza. The child would die a painful death, or at best, be horribly scarred for life!

Then the people gasped again, as they ran inside the courtyard. For the flames were no longer there! A fountain of pure spring water rose up from the center of the fire, drowning the flames, and drenching the boy who sat there, surprised and unharmed.

"That is the power of Lotus-Born," cried one of the wise women, a glowing woman of Dza. "Only he can bring fountains out of the solid earth." The aging but still beautiful woman pulled the boy out of the chilly water. "What's your name, child?" she asked him.

"Monkey-Song, ma'am," he stammered, with chattering teeth.

"I'll bet you're a mischievous little monkey," she smiled.

"Yes ma'am." Now I'll really get it, he thought.

The glowing woman put her arm around his soaked, shivering body. "I want you to do something for me," she said. "I want you to try to read these inscriptions on the golden tablet."

"But the boy can't read, madam," interrupted his mother. "No one here has that power."

"Let me try, Mother," said Monkey-Song. He looked at the tablet and squinted his eyes. The squiggly lines certainly meant nothing to him, yet as he stared at the tablet, a strange song began to form in his mind. Should he sing?

"Try," said the glowing wise woman.

The boy sang, "All the world is illusion, a magic show created by mind." His clear voice rang through the village. "That is the secret of *Chos.*"

Monkey-Song stopped singing, and looked around to see if anyone was angry. The wise ones were all on their knees, in their crimson robes, in the muddy, rutted street of Tser. Some of them had tears in their eyes.

"We want to take your son with us, to the Great Temple," said the glowing woman. "He is very special. We've been looking for him for a long time."

"Take Monkey-Song with you?" cried his mother. "He's only a child. He likes to run in the hillsides, and play tricks. He doesn't belong in a temple!" His mother and granny began to sob. Soon the whole family and the entire village were in tears.

"We'll take good care of him. He'll play with children of the nobility, and he'll come to visit often," promised the glowing wise woman.

"At least let me get him some dry clothes," cried his mother, "and pack his favorite blanket, and the food he likes."

"Do let me go, mother," begged Monkey-Song. "I want so badly to hear the music and see the Great Temple."

Monkey-Song loved the temple, at once. After the wise ones found the boy, the procession returned directly to the center of Dza Valley, chanting the doctrine triumphantly, in deep voices, blowing the mighty horns and beating the great drums all along the way. The people from all the farming villages gathered along the narrow, muddy roadway to stare in wonder. "They say that the successor to Lotus-Born has been found up the valley," they murmured among themselves.

Monkey-Song wasn't really sure what had happened, but he knew that he was having a grand time, as he danced along with the wise ones, adding his own clear voice to the chant, though he knew none of the words. They reached the temple late in the afternoon of the fifth day, when the sun made fiery glints on the golden rooftops. Monkey-Song's eyes widened, and he fell silent. It was more wondrous than he had ever imagined. If only his parents and cousins and granny could see it!

At first they wanted to take away his brand-new set of hand-me-downs, and dress him in red temple robes. But Monkey-Song began to protest and cry. He had just gotten these clothes, and they were practically *new*, with hardly any torn or worn places. Those red robes looked hot and cumbersome. How could he run around, burdened by all that wool?

"There won't be so much running around here, you know," said one of the wise ones.

94

The officials all looked at him in surprise. He should be in the temple, leading the ceremony, not in the courtyard, dealing with strays. The limping yogi looked at him with large, bulging eyes and made a pleading gesture. Suddenly, Monkey-Song realized that this was no yogi. The tiny ragged person was a woman, a rare yogini!

Small, round breasts peeked out of her torn clothes. Her filthy robe and grimy features were those of a young woman from one of the kingdoms near Dza. Her matted knot of hair was caught up with a woman's turquoise brooch. Yet the trident staff of Shiva marked her unmistakably as a wandering pilgrim, rather than a madwoman, or an escaped serf.

The yogini looked at Monkey-Song with those bulging eyes, and she smiled, revealing a mouth full of pointy little teeth. The smile made Monkey-Song feel very light-hearted and giddy. The strange little yogini seemed so *silly*, compared to the solemnity of the temple. Monkey Song began to laugh, a deep, hearty, joyous laugh. She looked so *funny*, standing there, with her big eyes, her tiny body, her limp, her rags, her staff. What a ridiculous person to interrupt the most important ceremony of the year! Monkey-Song laughed and laughed, until there were tears in his eyes. The temple officials watched him, alarmed, while the yogini looked at him with her wide eyes, and puzzled grin.

Suddenly, as he laughed, Monkey-Song felt the years of loneliness fall away. How could that be? Was this wisp of a girl the important person that had been missing all his life? Impossible! Yet the aching loneliness, the void that plagued him, was gone. Quite suddenly, it was filled by a little limping yogini with big eyes—*strange!* Unreal, yet it *was* real. He wanted to hug the girl, kiss her (perhaps make love to her—*very* strange!). All of Monkey-Song's sense of mischief suddenly returned. He wanted to take this girl by the hand, and run and romp with her on the hillsides. He wanted to get rid of these uncomfortable red temple robes. He wanted to laugh and play tricks, and be *free*.

He wanted to throw off his serious duties, and run with this girl, romp with her, and hold her tightly against his body. Why *this* girl, this funny-looking creature? There were so many beautiful young noblewomen in Dza, who wanted him, yet they never interested him. He was always so intent on his studies. Now he wanted to throw away his texts, forget his doctrinal debates, rituals, ceremonies, duties. He wanted to take this girl and run freely across the hillsides. Run. *Run.*

The temple officials, angered by the interruption, and worried by Monkey-Song's response, tried again to push the little yogini out of the temple grounds. Monkey grabbed onto the girl and shoved the officials away.

Just then, the aging wise woman, Yeshe, came out of the temple to see what was happening. The officials made questioning, uncertain gestures. Yeshe looked at Monkey-Song, and at the girl.

Suddenly, Yeshe also began to laugh with quiet joy. She hugged Monkey-Song, and hugged the puzzled girl. "Let them be," she said to the officials. "He's been waiting for her, for a long time."

The officials stared in amazement, as their young abbot and the ragged, limping yogini ran off together, hand in hand, through the great temple gates.

VII

Despite the limp, which caused her body to lurch to the side as she ran, the little yogini moved with quick grace, as she and Monkey-Song ran hand and hand out of the great east temple gate, both surprised and giggling.

They collapsed, laughing on a grassy meadow, outside the temple walls. "Thank you for rescuing me from those priestly bullies," she said. "I think this is a bad time to visit your famous temple."

Monkey-Song grinned sheepishly, "The temple is closed this week, but you couldn't know that. You're a wanderer from far away. They shouldn't push you around. Do you always travel alone, with just your bundle and staff? Isn't it dangerous? Aren't you afraid? Who are you? Where do you come from? How did you get that limp? Have we ever met before?"

"Wait, wait!" she cried. "One question at a time. I am Drolma. I come from a kingdom southwest of Dza. The *shen* of my kingdom say that my limp is from an arrow wound, in a previous embodiment. I heard about your wonderful temple, and I came on pilgrimage, to see it. It *is* lonely, wandering without company, but so far there has been no danger. I feel safer in the wilderness than among the people of my own kingdom." She grimaced. "But who are you? Won't you get in trouble for running away like that?"

"*Drolma?* The name sounds so familiar. . . . No, I can't get in trouble at the temple. I'm the abbot there."

"The abbot! You're the famous young abbot with the beautiful voice? I was hoping to catch a glimpse of you." The little yogini stared at him in awe, while Monkey-Song puffed up with youthful pride.

"But why do you say that it's safer in the wilderness

than in your own kingdom? Aren't you afraid of wild animals, bandits, avalanches and storms?"

"At least those things are honest," she sighed. "Wild animals want a meal, bandits want gold. Storms and rockslides kill without thought. But people are devious. They smile as they destroy you."

"You're so bitter. Why?"

"It's a long, dreary story. You should go back to the temple. I'll make my camp for the night at some caves nearby. I'll come back when the temple is open to pilgrims."

"I don't *want* to go back to the temple. It's stuffy and dull. I want to stay with you. Tell me your story, please!"

"If you can keep a secret."

Monkey-Song nodded assent.

"I am Drolma. I am princess of the small mountain kingdom of Thak, southwest of here."

"I've heard of your kingdom—it isn't so far away. I think our customs and ways are similar. But a *princess!* Why didn't you say so? You should request hospitality and protection from our king. Why sleep in caves? You'd be welcomed at the fortress!"

"I want no hospitality from your king. Nor would he be wise to take me in—unless he craves trouble."

"Trouble? How?"

"My father, the king of Thak, is worried by a political dispute on his northern borders. He decided to ask for aid and protection from the great Eastern Empire of Gyan."

"Gyan! No wise king invites soldiers from Gyan. Their empire is so huge and powerful—they come to help, and they stay on to rule."

"My father isn't terribly farsighted," said Drolma. "He thought he could get rid of Gyan when the northern borders were pacified. The Black Emperor of Gyan agreed to the alliance, and asked for a marriage bond as proof of my father's goodwill. The Black Emperor demanded my father's oldest unmarried daughter for his harem, as price of the treaty. *I* am my father's oldest unmarried daughter."

"The Black Emperor of Gyan! How awful! I've heard that he is an evil man."

"I've met him, and he's worse than that. I've never seen such a cruel face. He keeps a trained flock of huge black crows that follow him wherever he goes. Their scream is like death. I shudder to think of it. I'll never be in his harem—I'll die, first!"

"So you escaped?"

"I was learning the rites of Lord Shiva from a wandering yogi of Hind. When he heard of my desperation, he gave me his own mendicant's staff, and urged me to disguise myself, to flee and hide. The Black Emperor is searching for me. His spies are everywhere. So far, I've escaped, but I don't know how long I can stay free, even in yogini's disguise. The limp makes me conspicuous. Shall I still request protection from your king, now that you've heard my story?"

"I don't think our kingdom is eager to tangle with Gyan," said Monkey-Song, apologetically.

"I thought not," said Drolma. "Everyone fears the rage of the Black Emperor. That's why I must travel alone, and make my camp in the frosty solitude of caves. I'd rather risk the hot breath of a hungry snow lion than the hot breath of the Black Emperor."

"You're right," said Monkey-Song, slowly. "Except for one thing. You needn't make your camp alone anymore. I'll come with you. We'll fight off the snow lions, and hide from Gyan, together. You can teach me the secret rites of Lord Shiva. I've always wanted to learn them."

"But why?" cried Drolma. "This is crazy! You're very kind, but you're the abbot of the Great Temple. You belong there! Go back! I'm not so beautiful. I'm skinny, my eyes are too big, I was born with this terrible limp. You needn't lose your head over *me!* Why are you doing this?"

"I don't know why," said Monkey-Song. "Your presence feels so good to me, so right. I just want to be with you. As soon as I saw you, all my terrible loneliness disappeared. I don't want to lose you. I'll find a way to keep you here, somehow."

Monkey-Song flashed a wide grin at the girl. "Besides, it's time for some mischief. I used to be a very naughty farm boy, you know, always stirring up trouble. I haven't played any good tricks for a long time. I miss the fun. Now that I'm a learned abbot, I want to try a really *big* trick. Let's see if we can fool the entire Empire of Gyan!"

The big-eyed yogini grinned back at him.

It was nearly dark when they reached her cave, which was hidden behind a large outcropping of rock and wild rhododendron bushes, in the hillsides behind the Great Temple. Although Monkey-Song was quite familiar with these hills, this cave was so well concealed that he hadn't known it existed.

She had already transformed it into a cozy campsite, with rocks to build a fire, and a bed of soft grass. Using her flints, they lit a flame, and cooked a supper of hulled barley, which she had begged from local farmers. This was all very novel and interesting to Monkey-Song, but also quite uncomfortable. He wasn't used to hard stone floors, cold night air, and coarse, unseasoned food. He fidgeted in the narrow confines of the cave, whose ceiling was too low for him to stand up.

"You don't seem content here," she smiled. "Go back to the temple. I'll understand. You can visit me in the daytime, when it isn't so cold."

"No, no, I'll get used to it. Teach me some secret rite of Shiva, to take my mind off my chattering teeth."

"Something to warm you up?"

"Yes."

She giggled. "You'll think I'm wicked, if I show you how the Shivites really warm themselves."

"How? I don't understand."

She climbed into his lap, wrapped her arms tightly around his body, so that her small breasts pressed against his chest, and kissed him full on the lips. "Now do you understand?" she whispered.

"Monkey-Song, Drolma, are you there?"

Monkey-Song woke with a start. At first he didn't know where he was. Then he realized that he was lying on the bed of soft grass inside the cave, his arms and legs tightly twined with Drolma's. There was a woman's voice outside, calling him.

"Monkey-Song, Drolma, don't be afraid. Come out, I must talk to you."

It was the voice of the glowing temple wise woman, Yeshe. Well, better to go out and talk to her, since she already knew where he was. But he *wouldn't* go back to the temple. Not now.

He crawled out of the cave opening. Yeshe embraced him, and handed him skins filled with food and water, a wool blanket, and some of her handwritten texts. "Monkey-song," she cried, "I'm so glad I found you. I don't want to disturb you here—I know how much this girl means to you."

"How do you know, Aunty?"

"I *know*. I just want to bring you some food, and tell you to hide carefully. The news about the runaway princess of Thak is spreading all over Dza. Everyone knows she fled in this direction. It's so hard for her to hide, she's easy to recognize. No one outside the temple knows that she's here, with you. Stay inside the cave. Learn the rites of Shiva from her—it's said she knows them well."

Monkey-Song blushed.

"No, no, there's more to it than that. Persuade her to teach you while she can. The Black Emperor is searching for her. He knows she's in this vicinity, but he doesn't know where. He's sending *Rolangs* to hunt her down, so be careful!"

"*Rolangs!* Those horrible creatures that are walking corpses?"

"Yes. The Black Emperor is known as a sorcerer. He has raised an army of *Rolangs* from the cemeteries of Gyan, and sent them stalking through this region. The stinking monsters have been all over Dza, with their flesh peeling from their bones. They move mindlessly across the countryside, tirelessly searching day and night. They are only aware of the orders that were given to them by the Black Emperor who raised them from the dead—find the limping, large-eyed girl, and bring her back to Gyan."

"How can I protect her, Aunty?" asked Monkey-Song.

"First, stay hidden. The girl is smart—she found a good place to hide. Stay in there, and keep yourselves busy with the Shiva practice. I'll bring you skins of food and water when I can. And I want you to take this." The aging, glowing woman handed Monkey-Song a triangular-shaped dagger that flashed and gleamed in the bright sunlight.

"What is it?" asked Monkey-Song. "It looks familiar."

"Yes, you've seen it in the past. It's my *phurbu* dagger. If a *Rolang* finds you here, use it."

"But *Rolangs* are already dead. How can they be killed?"

"Not like ordinary people, but if you can find a mole on a *Rolang*'s body, and plunge a dagger through it, the *Rolang* will be destroyed."

"A tiny mole? That'll be hard. You've trained me in scriptures, never in combat."

"If you're frightened, come back to the temple."

"No, it's all right. I used to aim sticks when I was a farm boy. I'll find the *Rolang*'s mole."

"I hope so. I'll bring food. Take care and stay inside."

"Thank you, Aunty, you're very kind to me."

"I'm glad to see the two of you together again."

"Again? But she's from Thak. I've never been to Thak."

Yeshe was gone. Still puzzled by her words, Monkey-Song crawled back inside the opening of the cave, with the blanket and food.

Drolma was lighting a fire for breakfast.

"Look, books and good food!" cried Monkey-Song, happily unpacking the skin. "*Tsampa* flour, and dried meat. Tea! Cheese, fruit, butter and curds. We'll have a feast!"

Drolma looked at him with large, serious eyes. "Did she have any news?"

"News? Yes, there was news," said Monkey-Song uncomfortably. "The Black Emperor knows you're in this region, though he doesn't know where. He's searching for you—with *Rolangs*."

The little yogini's face went pale.

"But Yeshe showed me how to fight them," said Monkey-Song cheerfully, "so we don't have to worry. She said we should stay inside, well hidden, and practice Shiva rites. What we did last night, was that really a Shiva rite? I mean, it was *fantastic*, and I want to try it again—and *again!* But what was the rite?"

Drolma laughed at him, despite her own fears. "You've never really experienced a woman before?" she asked him.

"No, I was always so busy with temple duties, and I never met one before you that I really liked."

"Good," she said. "You're fresh and new. You can learn easily. I was also innocent, before I met the yogi from Hind."

"Was he your lover?" asked Monkey-Song jealously. "I mean, did you love him? Do you miss him?"

"No, I didn't love him, and I don't really miss him. He fascinated me because he knew so much. If a young girl wants knowledge, she must sometimes accept teachings through her body, rather than through texts and debates. That's how learning comes to girls. Ask your temple wise

106

woman. She'll agree. But now I'm so happy to be here with you, and I want to teach you what I've learned."

She quickly stripped off her ragged, torn chuba robe and gestured at him to do the same. They sat facing one another, naked, in the dim light of the chilly cave. Monkey-Song's body throbbed with excitement.

"In the rites of Shiva, we try to achieve ecstasy," she said.

"But we achieved ecstasy last night!"

"That was body ecstasy, over in a flash. In the rites of Shiva, we try to prolong the experience as long as we can, until two beings merge into one, and we reach *total* ecstasy, beyond the mind and the self. Then we can let go and enjoy the pelasure of our body."

"I don't understand."

"You will. First let's stroke our sensitive places."

Monkey-Song reached eagerly for her small, round breasts.

"No, not there. The *most* sensitive places are here, and here . . ."

She began to run her fingers lightly across the crown of his head, between his eyebrows, along his throat, at his chest, his navel. She lightly touched his hard, swollen penis, then gently massaged the soles of his feet.

"But those are the meditation points, the *chakras*," he murmured, breathing heavily.

"They can be pleasure points as well. Do it to me."

He felt exquisite energy running through his entire body, as his hands ran across the crown of her head, between her eyebrows, her throat . . .

They heard a loud, scuffling sound outside the entrance to the cave, and stopped, startled.

"Is that Yeshe again?" he asked, annoyed.

"I don't think so," said Drolma, with large eyes staring out of a pale face.

They quickly scrambled into their chubas, as the scuffling sound grew louder. Then suddenly, there it was! On hands and knees, staring at them in the dim light of the cave entrance—a tremendous *Rolang!*

The huge, stinking bulk was blocking the only cave exit, so there was no way to flee. They could only stay and fight the creature, who lurched towards Drolma with its arms outstretched, crawling on its knees. Sickened, Monkey-Song noticed that the rough rock of the cave floor snagged the rotting flesh of the creature's lower legs, and tore it away in long shreds.

Monkey-Song quickly took the *phurbu* dagger and searched desperately for some sign of a mole on the monster's body, but in the dim light he could find no distinctive marks on the Rolang's sagging flesh. Monkey-Song stabbed futilely at various spots on the creature, but the dagger sank uselessly into the lifeless muck, up to the hilt. The *Rolang* moved toward Drolma, who crouched at the back of the cave, frozen with horror.

Now the monster was upon her, and grasped her tightly with skeletal hands. Drolma began to scream as the vast *Rolang* dragged her tiny body out of the cave.

Monkey-Song followed them, blinking in the bright sunlight. The enormous walking corpse carried the crying girl down the hillside. Over his head flew a large flock of huge, screaming crows. Monkey-Song ran after them, with his dagger, and leaped upon the creature's back, feeling the flesh give under his hands. The *Rolang* stumbled, then continued down the hill with the girl in his arms, and Monkey Song on his back.

There, *there* on the back of its neck! There, visible in the sunlight, was a large black mole, sprouting bristly hairs! Monkey-Song climbed higher on the monster's back, raised the *phurbu* dagger, and plunged it deeply into the mole. Watery blood arched and spouted from the wound. The *Rolang* stumbled and fell, and was still.

The black crows wheeled around the fallen body three times, then flew screaming to the east, toward Gyan.

"To think it was once human, a person with feelings and a family!" sobbed Drolma.

They both ran hand in hand, panting with terror, back to their cozy cave.

They stayed inside the cave as the wild rhododendron bushes that hid the entrance burst into large, crimson blooms. They ate the food that Yeshe brought them, and passed the time with the rites of Shiva. The *Rolangs* were all gone, according to Yeshe, but they weren't at peace. From time to time, they could hear the big black crows of

Gyan, wheeling and screaming overhead. They were being watched. The death of the *Rolang* had allowed the Black Emperor to pinpoint their location. He knew where they were! Ominously, they waited to see what he would do next.

Again, it was Yeshe who brought the news. Her face, lined but still beautiful, looked grave in the pale morning light. She spoke quickly. "The glaciers have receded in the *la* pass, and troops from Gyan are pouring into Dza! They've surrounded the Great Temple, and are threatening to attack the fortress, unless the girl is surrendered. Gyan has declared war, and is threatening to conquer and destroy Dza!"

"Gyan is a thousand times more powerful than Dza. They'll crush us like fleas!"

"I know," said Yeshe. "The Black Emperor sent this message with his general"—she unrolled a long, elaborately written scroll—"I'll skip the formalities, and read the main text: 'It is unthinkable that a mere barbarian woman should try to reject and elude the Great Black Emperor of Gyan. This girl, unmarriageable due to a repulsive deformity, has been offered the protection of the Celestial Empire. She will accept that protection, whether she wants to or not, as a concubine in the imperial harem. It is unthinkable that the tiny, powerless kingdom of Dza should try to thwart the desires of the Empire. Dza will surrender the runaway girl at once, or the fortress will be occupied, the royal family will be killed, the people enslaved, and all of Dza will be absorbed into the vast and mighty Celestial Empire of Gyan.' "

Drolma began to cry. "If the emperor gets hold of me now, there'll be nothing to stop his cruelty, no end to his rage. Give me that dagger. Let me save Dza and myself. You can send me to Gyan as a corpse!"

"No!" cried Monkey-Song, "I won't let you do that. Please," he pleaded with Yeshe and Drolma, "give me a little time to think."

The faces of both women were streaked and reddened with tears. "Yes," said Yeshe, sadly. "Try to think of something."

In the afternoon, a delegation of temple priests and ministers from the royal fortress came to the entrance of the cave. The priests' red robes echoed the bright-crimson rhododendron flowers, but their faces were grim.

"More than a thousand troops of Gyan have already crossed the *la* pass into Dza," said the leader of the delegation. "Our militia can defend against bandit gangs, but not against the army of Gyan. They have large, vicious-looking weapons. They're ransacking the farmhouses for food. There will be famine in Dza! They are camping by the river, fouling the water, and cutting the sacred willows for firewood. We will be destroyed! Surrender the girl, before we take her from you. She has bewitched you, she brings nothing but trouble! You belong at the temple, as abbot and guide to the people. How important is the romantic whim of one girl, compared to the well-being of the entire kingdom? Many girls enter the harems of Gyan. They survive. They are well fed, and comfortable. *The Black Emperor, himself, is coming to Dza.* He travels swiftly, through sorcery. He will be here tomorrow morning. We must surrender the girl at dawn, or his troops will attack and destroy Dza. Give her to us, before we take her by force!"

Monkey-Song looked at the delegation, who looked back at him sternly, their red robes and the red flowers glowing in the bright afternoon sunlight. He looked at the large-eyed, pale face of the girl.

"You say the Black Emperor will be *here*, tomorrow morning?"

"That's right," said the delegation's leader. "We must surrender the girl at sunrise."

"Let me have one last night with her," pleaded Monkey-Song. "I'll bring her to the fortress, and deliver her to the Black Emperor myself at dawn."

Drolma gasped.

"Is that your sacred promise?" asked the leader. "None of your farm-boy tricks. If you try to escape, Dza will suffer."

"That is my sacred promise."

"Have your last night, then, and enjoy it as best you can," said the delegation. They departed.

Monkey-Song and Drolma spent all of that day and night locked mournfully in each other's arms.

"If only I could halt the sunrise, like the tales of Lotus-

Born," sighed Monkey-Song. "But I don't have such powers. I can only sing and chant scriptures."

"You'll take me to the Black Emperor tomorrow, with the dagger in my heart," cried Drolma fiercely.

"No, stop saying that," cried Monkey-Song, "We have all night. We'll think of something."

VIII

Toward midnight they dozed. While they slept, Monkey-Song had a strange dream of a glowing man, dressed in the robes of Hind. He was standing in a flowering forest of wild magnolia trees, next to a large outcropping of rock that spouted clear water. "Don't be afraid," said the glowing stranger. "Fight the Black Emperor. I'll help you."

Monkey-Song was filled with joy. He woke with a start, then he realized that it was merely a dream, a product of his own wishing. He felt total despair, and began to weep.

The night moved on inexorably. Drolma was also awake. They made love one last time, clinging together desperately, their tears mixing freely.

"Now give me the dagger," she demanded. "It's time to prepare the sacrifice to Gyan."

"Wait a little longer," he begged. "We still have time. There's still hope."

"Very little time, very little hope," she murmured.

Monkey-Song hid the dagger, and wouldn't give it to her, even though she screamed insults at him, and pounded him with her small fists.

Shortly before dawn, they heard a scuffling at the cave entrance. It was Yeshe, lighting her way with a small butter lamp. The wise woman had been running. She was panting, and her long gray hair streamed wildly around her head. But her face glowed in the tiny light.

"I had a dream!" she panted. "Lotus-Born came to me in my sleep, for the first time in *years*." Yeshe paused to catch her breath, and contain her excitement. "He said you should challenge the Black Emperor to a duel. He said you shouldn't be afraid, he'll help you!"

"I had the same dream, Aunty," cried Monkey-Song, "but I didn't believe it was real."

"Yes, yes it's *real!*" sobbed Yeshe. *"He* is real. Lotus-Born is still alive—still thinking of Dza!"

Monkey-Song and Drolma tried to comfort the older woman. Everyone knew the story of Yeshe and Lotus-Born. Everyone knew that she still missed him, still yearned for him. Even though she kept her extraordinary beauty well into middle years, she never accepted the attentions of another man after Lotus-Born left Dza. She devoted herself tirelessly to writing down his teachings of *Chos*. They had never seen her composure stripped away like this. The dream had moved and upset her.

Yet if the dream was real, then everything was changed! They were elated. As the first deep light of dawn began to appear, the three of them made their way down the hillside.

Monkey-Song was shocked by what he saw. The sallow faces of the soldiers of Gyan were everywhere. He could see their makeshift camp strewn along the banks of the river. He could see the grotesque stumps of the sacred willow groves, cut for firewood. He could see the big, scary weapons, and the huge cooking pots devouring the produce of Dza. He could hear the soldiers' horses whinnying with dissatisfaction, as they tried to digest the tough highland grasses of Dza. He could hear the trained crows of Gyan, circling and wheeling in screaming flocks.

The sun was rising behind the eastern mountains. Where was the Black Emperor? There, there! The people were pointing to the tall mountains that guard the *la* pass.

In the clear, thin air of Dza, details can be seen at great distances. The rock formations of the hills, bare except for colored lichens, stand out sharply against the dark-blue, cloudless sky. The ancient glacial caps gleam in the brilliant sunlight, as they gradually melt through the ages, to trickle down and water the Valley of Dza. There, against the tall ice-capped mountains, the people could see an extraordinary sight, etched in miniature detail.

A flock of four tremendous crows held the corners of a thick rug. On the rug lounged a figure dressed in gleaming black. The Black Emperor had come to claim his bride.

Drolma cringed.

"Don't worry," said Yeshe. "You'll be safe, believe me."

But it was *hard* to believe, even for Monkey-Song, who had dreamed the vision himself. The dream was just a fleeting fantasy. Here in the daylight, the black-jacketed soldiers of Gyan were so *real*, with their cold, mocking faces. The

114

crows were real, the weapons were real, the figure flying through the air was real. Was he actually going to challenge the Black Emperor? Was his entire dueling strategy based on a strange dream shared by a lovelorn old woman and a desperate youth? And if the dream was just a beguiling hope, then what would become of Drolma?

There was no time to reconsider. The huge crows swooped to a landing in the temple courtyard. The Black Emperor sat with his arms folded, upon his richly colored carpet. His face was hard and narrow. His skin was sallow, and his beard was a trailing wisp. He was dressed in black brocade, in the style of Gyan, and was heavily ornamented with gold and jewels. He stared with a sneer at Monkey-Song and Drolma, who looked fearfully back at him. He looked long and hard at Yeshe. "We all meet again," he muttered, "but now you're a wrinkled old hag, while I'm newly embodied with the vigor of youth—so much for your victory. Bow down!" he thundered. "Bow down to the Celestial Black Emperor of Gyan."

Everyone within hearing bowed down, except Monkey-Song.

"And who are you, that you don't bow to Gyan?" asked the emperor.

"I am the abbot of this temple," said Monkey-Song. "Here I bow to no one."

The priests and noblemen gasped and gestured at him furiously to bow.

"So you're the talented young abbot," said the Black Emperor. "I believe they call you Gopher-Squeak. Share your skill with us. I've had a long journey and want to rest. Sing us a little song."

"I'd be delighted," said Monkey-Song, stepping forward jauntily. He began to sing in a simple peasant tune:

"They call the emperor black, but he's gray like a rat,
He sneaks through the night, eating everything in sight.
He sends his hordes to attack peaceful lands.
They rob and destroy in ravenous bands.
But Emperor Rat never will fight.
He's afraid I'll chop his tail with my knife.
He can't win a bride, except by force.
'Cause his beard's like the tail of a dead horse!"

"Stop!" thundered the Black Emperor. "What rudeness! I should have you executed at once."

All through the crowd that was gathered around the temple, there were bursts of shocked laughter. One of the ministers of Dza ran to the emperor to bow and apologize for such provocative words. "He's gone mad," said the minister. "Please don't blame Dza."

"Yes," boasted Monkey-Song, "you'll have me taken by your soldiers—you'd never have the nerve to fight, yourself."

"Be quiet," growled the Black Emperor. "I've come to fetch my new concubine. Where is she? Silence, or your puny kingdom will fall with you. Where is the girl?

"Drolma is beside me, where she belongs," said Monkey-Song. "She is my bride. Our marriage was consecrated by love."

"You *love* that scrawny, deformed thing? Such love that she still limps from your own arrows! You're so scrawny, yourself, sitting hunched all day over gibberish scriptures, or whatever you priests do. Look, your robes are all torn, and you obviously haven't had a meal in months. How will *you* prevent me from taking the girl?"

"I challenge you to a duel," said Monkey-Song, loudly. "We will fight in hand-to-hand combat. The princess of Thak will be the winner's prize."

Everyone, even the nobles, priests and people of Dza, began to laugh. It was so pathetic, so ridiculous for this slight young man to challenge the mighty Black Emperor of Gyan.

"He's gone crazy," murmured some people.

"No, the girl has him bewitched, she's a sorceress," said others.

"Let them fight, let this be settled and the soldiers go back to Gyan. It's none of our business," said others.

"But he's our abbot, he'll be killed."

The Black Emperor guffawed. "*You* challenge *me* to a duel, Beetle-Buzz?"

"If you dare to fight with your own hands, instead of hiding behind your soldiers."

"Yes, I will fight you," said the Black Emperor, "because of your insolence. I will squash you, again, like vermin. Then I will take the girl, for my own pleasure."

* * *

The crowd buzzed with excitement.

"Hurry up," snapped the Black Emperor. "I don't have time to waste. I'm busy with the affairs of the empire, and want to be away before your frigid night comes. Choose your weapon, Mouse-Tune."

"My weapon, er, I . . ." Monkey-Song realized that he had no experience with weapons. The crowd began to laugh again. This was becoming a comedy show.

"What'll it be—swords, bows and arrows, spears on horseback?"

"You can use my horse, lad," said the king of Dza.

"Horseback!" blurted Monkey-Song. "Let it be on horseback." That was good—at least he remembered how to ride, from his childhood.

"Bring my horse," called the emperor to his general.

The general, dressed in leather armor, led a tremendous black stallion into the courtyard. Its mane and tail were plaited with ribbons of black brocade. Its black leather saddle glistened with jewels set in silver. The animal pawed at the ground and snorted, while the great black crows circled and screamed overhead.

The king of Dza's groom led the royal chestnut stallion into the courtyard, gaily decorated with ribbons of every color. The young abbot and the Black Emperor mounted, and rode to the long racing strip in front of the fortress, where tournaments and games were held. The crowd followed.

"My general and your king will decide the victor, do you agree?" called the Black Emperor, from his end of the raceway.

"Sure, why not?" called Monkey-Song, distracted. The horse was quite large and nervous, and he hadn't ridden for a long time. He was having trouble finding his balance in the saddle.

The Black Emperor and Monkey-Song took up their spears. The weapon felt clumsy and heavy to Monkey-Song. The Black Emperor twirled his spear rapidly over his head, so that the sharp point glistened and flared in the bright sun.

"Let the tournament begin!" called the general of Gyan and the king of Dza.

The Black Emperor started at a gallop. Monkey-Song urged his horse forward. It was a fast runner, but the black stallion of Gyan ran so swiftly that it seemed to fly without effort. Great sparks sprang out where its hooves touched the ground. Its breath became a cloud of dark smoke.

They met near the middle of the racecourse. The hooves of the black stallion were shooting lightning. As the black horse and rider approached, they suddenly grew larger. To Monkey-Song, clinging to his saddle and spear, they suddenly loomed large as a mountain. The black stallion's breath was a wreath of fire.

Monkey-Song almost cried out and shied away in fear. But at the last moment, he closed his eyes and charged, with his spear held high. The two weapons met with a mighty crack of thunder—and both spears snapped in two.

"The first contest was a draw!" cried the king of Dza and the general of Gyan. "Let the horses rest a moment, and we'll begin a second time."

The crowd was chattering with excitement. Yeshe and Drolma had tears streaming down their cheeks.

The horses sweated and heaved, and drank buckets of water. Then the two combatants mounted again, and rode to opposite ends of the track.

Again they charged. The hooves of the black stallion shot huge boulders of hail. The crowd ran for cover. As the two riders met, Monkey-Song saw the Black Emperor transform himself into a repulsive mass of writhing snakes and dripping entrails, which made him want to vomit. Again, Monkey-Song closed his eyes and charged. The two weapons met with the sound of a tremendous avalanche. Again both spears shattered.

"The *second* contest is a draw!" cried the king of Dza, excitedly. The general of Gyan scowled and agreed.

This time the people of Dza began to shout and cheer, despite their fear of reprisal by Gyan. Their spindly little abbot had matched the Black Emperor *twice*.

"The poor boy won't last much longer," said one old matron. "Let's show him our affection while we still can!"

The soldiers of Gyan, who were busy with routine preparations for the journey home, dropped their tent pegs and joined the people of Dza in front of the fortress, to watch the contest. "He's a spunky lad," they admitted among themselves.

The horses drank copiously, and the riders mounted

again. The black stallion shot bolts of flame at Monkey-Song's face as they met. He could feel the heat blistering his skin. He averted his face and charged. The spears crashed like a mighty waterfall—and snapped.

The third contest was a draw. The fourth contest was a draw, with the clash of splintering spears. Monkey-Song was shaking with exhaustion. The king of Dza's chestnut stallion collapsed, and was replaced. The fifth contest was a draw. A sixth contest was a draw. The crowd cheered wildly.

The Black Emperor demanded more spears from his soldiers. The seventh contest was a draw. The eighth contest was a draw. The crowd was tense with excitement. The ninth contest was a draw. The tenth contest was a draw, as the sun sank down, behind the western peaks.

As news of the contest spread through the valley, the crowd grew larger. By nightfall, many of the people of central Dza and all of the soldiers of Gyan were gathered in a great mob in front of the fortress, craning their necks to watch the two riders charge, and the spears splinter, again and again.

Nobody wanted to go home for supper, no one wanted to miss the excitement. People began to light small cook-fires, and roast skewers of meat in impromptu picnics. Large skins of barley beer were passed around the crowd. The people of Dza are always glad of any excuse for parties and celebrations. Soon the crowd had a festive, holiday mood.

The eleventh contest was a draw. The twelfth contest was a draw.

The people of Dza began to offer skewers of meat and skins of beer to the soldiers of Gyan, who stood in small groups, watching. The soldiers were suspicious and hesitant at first, huddled in their padded black jackets, but they were also hungry, thirsty and cold. They joined the people of Dza around the fires to eat and drink. The soldiers began to relax and smile, and enjoy the festive mood.

The thirteenth contest was a draw. The fourteenth contest was a draw.

Enterprising traders of Dza moved through the crowd, taking bets on the winner. Most were sure that the Black

119

Emperor would win soon, but a few placed their bets on Monkey-Song, out of sentimental loyalty.

The fifteenth contest was a draw.

The night wore on. During the lulls in the fighting, the soldiers of Gyan took bone dice from their packs and taught new betting games to the people of Dza. Soon the whole crowd was filled with gambling fever. Gyan against Dza, Dza against Gyan. Everyone felt jovial and relaxed. There was more barley beer and lots of laughter. The hostile strangers of Gyan were becoming fine drinking and gaming companions!

The sixteenth contest was a draw.

People were telling stories and jokes, "Did you hear the tale of the scoundrel who called himself Cock?" asked one old storyteller. "He robbed all the king's jewels, and the king shouted to his guards, 'Grab cock, grab cock!' The guards were confused and reached into their pants to grab their own cocks. The guards had a fine time, playing with themselves, and the thief got away with all the king's jewels."

The soldiers of Gyan roared with laughter, and the people smiled with pleasure, though they had heard this old story many times before.

The seventeenth contest was a draw.

It was very late at night. Most of the small children had lost interest in the fighting, and were fast asleep, wrapped in felt blankets. The soldiers were teaching the people some funny, dirty songs of Gyan, in their thick sing-song dialect. Everyone was drunk.

The eighteenth contest was a draw.

It was nearly sunrise. The Black Emperor was growing alarmed. This skinny barbarian boy resisted his powers and shattered his spears again and again, all through the night. Why? What sorcery did the lad possess? There was no sorcerer in Dza who could match the Black Emperor!

The Black Emperor felt weary and confused. He knew that his powers were growing dull with exhaustion. The limbs of the great black stallion were trembling. The tattered priest should have died before sunset. He should be back at the Celestial Palace in Gyan, taking pleasure—and revenge—with the girl. Something was terribly wrong!

The nineteenth contest was a draw.

The Black Emperor had sent a crow back to Gyan to

fetch his mighty ceremonial spear of solid bronze. Surely the little wretch didn't have the power to shatter a bronze spear with one of wood! As the sun rose behind the eastern mountains, it silhouetted a solitary crow, carrying an immense spear of solid, gleaming bronze.

It was the morning of the second day of the contest. Monkey-Song was so sore and tired that he could barely keep his seat in the saddle. He had worn out four horses, and shattered nineteen spears. He knew that he would collapse soon. How much longer could this go on?

"Please," he silently prayed to Lotus-Born, "help me."

The weary king and general called the twentieth contest. Monkey-Song groaned when he saw the emperor's giant bronze spear. Yeshe and Drolma stood near the raceway, their arms clasped around each other, fearfully.

The riders charged. As the black horse and rider approached, Monkey-Song could see nothing but a huge ball of flames and sparks—and that spear. The tremendous spear flew right toward him like a bolt of lightning.

Monkey-Song dodged and lifted his own spear to protect himself. The two weapons collided, and the bronze spear exploded like a mighty volcano.

The people stared in silent awe.

"The twentieth contest is a *draw!*" shouted the king and the general.

The Black Emperor got down off his horse. His face was pale and sweaty. His hands shook. He called his general to his side, and announced in a loud voice, "There is sorcery in Dza, vile, unwholesome sorcery. The Celestial Empire doesn't allow sorcery in the border kingdoms. Sorcery is evil and must be wiped out. Therefore I order my soldiers to attack and destroy the unscrupulous people and kingdom of Dza. *Attack!*"

"Attack, men!" echoed the general to the soldiers who were lounging in the crowd, in front of the fortress. "Take your weapons and attack!"

The soldiers looked bleary-eyed at the people of Dza, who looked fearfully back at them. The soldiers looked at the dying cookfires, the empty skins of beer, the dice, the storytellers, and the sleeping children wrapped in felt. Mothers began to gather up their babies and hurry away.

"No, don't wake the little ones," said one of the soldiers, in a slurred, drunken voice. He was a burly man, who had eaten and drunk and played heartily, all night long. The big soldier stood up, unsteadily, and faced the general. "Beg your pardon, sir, but we *won't* attack. These are good folk, they are our friends."

The Black Emperor and his general began to threaten and curse.

The people cheered and embraced the soldiers of Gyan. They invited them to stay in Dza and marry their daughters. The soldiers returned the embraces and accepted the invitations.

Yeshe, Monkey-Song and Drolma hugged each other and wept.

The Black Emperor stared at them, his face crimson with rage. He snarled between clenched teeth, and made an elaborate gesture with his hands.

Suddenly three huge crows dived down, out of the sky. Before anyone could stop them, the three birds snatched up the Black Emperor, his general—and Drolma, and flew quickly away to the east, toward Gyan.

The people and soldiers were stunned into silence. Monkey-Song looked up, toward the sky. He could hear Drolma screaming, see her struggling in the beak of the giant crow, until the birds flew over the eastern mountains, and were gone.

IX

Monkey-Song ran futilely toward the east, after the crows. But his body could no longer stand the ordeal, and he collapsed on the ground in a faint.

"He needs food and rest," said Yeshe.

The priests of *Chos* carried him back to the temple, where he slept and ate in gloomy silence. In a few days he felt better.

"I must go to Gyan, Aunty," he told Yeshe. "I must find her."

"The journey to Gyan is impossibly long and difficult, without the Black Emperor's sorcery to speed you."

"Perhaps Lotus-Born will help me again."

"Who knows?" she shrugged. "There have been no more visions, no more dreams. What will you do if you reach Gyan? You're no match for the emperor's guard."

"I *know* that!" he cried fiercely. "But what should I do, sit and chant scriptures?"

"*I* sit and chant and write scriptures," she sighed.

"You sit and chant, and write, and grow old," said Monkey-Song. "You should have followed Lotus-Born to Hind, years ago. Now you copy his prayers, and weep whenever his name is mentioned."

Yeshe gave him a hurt look and left Monkey-Song alone in his small, ornate bed alcove. He jumped out of bed, stripped off his temple robes and began to dress for a long journey.

A delegation of priests met him as he left the eastern temple gate. "Please don't go," they begged. "The people need you as their abbot. They respect you. You give them strength. They love you more than ever, since the battle. Don't abandon them."

"The people don't need an abbot who is wrapped in sorrow," he said, brushing them aside.

He sought out some of the soldiers of Gyan, who were settling into their new homes as sons-in-law and farmhands of Dza.

"Please," he said, "help outfit me for the journey, and tell me the way to Gyan."

"We'll gladly outfit you for the journey," they said. "We have no more need for this traveling gear." They filled his pack with dried foodstuffs and equipment, a tentroll, a small ax, a water bottle, flints, and the padded black jacket of a soldier of Gyan.

"But we can't tell you the way. We never traveled across the land by ordinary means. The emperor always whisked us through the night by sorcery. We've heard that the journey is terrible. You must cross the trackless northern desert!"

"Don't go!" cried the people, when they heard this. "We *need* you here. You belong to *us!* You'll never survive the journey. There are bandits and wild beasts. No one ever makes it across the northern desert. You'll die in the wasteland. You'll never find the princess, never rescue her, *never* come back to us. Don't go!"

"Please don't cry for me," said Monkey-Song, touched. "I can't sing any more songs for you, until I complete this journey. I'll survive somehow, you'll see."

The people followed him all the way to the foothills of the eastern mountains, pleading with him not to go. Then night fell. They became cold and discouraged, and returned to their homes.

Monkey-Song spent that first night camped in the foothills, mournfully enjoying the peace and solitude.

But the loneliness soon grew oppressive, as he tried to make his way over the eastern *la* pass. As he climbed higher into the mountains, the air grew thin, and very cold, even at midday, though the strong sun burned his face, and made his eyes water. His breath came in short, shallow pants. All vegetation was gone, except for the gray and rust-colored lichens. His body was weakened from the long months of hiding in the cave, and the ordeal of fighting the Black Emperor. His legs ached and threatened to give way under him. The big pack was an enormous burden on his back. He was used to carrying nothing heavier than a few religious texts or ritual implements. Yet despite the weight, it was obvious that his scanty supply of dried food would soon be gone.

"It's hopeless, go back," whispered a small, frightened voice, deep near the dark spot in his mind. But he ignored the voice and the fear, and trudged on.

At least water was no problem, here in the mountains, because the path followed along a steep-walled river canyon, with a thick rind of ancient glaciers on the upper banks. He was agile enough to scramble down to the icy, rushing glacial stream, and keep his water bottle filled. Occasionally, he saw fish in the water, but he didn't catch and eat them, for fear of offending the water *lha*.

Sometimes several streams of melted icewater converged in a series of mazes, so that he couldn't know if he was going in the right direction, through the tangled skein of narrow, rocky gorges. He only knew that if he went *up*, he was still approaching the *la* pass.

When he finally reached the summit, he found a frozen, inhospitable realm, so high that the sky was a luminous dark blue, and the stars shone brightly, even at midday. Gasping for breath, he added a stone to the small pile of rocks which rare travelers had placed as offerings to the *lha* of the pass. He could see the clouds of the valleys far below him, shot through with flashes of summer lightning.

He felt suddenly elated. How marvelous to see the storms from above! He felt like a *lha*. But his elation vanished as he plodded down the other side of the mountain range. Dza is a high, grassy valley, with flowering plants and sparse trees that are considered sacred gifts. Monkey-Song had never seen any other landscape. As he climbed down the last low range of flat-topped, tablelike hills on the other side of the mountains, he suddenly longed for the stark beauty of Dza—for here was a land that looked like a scene from hell. He had reached the northern desert.

The air was blazing hot in the daytime, and freezing cold at night. The ground was crunchy, gritty sand, with baked crusts of salt. A constant strong wind carried dust and sand swirling through the air. It burned his eyes, and made him choke and cough. Worst of all, there was nothing. No one. No villages, no field, no rivers. No trees or grasses, no animals or birds. There were occasional low clumps of spiny, grayish vegetation. There were scorpions and many stinging flies. There was the constant swirl of dust and salt, sometimes so thick that he could only see a few feet ahead. There was the sound of his feet crunching endlessly through the sand. There was the heat that made his head spin and the cold that made him shiver through the night, wrapped in his tent roll. There was *no* food and water. He was in the trackless northern desert.

There were only a few shreds of food left in his pack, yet it felt heavier than ever. There were only a few mouthfuls of water left in his bottle. He tried to ration it, a sip at a time. He hadn't sweated or urinated for more than a day. His tongue felt thick and leathery in his mouth. He kept seeing bright flashes of light. The sand grew soft and powdery underfoot, and he kept slipping and losing his balance, sometimes lying in the sand for many minutes before he could get up. He wasn't sure which direction he was going. The dust was so thick, and he was so confused. At times he came across his own tracks in the powdery sand. He was going in circles.

He hacked at the spiny vegetation with his ax, and tried to suck at the gummy sap, but the taste was so bitter that it nauseated him. He retched, though there was nothing in his stomach to vomit. The dust was coating his eyes and ears, his nostrils and the inside of his mouth, with a papery, stinging film. He grew delirious, and tried to keep up steady conversations with Drolma, Yeshe, his granny, cousins and Lotus-Born. This was hard because of the sand in his mouth. He stumbled, fell and landed in his own footprints of the previous day, nearly covered by blown sand. He had gone in a circle again.

They came moving across the sand like a vision, on stately camels, and found him lying there in the dust, babbling.

They were the vicious bandit tribe of Nor, who hide out in the desert. They slung Monkey-Song and his pack on one of the camels, and swayed off toward their stronghold in the east. They tried to revive the half-dead wanderer with some of their own water, in order to get news and gossip, before they robbed and slaughtered him.

Toward nightfall, they reached the strewn clumps of rounded boulders and low desert shrubs that marked their hidden oasis. They rode through an arch created by two tumbled, wind-sculpted slabs of rock, and entered the protected stone ring that held the camp of the bandit chief of Nor.

They unloaded Monkey-Song and his pack, as if they were skins of flour, and threw them at Nor's feet. Nor was a grimy, fat man, whose belly protruded out of his rough wool robe. One eye socket was an empty, dull-red pit. He had a scrubby beard, and very few teeth. The toes of one bare, crusted foot were missing.

Nor scratched his belly slowly and tried to brush away the thick flies of the camp. He burst out laughing when he saw Monkey-Song, and nudged at him with the toeless foot. "What's this?" he guffawed. "You're out wandering so late! Your mother will get angry when you're not home for your supper."

"I'm lost, sir," said Monkey-Song, weakly. "Please thank your men for finding me, and giving me water. I would've died out there."

"You might die anyway," said Nor, "and the contents of your pack will be fine thanks for the men. Let's see what you have in there." Nor tore open the pack greedily, obviously hoping for the gold and jewels of a trader. He rummaged around inside.

"Just an ax, flints—all with the seal of Gyan. Are you from Gyan, boy? You don't look it."

"I'm from Dza, sir. The Black Emperor of Gyan has stolen something very valuable from me. I want to get it back."

"Stolen from *you!* He also stole from *me*. Do you see my eye, do you see my toes? No, you *don't* see them, because that turd emperor took them in a petty dispute over a few trinkets. I *hate* him."

"Then perhaps you'll help me, sir," cried Monkey-Song eagerly. "I matched the emperor in a duel twenty times. I'm going to Gyan to challenge him again. Help me, please!"

Nor and his band roared and choked with laughter. "The sun has you babbling, boy," laughed Nor. "Twenty times, what a joke!"

"It sounds crazy, but it's *true*. Please, give me safe passage to Gyan."

"You're the best storyteller I've met in years," smiled Nor, belching and scratching his flyspecked beard. "I like a good tale, and you don't have *anything* in that stupid

127

pack worth taking. Sleep here tonight. Eat and drink with Nor. Tomorrow I'll give you some skins of water and food—and a camel. That should get you to Gyan. If you kill the Black Emperor, come back and tell me all about it." Nor laughed again, and fished around in his nose with thick, dirty fingers.

The moon was rising. "Come on, let's eat," said Nor.

Monkey-Song looked at Nor. The sun—or the moon—*had* affected his mind. Suddenly, instead of the filthy bandit chief, he saw a glowing man of Hind sitting in front of the desert campfire, his jeweled arm resting on a large rock that spouted clear water. . . .

Monkey-Song ate ravenously, pausing only to brush the thick clouds of buzzing flies from his food. His sleep was deep and dreamless.

At dawn, Nor yawned, stretched and scratched at the fly bites on his rank, sweaty body. He nudged Monkey-Song with his toeless foot. "Eh," he growled, "this isn't the day for a long gentleman's sleep. Get up and get going!"

Monkey-Song woke from a very sound sleep. He still felt exhausted. His body wasn't used to such rigors. His stomach rebelled at the bowl of flyspecked, curdled camel's milk that was given to him for breakfast. He suddenly felt very weak and nauseous. The dark spot in his mind throbbed painfully. He was quite ill from the ordeal in the desert. He wanted to rest, to sleep in the quiet, cool shadows of his own bed alcove at the Great Temple. But he was far away from Dza, and far away from anyone who could comfort or care for him. How miserable he felt! Nor nudged him again with his foot.

When the band finished breakfast, a large camel was saddled and loaded with provisions, and pointed to the east, toward Gyan. Monkey-Song thanked Nor and his men, weakly, and climbed onto the beast. The camel swayed with a sickening motion under him. Blackness kept passing in front of his eyes. Monkey-Song held on as best he could, as the animal moved east, into the heat of the desert. Nor and his band stood watching him go.

The bright sunlight and heat rapidly increased his vertigo and disorientation. Consciousness slipped away into darkness. With a low groan, Monkey-Song slid off the back of the camel and fell into the sand with a soft thud.

Nor cursed under his breath. "Saddle up another camel," he growled to his men.

They looked at him in surprise.

"Quit looking!" he bellowed. "Have I turned into a pretty girl, or something?"

The men guffawed.

"I feel like some action, that's all. Been sitting around the camp too long. Look at that baby. He'll *never* make it to Gyan, unless someone holds his hand all the way. Saddle up a camel, I'm going to Gyan!"

With Nor's help, Monkey-Song made it across the desert to the border of Gyan. There were no more fainting spells. Nor's cure was very simple. Whenever Monkey-Song swayed unsteadily in the saddle, Nor delivered a swift kick with the toeless foot.

"The baby can't even stay awake," Nor grumbled.

Along the way, Nor kept up a steady stream of vigorous scratching, and stories about the bandit's life—and lovelife. Monkey-Song haltingly tried to explain the doctrine of *Chos*.

"You see, it's all illusion, created by mind," he said earnestly.

Nor kicked him hard.

"Ouch!" cried Monkey-Song.

"Was that kick an illusion?" guffawed Nor. "Lemme tell you about a pretty little illusion that I kidnapped near Taxla . . ."

When they reached the border, Nor stopped. "Can't go no farther," he mumbled.

"Why not?"

" 'Cause if Emperor Shit catches me in Gyan, he'll take my other eye, and all my fingers, toes, balls, ears, nose. We aren't exactly chums."

"I know," said Monkey-Song, with forced cheer, "but don't worry about me, you can go back with the camels. We've passed through the desert now. Look, there are trees here, and streams. I'm feeling much better. Just tell me how to get to the palace. I'll be fine."

"Camel crap," said Nor. "What'll you do when you *get* to the palace, and the guards catch you? What about *your* fingers, toes, eyes and balls?"

"I don't know," said Monkey-Song, worried. "I guess I'll figure it out when I get there."

"Baby doesn't even have a *plan!*" cried the bandit chief, exasperated. "Nor has to do *everything* for baby."

Nor fished around in a crusty, ill-cured leather pouch, inside his greasy robe. He finally extracted a filthy little brown pellet. "Here, eat this when you get to the palace," he muttered.

"Dung?" asked Monkey-Song, looking at it, amazed.

Nor roared with laughter. "Just eat it, baby, and stay out of trouble. Gimme my camel back now. Gotta get to the camp before my men steal everything." With a final kick, Nor shoved Monkey-Song off the camel, threw the provision bags at him, and wheeled around to the west, back into the desert.

Monkey-Song watched him go. He suddenly felt very alone, and his eyes were still bothering him. In the distance, everything shimmered. Nor's dirty, tan robe took on the glow of a silken robe of Hind—and next to him appeared the mirage of an outcropping of rock, spouting clear water.

Monkey-Song looked at the strange pellet again, and tucked it into the little pouch that hung from his belt. At least he was out of the desert now, that was a relief.

The countryside of Gyan looked rather pretty. They had been going steadily downhill, losing altitude as they crossed the desert. As Monkey-Song climbed down the low line of jagged hills that marked the border of Gyan, he found himself in a pleasant, green, well-watered country, with none of the highland splendor of Dza.

The sky was a pale, watery blue, dotted with fat clouds. The sunshine felt mild and warm, and the lowland air was rich as thick cream. There were lush grasses, trailing vines and fragrant shrubs of delicious, cool green. Gnarled trees dotted the landscape. He could hear the songs of birds, the rustle of small animals, the drone of insects, and water trickling in creeks and streams. The air felt moist, though the hot winds that blew in from the west still carried the dry, acrid dust of the desert.

Dressed in the black padded clothing that he had borrowed from the soldiers of Gyan, Monkey-Song moved inconspicuously through the countryside. He passed mud-walled, tile-roofed villages, the pigsties, chicken coops, and flooded rice fields of Gyan.

Even though he wore the clothes of their country, no one spoke to him, or offered food or shelter. The people seemed quite aloof and suspicious of strangers. This was very different from Dza, where any outsiders—and their news and gossip—were always welcomed with warm hospitality. Still, he was glad that no one tried to talk to him, because his speech was quite different from theirs, and would give him away at once.

Frequently, the large black crows flew overhead in flocks, watching everything with their sharp eyes.

He traveled quickly. In a few days, he passed through the countryside, and entered the huge, bustling city. He was astonished by the thick, milling crowds, the constant noise, the smells of cooked food and the stench of open sewers, the swarming traffic. He had never imagined anything like this! It looked like an anthill. He was especially surprised by the small, three-wheeled handcarts, which allowed the people to move their bundles quickly. There were no such modern wonders in Dza, where all burdens were carried on the backs of people and animals.

Overhead, the black crows wheeled and spied, constantly. Their cries could be heard even over the roar of city noises.

Food vendors were everywhere, selling bowls of hot, steaming noodles, and fragrant little dumplings and rice cakes. Monkey-Song's mouth watered, hungrily. He had eaten so little recently, and his bones stood out sharply. He wished he had some of the little gold coins of Gyan, to buy a meal. But no time for feasting now. He moved through the thronging main streets, toward the center of the city. Soon he was at the mighty walls that guarded the palace of the emperor.

Even for one used to the Great Temple of Dza, this was an awesome sight. The immense walls, lookout towers, gates and pillars were made of thick slabs of black marble, veined with iridescent hues. The high rooftops were covered with gleaming black tiles, trimmed in gold work. Everything was decorated with ornate carvings and scrollwork of bright-crimson lacquer. On the huge gates, the emperor's crest was an immense shield of black, gold and lacquer.

Through the gates, Monkey-Song could see the black metal drawbridge that spanned a deep moat. Inside, there were magnificnet gardens, filled with large cypress and fruit trees, gurgling fountains and waterfalls, and flowers that wafted lovely scents. Monkey-Song could glimpse the charming pavilionlike buildings of the palace, made of black marble, with gold and lacquer work, set cunningly among the gardens. Trained flocks of songbirds flew among the large trees, guarded by crows who wouldn't let them escape.

It was like a scene from a heavenly park, set in the midst of the thronging city—except for the screaming, spying crows overhead, and the burly, fierce-looking guards, dressed in black, red and gold brocade. They ringed the palace, and stood clustered at the gate, with their hands held in readiness on their big, menacing swords.

One of the guards noticed him peering through the gate. "What are you doing?" he snarled. "You know the emperor doesn't like to be watched!"

Monkey-Song pointed to his mouth and shrugged, in the gesture of one who is deaf and dumb, and tried to walk casually away. But the guard followed him.

"Hey," he called, putting a thick paw on Monkey-Song's thin shoulder, "there are no dummies in the emperor's army. I don't believe you. I think you're a spy! The Black Emperor doesn't *like* spies. He eats their lying tongues for his supper."

At least I'm inside the palace, thought Monkey-Song glumly, as two large guards roughly tossed him into a tiny, windowless room at the base of one of the watchtowers. It was filled with the refuse and stink of previous prisoners. He tried to find a place to sit in the muck, but the ground in the tiny room was covered with filth. Monkey-Song pounded at the walls in despair. Then he remembered Nor's pellet. He nearly gagged on the odorous, gummy morsel, but forced it down.

Everything swirled around him, in rocking waves of light and dark. Then everything grew still. Monkey-Song looked around. The room had *changed*. It was a vast, immense cavern, covered with repulsive hills of excrement. But that didn't matter, because a long, low rectangular exit was suddenly visible beneath the tremendous door.

Monkey-Song ran quickly out of this opening, into the light and fresh air, before the room could change back to its original, confining shape.

He was outside now, in the fragrant air of the garden, but it was also changed. Each flower and grass blade was tall as a house, each tree the size of a mountain. The songbirds were larger than eagles, the fountains were like spring torrents. The delicate palace pavilions were the size of fortresses. Everything had grown, and was much, *much* bigger. How?

Two guards walked past him. Their footsteps were loud as thunder. They were the size of tall pine trees. Monkey-Song tried to hide. He didn't want to be captured again, and thrown back in that stinking room. But the guards passed him by, as if he didn't exist.

Then he realized. Everything wasn't bigger. Nor's pellet had made him much, *much* smaller, the size of a small insect, the size of a flea. Monkey-Song laughed a tiny little laugh, and scampered across the vast meadows of the palace lawns, toward the tremendous pavilions.

Running, running through immense caverns of black marble, massively decorated with lacquer and gold, and hung with enormous canopies of silk brocade. Running, running, looking for the emperor's harem. Monkey-Song scampered under locked doorways, climbed towering stairways, forded mighty puddles.

Then he found a golden door guarded by great fat, jeweled eunuchs—the harem.

Inside were huge, voluptuous women, lying partially nude on mountainous couches. Their breasts were round hills. Their hairy parts were vast meadows of long, black, shiny grass. Their arms and legs were stately tree trunks.

They gossiped and laughed with cavernous mouths, in deafening voices. They played enormous musical instruments, like crashing storms. They wallowed like buffaloes in black marble pools, the size of lakes.

Monkey-Song began to feel very aroused by these mountainous maidens, until he noticed their feet—their repulsive, deformed little feet. Each woman had the feet of a small child, swathed in white silk bandages, and stuffed into tiny black velvet shoes, decorated with embroidery. Monkey-Song noticed with disgust that the women couldn't walk on their miserable little appendages. They could only hobble painfully on the small, bound feet that are fashionable among the upper-class women of Gyan.

Where was Drolma? Monkey-Song scampered through the vast, echoing harem, searching. He finally found her, seated on a black velvet couch, in a simple room of very black marble, lighted by flaming torches that hung from the walls.

She looked very beautiful, but terribly unhappy. Her shabby, comfortable yogini's rags had been replaced by stiff, cumbersome robes of thick brocade. Heavy jewelry pulled at her earlobes and burdened her small wrists and neck. Her thick, flying hair was pulled into an elaborate, stiff knot. Her large eyes bulged with fear, as she stared at the two men who were kneeling on the floor, examining her feet.

Her feet. Why were they looking at her *feet?*

The two men were talking. The echoing effect of his tiny size, and the thick, sing-song court dialect of Gyan, made it difficult to understand what they were saying. Monkey-Song strained his ears.

"The emperor is displeased by the new concubine's gross, barbarian feet," said the older, larger man, holding up Drolma's small foot. "He wants her to be more beautiful."

"But how, honored doctor?" asked the younger man. "She is already grown. We can't shrink flesh."

"I want to try a little experiment," said the older man, who must be the court physician. "You will assist me. It will be good practice for you. You see, I think if we break the long bones of the feet in two places, here and here, we can fold the foot back upon itself, and bind it with silk. When it heals, her foot should be quite attractively childlike."

"But it might not heal," said the assistant. "Such things often gangrene."

"Then we amputate," shrugged the court physician. "She's only a minor barbarian princess, of no special beauty —and the emperor wants to make sure her wandering days are over."

The two men laughed.

"No!" cried Drolma.

With a panicked lunge, Monkey-Song leaped upon the
134

robes of the court physician and began to climb laboriously up the side of his body. It was the steepest, roughest climb he had ever made. The brocade robe gave no footholds. He could only cling tightly to tiny wrinkles and snags in the garment, and pull himself painfully up. Several times the doctor gestured eloquently, to illustrate a point, and nearly dashed Monkey-Song to the black marble floor, far below.

"Fetch the silver tools," said the doctor to his assistant. "We'll begin at once."

Up, up, bit by bit. Up to the hips, the waist, the armpit, the shoulder. Now he was at the doctor's neck. What could he do to stop him?

The assistant brought a small hammer, and silk bandages. Drolma began to cry.

In desperation, Monkey-Song leaped into the doctor's ear. He had no weapon but his voice. He would sing. Yes, he would *sing*.

"*Aaaaaaaaaaaah,*" sang Monkey-Song, long and loud.

"What's that?" said the doctor, startled and rubbing at his ear, nearly crushing Monkey-Song.

"*Aaaaaaaaaaaah,*" sang Monkey-Song, farther inside the ear canal.

"It's sorcery!" cried the doctor, alarmed.

"What's the matter?" asked the assistant. "Shall we begin the operation?"

"*Aaaaaaaaaaah,*" screamed Monkey-Song, as loud as he could.

"Stop!" cried the doctor. "I can't stand this. It drives me mad!"

"*Aaaaaaaaaaah!*" bellowed Monkey-Song, right at the doctor's pulsing eardrum.

"Stop!" screamed the doctor. "*Stop!*"

The worried assistant ran out of the room to get help. The eunuch guards came running into the room, and with them came the Black Emperor of Gyan.

"I was taking my afternoon pleasure," sneered the emperor. "What is this interruption? Unskilled doctors lose their hands, you know."

The court doctor ran around the room, bellowing and batting at his head.

"*Aaaaaaaaaaah,*" screamed Monkey-Song, over and over again.

"Has he gone mad, or is this some sorcery?" asked the emperor, grabbing the doctor to look at him.

"Sorcery, sir," gasped the assistant.

Monkey-Song saw his chance. He raced to the edge of the doctor's shoulder. Gathering all his strength, he made a long, agile monkey's leap across the huge gap, onto the emperor.

"I feel better now, thank you, sir," panted the doctor.

Monkey-Song rummaged quickly through his tiny pack. Where was his ax? He found the weapon, and swiftly climbed up a strand of the emperor's beard, to his ear. The emperor swatted, thinking it was lice, but Monkey-Song was already running up the tunnel of the ear, to the throbbing drum.

Hack, hack with the ax, into the eardrum.

The emperor screamed with pain and surprise. Monkey-Song was drenched and nearly carried away in a fountain of blood.

Hack, hack with the ax, into the taut membranes of the brain. Hack. *Hack.*

The emperor fell on the floor, writhing, blood gushing from his ear.

Hack. Hack. Hack.

The emperor was still.

In the confusion that followed, Monkey-Song made his way up to Drolma's ear, and whispered the whole story to her. She smiled slightly, her large eyes lighting up.

The entire palace was in an uproar, without the emperor's leadership. Confused people ran back and forth, bellowing orders that no one obeyed. During that chaotic night, they managed to slip outside the palace gates, the princess limping in stiff brocades, with tiny Monkey-Song perched, clinging to her neck.

When will I get my size back? he wondered. *Will I get my size back?* Did Nor forget something?

The leaderless crows screamed and flapped aimlessly in the dark sky. Drolma moved quickly through the city, hiding in the shadows of buildings. When they reached the sleeping suburbs, Monkey-Song suddenly spotted a figure lurking in a courtyard.

It was a fat, grimy figure, whose belly protruded from

a rough robe. He sat on a small pony, and led another horse by a rope halter. He stared at them with a single bright eye.

"Nor!" cried Monkey-Song in a tiny voice, jumping up and down on Drolma's shoulder. "It's Nor!"

Nor gestured at them from the darkness. "I heard Emperor Crap had a little accident," mumbled Nor. "I came to watch the fun. Also, I forgot to give baby a present. Where *is* baby, anyway?" Nor peered intently at Drolma's robes.

"Here, *here*," cried Monkey-Song, as loud as he could. "What about my size?"

"Your size? Yeah, baby, that's what I forgot. Good thing I remembered—I almost went off on a long raid. You could've stayed a flea forever—or until your girlie got mad and swatted you." Nor choked and coughed with laughter at his own joke.

"What should I do?" cried Monkey-Song, impatiently.

"Do? Oh yeah, eat this." Nor held out a minuscule bit of the same brown, gummy stuff. "Oh shit, I *dropped* it," cursed the bandit, searching in the dust of the courtyard with his toeless foot.

Monkey-Song clenched his tiny teeth and fists angrily.

Drolma found the bit on the ground and handed it carefully to Monkey-Song, who popped the odorous morsel quickly in his mouth.

Rolling waves of light and dark. Monkey-Song tumbled off Drolma's shoulder, and resumed his normal size.

"Thanks, Nor," sighed Monkey-Song.

They quickly mounted the ponies, the bandit chief on one, Monkey-Song and Drolma on the other. They rode swiftly through the countryside of Gyan, and reached the border before dawn.

Then came the long, hot ride across the desert, to the bandit camp.

"If I give you horses, food and water, can you babies make it back to Dza yourselves?" asked Nor. "*Your* king doesn't love me either."

"We can make it," said Monkey-Song and Drolma, "but we'll miss you."

"Horse dung, baby," snorted Nor. "You and girlie can have *lots* more fun without me around!"

As Monkey-Song and Drolma rode away from the bandit camp, the strong desert sun played tricks on their eyes again. When they looked back, to wave a final goodbye, they both briefly glimpsed a mirage of a glowing man of Hind, standing beside an outcropping of rock that spouted clear water.

X

They reached the sheer, scarp face of the mountain range that surrounds Dza Valley, and camped and rested before they began their ascent.

The climb was difficult. The little ponies were used to running swiftly through the desert sands. They had never climbed the narrow, treacherous mountain paths. This was work for goats or donkeys, not ponies! Several times, their hooves slipped as loose shale gave way under them.

They reached the thin, cold air of the summit, and added two stones to the little mound of rock offerings, to thank the *lha* of the pass. Monkey-Song noticed that his stone, placed on the journey to Gyan, was still at the top of the pile. No one had traveled this way since then. They both felt the light-hearted exhilaration of climbers who finally reach a remote mountain peak.

Because the pass is considered the border of Dza, Monkey-Song impulsively used his ax to carve a small inscription into an impressive solitary pillar of rock. It commemorated his victory over the Black Emperor of Gyan.

"Few people will ever see this," he said to Drolma, panting with exertion in the thin air, "but let the border of Dza be properly marked, so Gyan will show more respect in the future."

They began their descent into the winding maze of gorges that led back to Dza. It was late summer, and the thick, ancient rind of ice that covered the mountain peaks was melting rapidly. It flowed in small riverlets and waterfalls, down the sides of the canyons, to the rivers at the bottom, which were deep and rushing with fresh water.

At times, the canyon walls were so high and steep that the swollen river was a small, meandering blue ribbon, far below.

"Do you know the way through these canyons?" asked Drolma apprehensively, as her pony cautiously picked its way along the narrow trail that gradually went down toward the river. "I hope we're not lost."

"There's no *right* way," said Monkey-Song. "You just follow the trails *down,* and finally you get to Dza."

As though his words had triggered a response in the bowels of the mountain itself, there was a sharp, sudden jolting movement of the ground. An earthquake. Drolma cried out, startled. Then the shaking stopped, and everything was still—for a moment.

Suddenly they heard a rumbling sound up above. The earthquake was sudden and quick. It was over now. But it had loosened a tremendous chunk of melting ice, which came bouncing down the side of the mountain, tearing loose rocks and boulders as it fell. *An avalanche.*

The ponies whinnied and shied as the mass of ice and rocks fell from above, and threw horses and riders off the trail, over the edge of the cliff, into the river canyon—into the abyss.

Falling, *falling . . .*

Hitting the water with a loud, painful *thawk,* that caused every bone to cry out in agony.

Choking, gasping under the churning, rushing river water, unable to breathe, unable to fight to the surface with battered, broken limbs.

Suddenly something soft and gentle wrapped itself around Monkey-Song and Drolma, and dragged them down, down, to where it was quiet, dark and deep. Down, down, struggling and suffocating . . . down, down until blackness overtook their minds.

They awoke somewhere silent, dim and soft. They couldn't really see, hear or feel anything. It was a deep, gentle limbo.

Was this the realm of Shinje, lord of death?

Something pale and shapeless came slithering through the deepness, and wrapped itself gently around their bodies. They floated, cradled in the quiet dim. Now some sensation was returning. They could feel pain shooting through their limbs, which had been badly injured by the fall. As if aware of their discomfort, the soft shapeless thing began to gently massage all the muscles of their arms and legs. It uttered a low, crooning hum.

Monkey-Song lay back, and began to relax. Where were they?

They felt no craving for food, drink, breath, or each other. They felt no cravings at all. They were aware that their limbs were gradually growing less sore. They were healing. The creature was taking them somewhere, but where? Why?

The serpentine thing floated them through endless caverns and passageways. Time passed, timeless time. They could dimly sense their pathway, by watching the vague shadows grow slightly lighter, then a bit darker. But they had no idea where they were, where the shapeless creature was taking them. They relaxed in the softness of the dim, gentle deep.

Occasionally they saw other pale, sinewy things floating past them—mostly they saw nothing. They rested and relaxed. Time passed. Timeless time, as shapeless as the thing that carried them along, humming a soothing, tuneless croon, all the while.

Swaying back and forth, cradled in soft folds, swaying and flowing through timeless time. The creature seemed to have a head that guided its direction, but did it have a mind? Where were its eyes, feelers, mouth, some semblance of animal life?

Then Monkey-Song realized that this was no animal, no beast of the river. This was a *naga,* a serpentine water *lha.* They were floating through the *naga* realm.

When any land creature falls into the water, it is the *naga* spirits who decide whether it will perish or survive. When a fisherman goes out in his boat, it is the *nagas* who give him a bountiful harvest to feed his family—or give him only an empty net and an empty belly. It is the *nagas* who rule the waters of the universe, and a *naga* that cradled them in soft folds. But where was it going, and why? How long had they been floating in the *naga* realm?

Time passed. Soft, healing, timeless time.

Suddenly, without warning, the creature released them. They floated upward, rapidly. Up through the quiet deep —into a torrent of rushing river water.

Water. Harsh and churning, burning their lungs. They gasped and choked, and began to thrash with their arms and legs. Their limbs were strong and whole again. The creature had healed them! Quickly, they swam to the surface of the river, and made their way to a grassy bank, lined with old willow trees.

Wet, but not tired (for they had rested *so* long), they climbed onto a small, sandy beach, strewn with rocks.

Where were they? They looked around, and suddenly realized that they were near the center of Dza, on the banks of the river that nourished the whole valley. The *naga* had healed them, and brought them home.

They threw their arms around each other, filled with joy. Monkey-Song looked happily into Drolma's face, and she looked at him. Then they both stepped back, startled by what they saw.

Drolma's face suddenly reminded Monkey-Song of Yeshe. Why? Then he realized. Drolma's hair was streaked with gray. There were small wrinkles around her eyes and mouth, creases along her forehead and neck.

When Drolma looked at Monkey-Song, she saw the same thing. Gray hairs, and the lines and wrinkles of age.

Much time had passed in the *naga* realm. They were *both much older now.*

"We're *old!*" cried Drolma. "What should we do?"

"I don't think there's anything we *can* do," said Monkey-Song. "The most powerful sorcerers have no cure for passing time. Let's go to the temple. I want to see Yeshe."

"We don't know how much time has passed," said Drolma, "or if she's still alive."

Apprehensively, they walked to the temple, not sure what they would find. Yet it felt good to be on the land again. It felt good to be home. Despite their sudden aging, they both felt strong and energetic. Their spirits began to rise. They were safe. They were alive. They were home.

The gate of the temple was guarded by a young priest in red robes.

"Who are you?" he asked the disheveled pair, suspiciously.

"I am Monkey-Song, abbot of this temple."

"Don't make crude jokes," said the young priest. "Monkey-Song went to Gyan decades ago, and never came back. If you're beggars looking for a meal, go around to the kitchen in back."

"How many decades have passed since Monkey-Song went to Gyan?" asked Drolma.

"You want a history lesson with your meal?" asked the young priest. "Nearly thirty years have passed since our beloved abbot left Dza. No one has ever replaced him."

"Thirty years!" cried Drolma, mournfully. "Then I'm a woman over fifty years old! My entire youth is gone."

Monkey-Song hugged her consolingly. "What about Yeshe?" he asked. "Is she still alive?"

The young priest looked at them, puzzled. "Why so many questions? What *do* you want?"

"I want to see Yeshe," said Monkey-Song.

"Yeshe sees no one, she's in retreat. She's too feeble to receive strangers."

Monkey-Song was so relieved to hear that she was still alive that he couldn't wait any longer. He grabbed Drolma's hand and ran with her through the temple gates, just as they had run *out* of the temple, so many years before. They raced straight toward Yeshe's rooms.

"Hey, I said the kitchen's in *back!*" called the young priest, scrambling to his feet to summon the guards.

But Monkey-Song and Drolma were already inside the magnificent, echoing *puja* hall of the temple. They ran down a small side corridor, and pushed past an ancient servant woman who sat at Yeshe's door.

"Aunty," he called, "it's me, Monkey-Song. I'm back!"

They both stopped suddenly, silenced and surprised by the tiny, glowing, white-haired figure who sat propped in a bed of soft carpets. Her flesh was shriveled like dried fruit. Yet she had the luminous, fragile quality of a delicate ivory figurine. Her shrunken body was wrapped in a robe of warm wool, and she was dozing, with her head lolling to one side.

Monkey-Song reached out his hand to caress her warm, dry cheek. She woke with a start, and they were both relieved to see that her black eyes still held their quick intelligence.

"I dreamed that Monkey-Song came back," she mumbled to herself, in a cracked, feeble voice. Then she noticed them and stared for a long moment. "Who are you, what do you want?"

"It's Monkey-Song," he said, "and Drolma. We've come back!"

The ancient figurine began to weep softly. "I knew you'd come, I *knew* it, and just in time!"

They all began to laugh and cry and embrace one another.

"But you've been gone so long," said Yeshe. "What happened? I heard that the Black Emperor was killed, years ago. I was so happy, I knew that *he* must have helped you. Lotus-Born came to your aid again, didn't he?"

"I . . . I think so. I'm not sure."

"*I'm* sure," said the old woman, firmly. "*He* was so powerful . . ." She began to reminisce in a dreamy voice. "Once he made me meditate in a dark cave for six years. He said I was too proud of my beauty and intelligence. But when *he* was with me in the cave, the time passed like six minutes."

Monkey-Song and Drolma listened respectfully.

"I expected *you* back any day," she said. "I waited and waited, but you never came. What happened?"

They told her about their time in the *naga* realm.

"So long!" she said, surprised. "I never heard of *nagas* keeping anyone that long. I suppose you needed the time to heal. But how sad, eh, Monkey-Song? You were always worried about wasting your precious youth chanting scriptures. Now your youth is gone forever."

"It was worth it, Aunty," said Monkey-Song. "Anyway, I don't feel *so* old."

"I do," sighed the old woman. "I'm more than a hundred years. Maybe two hundred—who knows? It's nearly time for me to be gone, gone to the other shore. That's why I'm so glad you came back now, just when I need you."

"Why, what happening?"

"There's a great threat to Dza and *Chos*. I'm too weak to defend the doctrine any longer. You must forget your childish games now, and resume your duties as abbot and protector of *Chos*."

"I'm willing to do that, Aunty, but what is the threat?"

"The old king has just died, and there are two rival youths claiming the throne. One is the young prince, Tashi Palchen, the boy with the arrow-shaped scar over his heart. He is a beautiful lad, with a quick mind and a kind, gentle disposition. You must guard and protect Tashi *like your own son!* You must be sure that Tashi Palchen takes the throne, not his evil young half-brother, the Black Duke of Lang!"

Yeshe spoke so vehemently that it took all her feeble

strength away for a moment. She lay back on her cushions, gasping for breath, and seemed to become even smaller.

"The Black Duke of Lang?" asked Monkey-Song, when she had recovered.

Her shriveled, translucent face twisted with anger. "Yes, Lang. That's what he is called *now*. But you will recognize him at once. Because he is a new embodiment of our old enemy, the Black Emperor of Gyan! That monster, he couldn't *wait* to enter a new cycle of human rebirth. He was so eager to return to Dza, and seize power over us. He is a bit less powerful, and his memories of the past are mostly gone. He really doesn't remember who he was, or why he is here. But he's evil as always, and terribly hungry to rule over Dza. He spends all his time plotting and scheming with his gang of supporters—and training his screaming black crows."

"Black crows!" cried Drolma.

"Yes," said the old woman. "I know you'll recognize him at once. If only you had been here *before* he became powerful, you could have stopped him! He's wicked as ever, cruel, and grasping for power. He'll destroy *Chos* if he takes the throne. He wants to restore the old ways of the *shen!* He'll plunge Dza into internal warfare, famine and chaos. You *must* be sure that your beautiful godson, Tashi, takes the kingdom. You must!"

"But how, Aunty?"

"Do you remember your dream of Lotus-Born? He stands beside a large rock, spouting clear water."

"Yes, I remember."

"Inside that rock is another gold tablet, legendary twin to the one that's enshrined in this temple. That rock fountain, and the second gold tablet, are *real*. They are hidden in a wild magnolia grove on the western slopes. I'll tell you how to find them. After you've taken your place as abbot, you must tell Tashi how to find the tablet. You and he will go there, with all the nobles and priests. When he finds the tablet, they will declare him king. Then *Chos* can continue to rule in Dza, and Lang can sulk with his trained crows."

Yeshe told Monkey-Song how to find the rock fountain, in weak, halting whispers. Then she fell back on her pillows, panting and shrunken from the effort and excitement.

Monkey-Song sat thoughtfully for a few minutes, watching her. Then he said, in a voice full of wonder, "Yes, I *do* remember. I remember the beautiful baby, Tashi, with the arrow in his heart. I remember the fountain of solid rock, with the gold tablet inside . . . I remember."

"Good," smiled Yeshe, weakly.

Just then, the temple priests broke into the room, to eject the intruders.

Yeshe lifted a pale hand, "Your abbot, Monkey-Song, has returned, with his wife. Greet them with proper respect."

The priests stared. Then the older ones, who remembered him as a boy, embraced him warmly, one by one, with a scent of incense and musty red wool. The younger priests looked awed, and stuck out their tongues in the gesture of respect.

Suddenly, Yeshe's breath rasped out hoarsely. Her head fell to the side, and her skin took on the frozen sheen of antique ivory. Her wide-open eyes lost their shine.

Then, to everyone's great astonishment, her entire body became gradually smaller and smaller—until she finally disappeared in a rippling wave of rainbow-colored light.

Yeshe was gone, gone to the other shore. She was one of the few who truly understood the secret of *Chos*—and she would never be born again.

Monkey-Song resumed his position as abbot of the Great Temple, and Drolma easily slipped into Yeshe's role as a wise woman. She began to study the lore of medicinal herbs. They enjoyed the comfort, relaxation and beauty of temple life. Their big, soft bed where they could snuggle together, the warm, rich foods, the calm, sonorous chanting of scriptures, the thrilling temple music and the magnificent art. It all felt marvelous after their long, frightening journey. Everyone was glad to have the abbot back. They were welcomed warmly throughout the temple, and wherever they went in Dza Valley.

But they couldn't rest too long. Shortly after they settled in, they were visited by a delegation of nobles, asking their advice.

"The old king is dead, and we must choose a new king of Dza," said the leader of the delegation. "The young prince, Tashi Palchen, is the favorite. He is an intelligent, gentle lad. But his half-brother, the Black Duke of Lang, is very powerful. He has gathered many supporters who demand that he be king. How can we decide?"

"I can help you," said Monkey-Song. "I recently had a vision of Lotus-Born, saying that there is a second gold tablet, hidden somewhere around Dza, filled with the inscriptions of *Chos*. Lotus-Born said that whoever can find the other tablet will be the next king of Dza."

The nobles buzzed with surprise, and hurried to tell the news to the two young contenders.

Sallow Duke Lang sneered petulantly, and pulled on his wispy beard. "I don't believe this new abbot of ours. I think he's an impostor and a fool. When *I'm* king, I'll get rid of him. I don't believe that there's any hidden tablet. Why hide something so valuable? But if there *is* such a thing, my trained crows will find it quickly."

Soon Lang's screaming crows were seen searching in every nook and cranny of the kingdom, harassing the people in their homes, and the flocks in the fields, annoying the *lha* and spirits of rocks, streams and trees.

Tashi Palchen's response was quite different. He smiled at the delegation and said, "How exciting that our abbot had a vision; I have no idea where the tablet is, but it'll be great fun to look."

During a cold, dark, moonless night, Drolma limped hurriedly to Tashi Palchen's rooms in the fortress, and told him where the tablet could be found—inside the rock fountain, in a grove of wild magnolia trees, on the western slopes. She didn't notice the silent shape of a black crow, following her and listening at the silk-covered window.

The next morning, Tashi Palchen announced to the court that he had a vision, telling where the tablet could be found. A caravan was quickly arranged.

Monkey-Song and Drolma couldn't help laughing at this elaborate caravan of aristocrats, so very different from their own simple trek through the mountain passes. The nobles and temple priests gathered a long line of yaks to travel through the western mountains, carrying large storage skins of foods and water, tea and barley beer, meats, cheeses, *tsampa* flour, salt, butter and fruits, warm, dry clothing, fresh boots, clean robes, furs, ritual implements, musical instruments, incense, banners, drums, tents, tent posts, cooking pots, butter churns, weapons, flints, axes and trade goods for nomad tribes.

147

"They're carrying all of Dza!" cried Drolma, as she and Monkey-Song mounted their ponies.

Tashi Palchen eagerly led the caravan onward. No one noticed the tiny black speck in the sky—a high-flying, silent crow, following them to the western slopes.

Still, the journey *was* far more comfortable than the travels of their youth. The weeks passed by, as they rode lazily on their ponies, watching the changing landscape under the dark-blue sky. Guides from local tribes led them through the maze of canyons, and over the magnificent *la* pass, in return for gossip and trade goods.

When they camped, the servants set up tents, and cooked large pots of hot *thukpa* soups. The priests chanted, and the nobles hunted on the barren hillsides, while Drolma walked with her limping gait into the secret valleys, to collect rare and precious medicinal herbs.

For the young prince, Tashi Palchen, this was the most exciting adventure of his life. Up to now, he had been content as the most popular young aristocrat of Dza, playing at dice games and horse races, tournaments and hunts, and occasionally attending to his studies. Then the old king suddenly died, and the throne was almost his—until Lang and his followers put forth their false claim. Lang, damn him! He had always been a cruel bully, even when they were children. He played too roughly, and enjoyed torturing small, helpless creatures. Now Lang was trying to steal his birthright!

Until the strange, limping old wise woman, Drolma, came to him one night, and whispered the secret of the tablets. But could she really be believed? Older women sometimes have strange ideas. What if she was wrong—or lying? She admitted she'd never seen the second tablet herself. What if this were a trick, instigated by Lang? If this elaborate caravan found no golden tablet, he would be laughed at and discredited throughout Dza. Tashi Palchen's tension mounted, as they crossed the pass, and headed down to the western slopes.

Everyone's excitement was growing. Would the cheerful prince find the tablet, and become the next king? Or would he be proved a fool, and go home ashamed and empty-handed? Yet there was the magnolia grove, just as the young prince described it—with a large crevice through the

148

center. And there was the outcropping of solid rock, spouting clear water!

Tashi Palchen leaped off his horse and rushed eagerly to the rock. He thrust his hand inside, there, where the water gushed freely.

Suddenly something soared down, out of the sky, screaming. It was one of Lang's huge black crows, aiming at Tashi's hand with its long, sharp beak. The bird dove down, and Tashi felt a sharp, searing pain in his hand, as the crow pierced it right through. He instinctively withdrew his torn, bleeding hand from the rock, to protect it. The big bird jumped into the water and emerged with something in its beak—something large, shining and gold.

The tablet.

The crow wrestled with the heavy object. At this moment Tashi Palchen was filled with great rage. It wasn't enough to be smart, gentle and popular, he realized. If he didn't *act*—now—this nasty creature would snatch his throne, his heritage, from him forever.

With a loud cry of anger, Tashi grabbed the bird with his uninjured hand and tried to wring its neck. The crow dropped the tablet and pecked and clawed at Tashi's hands, face and eyes with unnatural strength. Tashi held on tightly, even though the creature tore and tore at his bleeding flesh. Finally he felt the bird's neck bones snap in his grasp. The crow's head fell limply to one side, and the creature died.

Shakily, Tashi Palchen picked up the golden tablet, cleaned and dried it carefully on his robe, and began to read the inscriptions of *Chos*.

The caravan returned, and Tashi Palchen was declared the forty-first king of Dza. The people cheered and celebrated, drank and feasted. Everyone liked the handsome, friendly young king.

Everyone except Duke Lang, who sat sullenly, drinking strong barley liquor, with his supporters, a trained crow perched on his shoulder. "Let the stupid boy enjoy the throne," muttered Lang. "He won't have it long." Lang's men gulped down their barley liquor and nodded their heads in angry agreement.

Yet for a while, all was peaceful in Dza, despite the underlying discontent of Lang and his faction. Tashi Palchen was a good and strong king who kept the peace and propitiated the *lha,* so that the crops and harvests were rich and bountiful. He protected and patronized the Great Temple of *Chos,* so that the doctrine grew and flourished.

Under the leadership of the abbot, Monkey-Song, and the temple doctor and wise woman, Drolma, new copies of the scriptures were made, and great teachers were invited from Hind. The beautiful *puja* hall of the temple housed elaborate ceremonies, with wondrous music that could be heard for miles around. The priests chanted, and debated fine points of doctrine, such as the esoteric meaning of a double set of tablets. The beauty and mystery, the rituals and artwork were a source of inspiration and entertainment for all the people.

They loved their gentle new king, and ignored the disgruntled minority that still supported Duke Lang. They loved their abbot, with his wonderful voice, who chanted the scriptures so beautifully. They loved Drolma, who gathered medicinal herbs on the hillsides, and made every effort to care for the sick and the poor.

The couple continued to enjoy each other, in a quiet, gentle way.

For over ten years, Dza was a peaceful, prosperous place, despite the constant plotting of Lang.

At last, Monkey-Song and Drolma began to feel their years. Their strength and vigor were steadily declining. They were bothered by pains of their old injuries, from the fall in the mountains. The dark spot in Monkey-Song's mind was troubling him.

In the eleventh year of Tashi Palchen's reign, a virulent pox fever swept wildly through the valley, killing many children and older people. The aging abbot, Monkey-Song, was unable to resist the infection, despite Drolma's medicines and all the prayers of the priests and the people.

Drolma worked tirelessly, day and night, distributing medicinal herbs throughout the valley. Then, saddened and exhausted, she also fell prey to the disease. It was time for them to be gone, gone. . . .

Back to the realm of Shinje, lord of the dead.

Dissolving, dissolving into death. Earth sinking into water. Water into fire. Fire into air. Air into ether. Ether
150

sinking into air. Air into fire. Fire into water. Water into earth. Earth sinking into water. Water into fire . . .

Blackness. No thought. Nonbeing. Death.

Then a great burst of colorless light, filling the entire universe.

So bright that Monkey-Song briefly glimpsed the shadowy figure of Shinje, the black, bull-headed lord of death, seated on his mirrored throne, playing dice games to determine the fate of souls. Then the light faded and dissolved.

Dissolving. Dissolving into a perfect peace.

A calm, silent center.

Merging.

Resting.

Timeless time.

Death.

Then a shimmering disturbance in the silent calm. A swirl of color and form. Monkey-Song awoke, startled, from the blissful peace of timeless death. A vision was forming. A vision of the Great Temple of Dza, surrounded by shimmering green light. An elaborate funeral was being held in the courtyard, with rings of chanting, red-robed priests. But the corpses were weird and scary—a large male ape with a stump of a tail, and a small female demoness with bulging eyes!

Suddenly, a flock of screaming black crows came flying around and around the temple. Frightened, Monkey-Song lunged toward the vision. It disappeared.

Another vision appeared, in the same shimmering green. It was Drolma, wide-eyed and looking like a young girl again. She called and beckoned to him. *Drolma.* He felt a great wave of sadness. He felt terribly alone. How could he rest in the peace of death without her? He *couldn't!* He tried to reach out and grab at her. The vision disappeared.

A third vision formed. It was a beautiful, prosperous young matron of Dza. She lay on a bed of soft carpets, naked except for a necklace and earrings of very large turquoises. Her breasts were large and shapely. Her skin was tawny and smooth. The expression on her high-cheeked face was languid and inviting. Her legs were spread wide.

Monkey-Song felt a sudden surge of passion. His body strained to reach the woman. Suddenly, from between her thighs came a bolt of bright-green light that hit him just

151

above the navel, filling him with a tremendous surge of energy.

The powerful light caused his semen to spout freely, into the void. He grunted with a sharp *HA!*

The light, the vision, and everything disappeared into emptiness. He dissolved into himself, to enter the woman's womb—and begin a new cycle of human life.

Part III

According to Tibetan history, the mighty Khans came to attack and conquer. When they learned the way of Chos, it calmed their violence.

XI

The beautiful young woman was sprawled on a thick bed of soft carpets, in the rambling stone mansion, near the center of Dza Valley. Her high-cheeked face was rosy and moon-shaped. Her loose woolen chuba robe hung partly open, revealing smooth, tawny skin and large, shapely breasts. She wore a necklace and earrings of very large turquoises.

She was playing with her small son, named Garpa Lobsang Wangchuck Sangay Jamyang Gyalten. The child's name was long and complex, because the Garpa family was old and important in Dza. The Garpas were a clan of wealthy, influential merchants. Although they didn't control huge tracts of land, like the nobility, the head of the Garpa clan was treated with deference and respect—even by the king.

The stone mansion of the Garpa family was large and imposing, perched on a low hill. It dominated a small, fertile and well-watered valley that held the family farmlands and serfs. In the distance, the Garpa family could see the prayer flags and stupas and the shining golden rooftops of the Great Temple of Dza. They could hear the eerie roaring of the big horns in the thin air. They could see the huge snow-capped mountain peaks, and the king's stone fortress, that guards the *la*-passes—and the dark-blue sky, above.

The little boy joked and teased with his beautiful young mother inside the mansion. It was sumptuously furnished with silks and brocades, colorful carpets of rare beauty, ivory and jeweled inlays from all the great kingdoms, beyond the sky-high mountains. For the Garpa clan were traders. As long as anyone could remember, the Garpa men had organized large caravans, laden with trade goods. They loaded the yaks and horses with salt and rough turquoises, yak tails and furs, dried meat and wool. They

155

traveled across the tortuous and dangerous pathways and *la*-passes, over the mountains to the kingdoms beyond Dza. In a few years, if all went well, the Garpa traders returned with yaks and horses burdened with silks, brocade, tea, rice and all the exotic goods loved by the wealthy of Dza. As these goods changed hands, the Garpa traders took a profit. The family grew rich—very rich. Their storerooms were filled with rotting bags of surplus food—a symbol of their status. Although they weren't nobility, they lived like nobility.

The child, Garpa Lobsang Wangchuck Sangyay Jamyang Gyalten, tumbled and played with his laughing, beautiful mother. The Garpa men always chose the most beautiful girls of Dza as their brides. This was their custom. Because, as traders, they might not see her for many years. They needed something to urge them forward, on the long journey home.

The young mother on the bed was proud and lucky to be a Garpa wife, for she would live a life of luxury and ease. And although her husband was a trader, she needn't fear long years of loneliness. For a Garpa bride has not one but several husbands.

She formally married the eldest brother of this family branch—and all the younger brothers automatically became her husbands, too! This system of polyandry meant that the family property wouldn't be fragmented between quarreling relatives. It would remain intact, inherited through one line of grandchildren. When some brothers were off trading, others could stay home to care for the wife, family and Garpa estate.

It was a fine arrangement that suited everyone, including the young mother on the bed. She had five husbands altogether. They shared her favors in an amicable, brotherly way. She was energetic, and able to satisfy them all. Besides, two of her husbands were currently away on a caravan. So her task wasn't *too* overwhelming.

Her son was officially the child of the eldest brother, Garpa Lobsang, a hearty and good-natured man. But actually, he could be the son of any brother that was home during his conception. And by informal custom, he was considered the son of *all* the brothers.

That's why the child had so many names. Five fathers—
156

five names. The smiling young woman watched her child romping on the bed of carpets. Which husband did he resemble—who was the actual father? It was hard to decide.

The boy, now aged five, was quite distinctive-looking. He had long, thin and agile limbs, covered lightly with soft black down. He had a curious round scar at the base of his tailbone. He had a clear and pleasant voice. He was active and energetic, full of mischief and fun. He loved to play little tricks.

That's what earned the boy his nickname. No child of the Garpa clan is ever called by his full, long name. It's too much for a child to handle. A pet nickname is always used. Because of his long limbs, and love of mischief, this boy was nicknamed Monkey-Trick.

It was an icy, wintry day outside the stone mansion. But Monkey-Trick didn't mind. He played happily on the colorful bed of soft carpets, and babbled to his beautiful young mother.

"Mama, watch me somersault!"

He did a series of flip-flops on the bed.

"Good! Where did you learn that so well, Monkey-Trick?" asked his mother.

"I don't know. You wanna hear me sing?"

"Sure."

Monkey-Trick sang a child's song, in his clear voice.

"Where did you learn that song?" asked his mother. "I didn't teach it to you."

"At the big temple. I learned it at the temple."

"What a silly boy! Some servant taught the song to you. We haven't been to the temple since summer. They chant prayers there—they don't teach little boys to sing!"

"Yes they *do*. Anyway, I used to live in the temple!"

"Oh, what stories! You never lived there."

"Yes, I *did*."

"What did you do at the temple, you naughty liar?"

"I sang nice songs there, and I had a pretty aunty. And I had a friend."

Monkey-Trick's face looked sad, and he began to cry.

"What's wrong, baby?" asked his mother, worried. The boy sometimes had strange fits of tears and gloom.

"My *friend*. I miss my friend!"

"What was your friend's name?" she asked, trying to cheer him up.

"Drolma—with great big eyes."

"But Drolma is a girl's name, and you don't like to play with girls."

"I don't *care*. Drolma is my best friend. I miss her. Where is she? *I want her!*" wept Monkey-Trick.

His mother tried to hush him. The boy was working himself into another tantrum. They happened more often lately. The doctors and priests said he'd outgrow it soon. She hoped so. He was her first son, so she wasn't sure if this was normal. Mostly, he was such a playful, cheery little scamp—lively, curious and full of fun. Then suddenly he would grow cranky and irritable. He complained that his head bothered him. Or he would make up these strange stories about the temple, or his imaginary friend, Drolma. She *hoped* he'd outgrow it soon.

She sighed and adjusted her chuba. It was probably the weather. Everyone knows that bad weather makes children whine. They have too much energy to be cooped up inside. Maybe she should get him a fluffy little terrier. Or she should invite other children of the Garpa clan to come to her quarters and keep him company. They could romp together, eat dried fruit, and play games in the warm, cozy room. Then he wouldn't have time to complain about his head, or invent strange stories. He wouldn't need to beg for imaginary friends.

Suddenly, a black shadow flitted across the small, silk-covered window. They heard a hoarse cry. The child began to scream and thrash around on the bed.

"Bad bird, mama, *bad!*" cried Monkey-Trick. "Scares me!"

"Hush," said his mother. "You mustn't be afraid. That's only a crow outside our window. One of Duke Lang's trained, funny crows, flying around to make us laugh! I know they frighten you, but don't worry. They can't hurt you. Mama is here to protect you. A big boy like you shouldn't be frightened by silly little birds. Come on, cheer up. Let's go into the kitchen, and see if cook has made mo-mo dumplings."

The crow flew away, and the fit gradually subsided. Monkey-Trick stopped crying and regained his normal, active mood.

"Oh goodie! Mo-mo dumplings! Come on, mama, let's hurry, before my papas eat them all."

Monkey-Trick grew rapidly, in the big stone mansion. He was tall and thin, agile and full of fun—usually. But sometimes he felt confused, as if there were two people inside him. Ordinarily, he was the cheerful and active young heir of the Garpa clan, who enjoyed riding and gaming with the other upper-class lads of Dza. But sometimes he was aware of strange thoughts, that felt like vague memories of another self.

He would experience sudden flashes of recollection that had nothing to do with the comfortable life of Monkey-Trick of the Garpa clan. He would see the inner rooms of the Great Temple—rooms that only priests are allowed to enter. He would fantasize about a large-eyed girl named Drolma—whom he missed, terribly. He experienced troublesome feelings, deep inside his mind. He remembered chanting scriptures in a deep, sonorous voice—scriptures that he didn't know, and a voice that was far more powerful than his own. He recalled a glowing man of Hind, standing beside a rock fountain. He remembered terrifying black crows.

The crows were the worst, because they were real. The Black Duke of Lang now led a powerful political faction in Dza. His trained black crows flew constantly around the kingdom—watching and spying. The doctors assured Monkey-Trick and his mother that there was a simple explanation. A bird must have frightened the child when he was still a tiny infant, basking in the sunshine. And the fear remained, like the scar of an old wound. But Monkey-Trick knew that the doctors were wrong. The crows were evil. Lang was evil. Somehow Monkey-Trick *knew* it.

Yet there was nothing he could do. He was only a boy, just into adolescence. He wasn't supposed to meddle in politics. He was supposed to ride and play, and attend to his studies. Although he was a doer, not a scholar, he learned easily. His tutors found him especially quick at memorizing the prayers of *Chos*.

Soon Monkey-Trick was fifteen years old. The wise and gentle king, Tashi Palchen, held the throne of Dza, and guarded the *la*-passes. The people of Dza loved their king, yet there were restless stirrings in the land.

159

Lang's faction was growing more powerful. He was very clever at manipulating the minds of the people and stirring up latent discontent. Whenever any trouble came to Dza, such as hailstorms, crop failures or epidemics, Lang would seize the opportunity to point an accusing finger.

"The old *lha* and spirits of Dza are angry!" Lang would shout, with a trained crow perched on his shoulder, and a sneer on his sallow face. "They hate being usurped by the alien religion of *Chos*. The old *lha* and spirits of Dza don't want the Hind priests here, with their shaven heads, their foreign religion and foreign ways. Remember how the singing abbott of the Great Temple was struck down by a pox. That was a sign of the gods' rage. Every hailstorm and crop failure is proof that the *lha* and spirits are *angry!* The old *shen* were men of Dza, not foreigners from Hind. The gods of Dza are furious! They don't want a king who supports foreigners. There will be trouble in Dza—famine and plagues, until the *lha* and spirits are appeased. *The foreigners and their religion must be driven out of Dza! The king must be deposed! The way of the shen must be restored!"*

Thus spoke Lang, whenever there was trouble in the land. And when there was trouble, the people were ready to listen, and eager to find scapegoats.

"Perhaps Lang is right," the people would mutter quietly among themselves. "Perhaps the *lha* and spirits *are* angry with the fancy foreign religion. If the way of *Chos* were truly powerful, why *was* the singing abbot of the Great Temple struck down by pox? Why didn't the scriptures of *Chos* protect him? Perhaps *Chos* is merely a fine show, with no power at all. Perhaps the old ways of the *shen* are better. The *shen* had power. The *shen* were people of Dza. The *shen* knew how to pacify and extract favors from the gods. Perhaps Lang is right."

The Black Duke of Lang spoke—and the people listened, as they passed the cold nights in their stone huts, drinking barley beer by the flickering light of the butter lamps. There was a swelling undercurrent of discontent throughout Dza. Monkey-Trick also listened, with a deep and growing feeling of alarm.

"Lang is poisoning the minds of the people!" he cried.

The Garpa men laughed. "Hush, boy," said one of his fathers. "What does a fifteen-year-old sapling know about such matters? You should be thinking about horse-races, not politics!"

Monkey-Trick fell silent. He listened and felt afraid.

The king, Tashi Palchen, with the arrow-shaped scar over his heart, also listened. But he wasn't too worried. Lang was always a power-hungry malcontent. That would never change. The people were fond of their king. There was peace and prosperity in Dza. The Great Temple was flourishing. True, there were occasional problems with the crops, bad weather, or disease, but what land is without its share of troubles? Only the Paradise Realms live in unending bliss. Tashi Palchen felt confident. He ruled the kingdom ably and well, with a firm but gentle hand. Dza was orderly and content, and the king felt secure on his throne.

The big Garpa mansion was bustling with excitement, as the first buds of early spring appeared in the frozen river valleys. A grand wedding was taking place. One of the Garpa daughters was marrying into a powerful aristocratic family of Dza.

The wedding celebrations had been going on for nearly three days. First, go-betweens from the groom's family came with gifts, and many hours of prolonged, flowery speeches. They praised the virtues of the young man and his family, and the great luck of the girl who had made such a match.

Although everything was arranged months in advance, the go-betweens were met with good-natured insults—and lots of good food and strong barley beer. Finally a bride price was formally set, and the go-betweens departed.

They were followed by a mounted troop of young men, dressed in their finest chubas, fur hats and felt boots, jewels and swords. They rode on horses decorated with silver and ribbons. They serenaded the young bride in loud, raucous voices, praising her future husband. Suddenly a troop of elaborately dressed Garpa men rode out of the stone mansion, and challenged the visitors with loud insults. The two bands of men began a series of mock duels, tournaments and games that lasted until everyone was exhausted. Then came the long day of feasting, with vast amounts of food and barley liquor.

Nearly every important person in the kingdom was attending the wedding feast. The people of Dza loved parties and celebrations, and a wedding between a Garpa and the nobility was an important event. People were dressed in their finest brocades, their most magnificent jewels. Great cooking pots steamed at one end of the large courtyard, filled with mo-mo dumplings, *thukpa* stews, sweetmeats, buttered tea, costly rice and every tempting delicacy. The succulent odors drifted across the courtyard to entice the guests, who stood tipsy, talking and laughing, and watching a band of wandering players.

The minstrels were a ragged bunch, but clever. Their big masks seemed so real that the guests could almost believe that the mimes were demons, *lha*, animals and birds. They moved to the beat of a large drum, and the reedy wail of small horns, and the tinkling of bells and finger cymbals. The dancers stepped, bowed and twined gravely, or leaped into the air with piercing yells, as they acted out an ancient tale of battles between demons and *lha*. Sometimes the dance was slow and solemn. At times the drums and dancers moved in an exciting, fiery pace. The drama had gone on all day, and no one was in any hurry for it to end. The wedding guests talked, laughed, feasted and drank. They watched the players perform, and occasionally tossed bits of silver and gold, to applaud a skilled move.

Monkey-Trick stretched his neck to peer over the shoulders of the adults. He watched the show with excited, shining eyes—and sticky, greasy fingers.

In the background, they could hear the sonorous chanting of the priests of *Chos*, who sat in a spacious room, off the courtyard, praying for the happiness, health and prosperity of the young couple.

Members of the Garpa clan and the groom's family joked and traded insults, but the bride wasn't among the crowd. She sat in a gaily decorated room, with her sisters —waiting. Later in the day, her new husband would arrive on horseback, with a mounted troop of elegantly dressed and armed men. They would carry her off, in a mock kidnap, to her new home. There the groom's family would host another day of celebration and feasting, and the wedding would be complete.

At one end of the courtyard, drunkenly watching the spectacle, stood the Black Duke of Lang, and his followers. Lang was sallow-faced, with a long, wispy beard. He wore a chuba of black brocade, and a tall hat and boots of black

162

felt. His hands and neck glistened with jewels. A trained crow was perched on his shoulder. Lang wiped barley liquor off his lips and sullenly eyed the festivities.

Monkey-Trick glanced at him, nervously.

Then a murmur rose from the crowd. "The king is coming, the king!" The crowd parted to make way for the king, Tashi Palchen, and his retainers.

King Tashi wore a broad, friendly smile, and a magnificent chuba of blue-and-white brocade. He carried a large gift, wrapped in the traditional white greeting scarf of Dza. The leader of the Garpa clan hurried to greet him, with flowery speeches of welcome. The servants scurried to bring silver trays, filled with food and drink.

All of the nobles moved toward the king, to greet him with the traditional extended tongue. The king returned their welcome with friendly jokes.

Lang swaggered to join the other nobles. They all made way for him, and Lang confronted the king, face to face.

With a sneer, Lang stuck out his tongue and said, "Greetings, regal half-brother."

Just at that moment, the king bit into a large, steaming mo-mo dumpling. Because his mouth was filled with hot food, he was momentarily unable to talk.

Lang growled, "Have you grown too proud to speak to your half-brother?"

The king looked at him in surprise and hurriedly swallowed the food.

But before the king had a chance to reply, Lang whipped a long dagger from the folds of his chuba, and held it high. The crowd gasped.

"The Black Duke of Lang doesn't tolerate such insults," he snarled. "Offenses to my pride will be avenged!"

Without any further warning, Lang plunged the dagger into the king's chest. The people watched, horrified. Blood gushed onto the king's beautiful blue-and-white chuba. He staggered and fell.

Monkey-Trick cried out with rage and surprise.

Lang adjusted his robe and stared at the crowd, daring anyone to challenge him. No one moved—except Monkey-Trick.

With a flying leap, the boy threw himself at Lang and began to pound him with his fists. Lang gave a short laugh

163

and kicked the sobbing boy aside. Two of Monkey-Trick's father's grabbed him by the arms and dragged the boy away, telling him to hush.

With another challenging look at the crowd, Lang gave a drunken lurch and stomped away from the Garpa mansion. His retainers followed him, silently. The crow gave a single long cry, overhead.

No one moved. The people watched him go, and stared at the fallen body of their king with shock and disbelief.

The news flashed through the valley like summer lightning. Lang had murdered King Tashi over a petty insult—and no one dared to challenge him! Now Lang was clearly the most powerful man in the kingdom. After a brief period of mourning, a subdued and nervous council of nobles declared Lang the forty-second king of Dza. The priests of *Chos* and Monkey-Trick watched apprehensively, fearing trouble. They didn't have long to wait.

The coronation rituals were drunken and gloomy. The weather was dark and stormy, with chilling winds. Lang's big crows flew overhead, all day and night, frightening the people with their shrill, mocking cries.

Lang quickly issued his first proclamation: "The royal treasure chests have been ransacked for years by the foreigners of Hind. The royal purse will no longer feed the useless priests of *Chos*. If they want to eat, let them work as serfs on the land, go begging—or starve!"

With fear and sorrow, the teachers and wise ones of the Great Temple prepared for the long and dangerous journey, over the sky-high mountains, to Hind. Many of them were quite old and feeble, and knew they couldn't survive the ordeal. Monkey-Trick hurried to the temple and mournfully watched them go.

On their backs, they carried a few provisions, and as many of the precious scriptures and relics of *Chos* as they could manage. Many of these texts had been handwritten by the legendary wise woman Yeshe, the scribe. Fearing more trouble, the remaining priests of *Chos* hid many texts and relics during the night. Monkey-Trick stayed with the priests, helping them to find safe niches for these priceless objects. The job was hard, because the big screaming crows flew overhead constantly, watching and spying.

After the wise ones of Hind were gone, Lang issued another proclamation: "Now the Great Temple belongs to the people of Dza—and it will follow the old ways. Let the handiwork of the foreigners be destroyed! Let the Great Temple become the meeting hall of the *shen!*" Adding weight to his words, Lang now wore the bone ornaments of the old *shen*. Rumors spread through the kingdom that he was learning the ways of black sorcery.

Lang's troops rode to the temple, dressed in black leather armor, and began to loot and destroy everything in sight. In one dreadful day, they burned and mutilated the remaining precious texts. They knocked down the big brick stupas and reduced them to rubble. They slashed at the artwork, banners and prayer flags with their swords. They smashed the big musical instruments, the horns and drums, and ritual implements of silver and bone. They stripped the golden tiles and jeweled inlays, and carried them away. Monkey-Trick watched, helpless and horrified.

When Lang's men approached the altar, which held the twin golden tablets of *Chos,* the priests finally made their stand. Armed with a motley collection of kitchen knives, farming tools and sticks of firewood, the priests defended the tablets. Monkey-Trick was among them, with a small hunting lance.

"You must stop!" cried a feeble old priest. Lang's men guffawed and began to hack at the priests with their knives. Many fell to the tiled floor, gushing blood. Others fought as best they could. Some stared or fled in terror. The vast *puja* hall of the temple was a nightmare scene of bloodshed and destruction.

Suddenly, in the confusion, Monkey-Trick *knew* what he must do. He didn't think—he just knew. He grabbed the heavy golden tablets of *Chos,* and managed to slip out a side door of the temple. He ran down a great, echoing corridor. He had never been here before, yet somehow he *knew* the way. He could hear the shouts and heavy boots of Lang's soldiers, chasing after him. Yet somehow, he knew how to elude them. He slipped through the bowels of the temple, into secret rooms and passageways. He found a tiny, hidden gate in the big wall. He scurried behind the temple and headed into the foothills.

There was a secret, hidden cave up there somewhere—

he just *knew* it. The entrance would be hidden by a large rhododendron bush. Hiding in the underbrush, to avoid Lang's soldiers and the flying, spying crows, Monkey-Trick climbed into the hills. The thorns of the bushes tore at him, but he continued to follow his strange intuition, until *there* —he found it! There was the big rhododendron bush, just beginning to bud. There was the hidden entrance to the cave.

Exhausted, Monkey-Trick sank down on the damp, hard cave floor. He would hide the tablets here, buried safely under layers of dried leaves and grasses. The tablets of *Chos* would remain snugly sleeping, in their hidden cave, until Lang could be destroyed.

Working furiously, Monkey-Trick buried the tablets. Then he hurried back down the hillside to the temple. But when he arrived, he found no one—nothing. The battle was over, and Lang's men had won. The ruined temple of *Chos* was charred, smashed, destroyed. The bodies of the priests lay in a bloody tumble on the tile floor. Everything of value had been stripped. The big crows wheeled and circled overhead, screaming in triumph.

With tears in his eyes, Monkey-Trick looked at the destruction, as the last dreary rays of daylight entered the jagged, torn silk windows. Now the Great Temple of *Chos* was only a memory. There would be no more rituals, no more processions, no more eerie music echoing across the valley. Sweating and trembling with shock and exhaustion, Monkey-Trick left the ruined temple, feeling completely lost.

As he wandered aimlessly back toward the Garpa mansion, he caught sight of a small figure huddled against a rock. The figure shrank back as he approached, yet there was still enough light for Monkey-Trick to see the red robe of a young priest of *Chos*. Here was one of the survivors —one of the few who had escaped.

"Greeting, brother, don't be afraid, I am a follower of *Chos*," said Monkey-Trick, softly. The two men embraced. The priest was shivering noticeably with cold and fear.

"Come back with me to my family's mansion," said Monkey-Trick. "I'll hide you there, and feed you. It'll be warm."

"No," said the young priest, his teeth chattering. "Dza is no place for the people of *Chos*."

"Then what will you do?" cried Monkey-Trick. "Freeze to death out here, or wait until Lang's crows spot you?"

"I'm going to leave Dza," said the shivering priest. "I'll follow the wise ones to Hind."

"Then let me fetch warm clothes and provisions, and I'll come with you," said Monkey-Trick promptly, without further thought. "We'll journey together to Hind."

So Monkey-Trick joined the ragged band of temple refugees that made the difficult and dangerous journey across the southern sky-high mountains to Hind.

The trip took nearly a year. Many didn't survive the sudden rock slides and avalanches, the storms and bitter, freezing winds. Their food was soon exhausted, and they were forced to chew strips of yak leather, to fool their stomachs. The pathways were slippery with ice and loose gravel. The way was unmarked, through tortuous mazes of gorges and canyons. They were stalked by a solitary and hungry snow lion that haunted their makeshift camps at night. Their hearts pounded and they panted and gasped in the thin air of the high passes. Many fell, and could go no farther, or were injured and couldn't move.

Monkey-Trick tried to help his traveling companions. He carried one old priest on his back, over a treacherous bridge of rotting rope. As they journeyed, the tall, agile young man became wiser, and more mature. The ordeal forced him to grow up—rapidly.

A handful managed to survive, carrying the precious relics and texts of *Chos*. The stronger ones continued onward, without food, without sleep, without guides. Monkey-Trick was among the starving, hollow-eyed little band that finally crossed the last *la*-pass, and headed downhill, into the hot, steaming, fruit-filled jungles of Hind.

They could hear the chattering of monkeys, the screeching of bright-green parrots, the tinkling of tiny streams. A thousand new sights, sounds and smells greeted them. The air was warm and rich and humid. The scent of wet vegetation filled the air. They began to sweat under their thick furs and wools, which attracted myriad biting mosquitoes and flies. They sloshed through muddy marshes, filled with

167

slithering poisonous snakes. They gorged themselves with ripe, wild fruits.

They were alive. The texts were safe. They had escaped Lang. Their journey was successful—and there was the whole new world of Hind to explore.

XII

Attracted by the crowing of roosters, the little band of refugees found a hot, dusty village, built of mud and the dung of water buffaloes. Naked children and ragged chickens and dogs nosed listlessly in the muck of the courtyards. The people were small, lithe and dark, with round black eyes. The women wore tremendous gold rings, dangling from their nostrils and ears. These people had no speech in common with Dza—but the language of starving beggars is universal. Soon their bowls were filled with kitchen scraps. Monkey-Trick and his companions settled into the shade of a huge mango tree, twined with fragrant white orchids, and enjoyed their first cooked meal in months. They slept soundly there that night.

One of the surviving wise men of Hind could communicate with these people. Following their directions, and helped by other villagers and tribespeople along the way, the ragged band journeyed for months, to reach the tree-lined banks of the vast river—holy mother Ganga.

They made their pilgrimage to the peaceful deer park, nearby, where the wise *śramana* taught the secret of *Chos*, many centuries before. The priests and wise ones decided to end their journey here. They would live out their days in meditation, in the quiet and holy grounds of the deer park, contemplating the secret of *Chos*.

Monkey-Trick stayed at the deer park, with the priests, for a while. He meditated, begged for his food, and learned some speech of Hind. Then he grew restless. After all, he wasn't a wise man, like the others. He had never been trained in priestly rituals and ways. He did have those vague memories of life in the Great Temple—echoes from another time. But he was still Monkey-Trick, an inquisitive, lively lad, who had escaped Lang, left his family, and journeyed on a great adventure. He wasn't ready to stop now, and devote his life to contemplation. He wanted to explore Hind! With warm farewells, Monkey-Trick left the priests of *Chos*. Traveling alone, he walked the short distance to the teeming holy city that sits on the banks of Mother Ganga.

The energy and excitement of the vast city hit him like lightning. Feeling almost drunk, he reeled along the narrow, cobbled streets, watching everything with amazement. He'd never seen so many people at once! The center of Dza Valley has some muddy streets, lined with merchant's shops, drinking houses and large homes. But those are only a few streets, with only a few busy people.

Here in this sprawling city, there were countless narrow winding streets, stinking of sewage. There were myriad shops, houses, inns, merchants, vendors, and innumerable throngs of bustling people, mingling with wandering water buffaloes and dogs, and long caravans of horses, camels and elephants. Bearded men in elaborate silks and turbans mingled with filthy beggars in loincloths. Women, wrapped in silks, with tremendous nose rings and earrings, escorted bands of screaming, playing, dark-eyed children. Elegant military men, with big curved swords, led their mounted troops in processions along the main avenues.

Monkey-Trick watched, fascinated. Most impressive of all were the temples. Dza boasted one tremendous temple. But this city had a temple on every street! Huge, ornate temples, tiny temples barely as wide as doorways, elaborate temples, simple temples. Each temple was devoted to a different deity. Monkey-Trick glimpsed images of elephant-headed gods, monkey-headed goddesses, gods and goddesses of monstrous shapes—and a god who was represented only by a big stone phallus. He could hear the chanting of priests, and the wailing of horns, the beat of drums, bells and cymbals. It was very different from the slow and sonorous temple music of Dza. Here the mingled chanting and music was fast-paced and exciting, a throbbing babble of sound that made Monkey-Trick's heart race. He could smell the incense wafting through the temple doorways.

One huge temple seemed to attract an especially large crowd—and he heard weird screaming inside. Curious, Monkey-Trick wriggled and peered through the crowd, and gasped when he saw the temple altar. It was dominated by

170

the immense image of a monstrous goddess, with matted hair, and the face and body of an ugly hag. She was wreathed in skulls, and chewing bloody gobs of human flesh. At the base of this grotesque altar were the shaven-headed priests, dressed in white robes, but covered with hot blood. With crazed eyes and sharp knives, they slit the throats of screaming goats, chickens, rams—and yes, *even small children,* brought as offerings by the frenzied devotees.

Sickened, Monkey-Trick stumbled away from this gruesome temple of *thugs,* and made his way to the riverbank. The river was wide but foul-smelling—for it served as the refuse dump for the entire teeming city. Despite this, it attracted countless pilgrims. For the holy river, mother Ganga, has the legendary ability to heal all who worship at her banks and bathe in her waters.

They came from all over Hind, the cripples, the blind, the diseased, the lepers. They dragged their bodies on makeshift crutches, stumbled with sightless eyes, gestured with the rotten stumps of their leprous hands, and coughed out their last bloody breath. They swarmed along the banks of the holy river, mumbling prayers, trying to win the favor of the gods, bathing in the waters of the odorous river. All of the human refuse of Hind made pilgrimage to holy mother Ganga, to be healed—or die.

Many died, there along the banks of the river. Alone and friendless, gasping in the hot sun, with no food or medicine to sustain them. Yet they died with honor, for their pilgrimage was complete. Death along the shores of mother Ganga is a noble ending, which will guarantee a favorable rebirth. They dropped along the muddy shore, unnoticed. Their cycle in this body was complete. Gangs of young boys stripped away their ragged clothing and sold it for a few coins. The shallow waters of the river's edge lapped around their naked bodies. Dogs nosed at their flesh. Carrion-eating birds pecked at their eyes. Flies settled on them in thick droves.

Eventually the corpses were gathered and carried in carts to the great funeral pyres that dot the riverbank. At dawn, the bodies are burned in large heaps. The oily, foul-smelling smoke drifts down the river. Monkey-Trick could smell the scent of charred flesh, and he could see the glowing embers of the pyres along the river.

Although many died, the crowd wasn't diminished, for new ones arrived constantly, to pray and bathe at the holy river—to be cured, enlightened, or die. Among the crowd were many mendicant yogis and holy ones, neither diseased nor lame. They were naked, or nearly so. Their hair was long, matted tangles. Their bodies were smeared with ashes, or pigments worked in elaborate designs. Some carried the trident staff of Shiva, others carried a small musical instrument, or a pipe of hashish. Many carried nothing. Their eyes were vacant and vague, looking beyond this world. They contorted their bodies into elaborate postures and held them for long hours, days, months or years. They drank the filthy river water, starved themselves, chanted and mumbled prayers. Or they merely mumbled. They stared at the strong sun until their eyes burned out. Monkey-Trick watched them, puzzled. Were they evolved—or merely crazed?

Weak with hunger, and the excitement and strangeness of it all, Monkey-Trick begged some scraps from nearby houses, and found a quiet shrine where he could eat a few morsels and rest. What should he do now? Should he rejoin the priests of *Chos* in the calm (but dull) deer park? Should he try to find lodging and work, and learn the ways of this vast, chaotic city?

Suddenly a small boy approached him and tapped him on the shoulder. Monkey-Trick jumped up, startled. The child spoke in a clear voice: "Please come with me, sir. My master wishes to have words with the visitor from Dza."

Astonished, Monkey-Trick followed the boy through a winding tangle of narrow, dirty streets. "How do you know I'm from Dza?" he asked.

"I don't know, sir. My master saw you wandering around the city, and ordered me to fetch you."

The boy led him to the quiet outskirts. Monkey-Trick grew nervous. What if this was how the *thugs* kidnapped newcomers, to sacrifice them on the altar of their blood-loving goddess? He could be waylaid and killed here, and no one would notice. The child grinned mischievously at him, which made Monkey-Trick more anxious.

They turned into a very narrow alleyway and knocked at a small wooden gate. An unseen person let them into a small court yard, filled with flowering shrubs. The scent of night-blooming jasmine and the trickling of many fountains filled the air. They walked through the garden and entered a small, candle-lit shrine room. Monkey-Trick was surprised and slightly embarrassed, for the walls of this room were made of carved stonework that graphically showed muscular men and voluptuous women in every form of sexual embrace. In the flickering candlelight, the stone men and women writhed and coupled in every imaginable position—and some that Monkey-Trick had never imagined! However, his fear began to vanish. It might be *fun* to be kidnapped for the rites of this temple!

Monkey-Trick stared at the sensuous carvings in the dim light. Then something moved in one corner. Startled, Monkey-Trick glimpsed a small figure seated in the corner, who laughed softly, in the high-pitched, quavering voice of a very old man. A sticklike arm beckoned Monkey-Trick to come closer.

He approached the old man on the floor. As Monkey-Trick drew near, he realized that the figure radiated a strange, luminous glow, as if he was filled with some inner light. The old man looked up with his face glowing, and his eyes sparkling—and extended his tongue in the traditional greeting of Dza.

Monkey-Trick was astonished. "Where did you learn that gesture, old uncle?" he stammered.

The glowing old man laughed again. "I was in your country once, long ago. The air was thin and the nights were bitter cold. But I had a fine wench to keep me warm. Ah yes, I still miss her. *Yeshe.* Her name was Yeshe. I never found another one like her. Lovely wenches in your land of snows."

"You mean Yeshe, the wise woman, the scribe?" exclaimed Monkey-Trick.

"*Scribe?* Is that her title now?" laughed the old man. "She was always scribbling down notes, whenever I gave teachings. Is she still alive?"

"No," said Monkey-Trick. "She died long before I was born. I've only heard tales of her. They say she attained the rainbow body—at the end of her life."

The glowing old man slapped his knee and chuckled, "Good girl! She learned the teachings well. But what are *you* doing in Hind, lad?"

Monkey-Trick quickly poured out the tale of Lang, and the destruction of *Chos*. The old man looked grave. "The black one and his crows have returned and taken power in Dza, eh? We'll have to take care of that."

"But who are you, sir?" asked Monkey-Trick.

"*Me?* Don't you remember Lotus-Born?" asked the glowing old man.

"I *think* I remember you," said Monkey-Trick, slowly. "From another time—long ago."

"Of course you remember me!" cried Lotus-Born. "And you needn't worry whether your memories are from this time, or some past time. Time is just a great circle, after all, a spinning wheel. It goes around and around, repeating itself again and again. And we go around and around on the wheel of time, repeating the same karmic patterns again and again—until we finally achieve the rainbow body, like Yeshe, and leave the wheel of time forever. Your memories are merely the same memories, again and again."

"I'm confused," said Monkey-Trick.

Lotus-Born sighed. "You never were a very quick student. Your monkey mind keeps jumping around. But you have more power than you realize. I'm glad you came back to me, to learn the Secret. I'll try to explain it, so you can understand. Last time we spoke, you were in terrible shape. We were on the western slopes of Dza. Yeshe was with me . . . such a beautiful girl . . . such a sharp mind . . . never met another one like her . . . then we went to build the Great Temple . . . then I left Dza, and went to the copper-colored mountains in the southwest, to subdue the red-faced ogres . . . never saw her again, pity . . . then . . . Ah yes, *mind*—the last time we were together, we spoke about mind! You're always troubled by that dark spot in your mind."

"That's true, sir! How did you know?"

"Come with me, and I'll show you the nature of mind," said glowing old Lotus-Born, hobbling out of the dancing shrine room and through the garden, bubbling with fountains—and out toward the holy river.

Monkey-Trick followed, wondering. The riverbank was crowded with people, even during the sticky, mosquito-filled night—chanting, praying, bathing and dying. With an astonished stare, Monkey-Trick noticed a pair of strange beings. They were obviously human, but taller than any

174

man. Their skin was a pale, ghostly white. Their eyes were very round, with the watery blue color of blind men. Their beards and hair were a startling halo of frizzy reddish gold. Their clothing was weird, unlike anything Monkey-Trick had ever seen.

"What are those monsters?" he whispered to Lotus-Born.

The glowing old man burst out laughing. "They are men, just like you and me. They call themselves 'men of the west' because they sailed on a great ship, from a mysterious island, far to the northwest. Don't be frightened. They're harmless. They come to barter and trade their amber and tin for our spices."

Relieved, Monkey-Trick followed the old man along the river, until the crowd thinned out. There was a sickening smell in the air that grew noticeably stronger. With a gulp of nausea, Monkey-Trick realized that they were entering the cremation ground. The embers of the fire still glowed. Skinny, scavenging dogs poked at long bones that lay half-buried in the muddy riverbank. A nearly full moon illuminated the eerie scene.

"What do you see here?" cackled Lotus-Born. "Is it beautiful, or ugly? Is it real—or an illusion, created by mind?"

"It looks real ugly to me," blurted Monkey-Trick.

Lotus-Born smiled and moved his glowing hands in an elaborate gesture. Suddenly the cremation ground was *gone*. In its place was a lush garden, with tall trees heavy with fruit, many gurgling fountains, singing birds, and sweetly scented flowers. Monkey-Trick looked around with surprise and pleasure.

"Some of our girls are quite lovely, too, though I'm too old to get much use of them," cackled Lotus-Born. "Would you like to meet them?" He moved his hands again.

On a grassy meadow, in the center of the garden, there appeared a troop of veiled dancing girls, of the untouchable caste. They danced gracefully, the filmy veils revealing their luscious bodies. Bangles jingled at their wrists and ankles. There were garlands of scented flowers in their hair.

Another girl sat on the ground, playing sweet music on a stringed instrument. She was a small creature, with large, bulging eyes.

Large. Bulging. Eyes.

Monkey-Trick grabbed Lotus-Born's frail arm. "Who is that girl?" he demanded.

"Does one of our dancing girls please you?" asked Lotus-Born, sweetly.

"No, no, not the dancers—they're very lovely, but I want to know about the little girl playing the music. The one with the big eyes—she looks familiar to me."

"Ah yes," said Lotus-Born. "Her name is Tara. She can't dance, you know, because she has an unfortunate limp from a past injury. The wheel of time plays jokes on us all."

"Her name is Tara?" asked Monkey-Trick, disappointed.

"Yes, Tara—in the language of Hind. Translated into your language, her name would be Drolma."

"Drolma!" With a loud whoop of pure joy, Monkey-Trick raced onto the grass, to embrace and hug the large-eyed girl.

She cried out with delight and surprise, and returned his embraces, eagerly.

Lotus-Born cackled softly, and waved his hands again.

Suddenly the garden was gone, the dancing girls were gone, the fountains and music were gone—Drolma was gone. Monkey-Trick found himself back in the cremation ground, kneeling in the muck of the riverbank, hugging a gnawed thighbone.

"Form is empty illusion," laughed Lotus-Born, "illusion is empty form."

Monkey-Trick bellowed with rage. He rushed to Lotus-Born and clutched at his frail shoulders. *"Bring her back,"* he demanded, "or you won't live to see the dawn! Bring her back, *right now!"*

Lotus-Born smiled sweetly. "Don't get so upset at an old man," he said. "I was only giving you a little demonstration of the nature of mind."

"Bring her back!"

"But she doesn't belong here—she's no longer part of the human realm!"

"I don't care. *I want her!"* Monkey-Trick grabbed at the old man's shriveled throat.

"All right, let go of me and calm down." Lotus-Born moved his hands again.

Drolma stood beside them, still dressed in veils, bangles and sweetly scented flowers. She held the stringed instru-

176

ment in her hands, and she was laughing. They hugged each other joyously.

"Is she real, or is she an illusion?" smiled Lotus-Born. "But enough of that, for now. She's obviously real enough for you, and we've got important work to do."

Monkey-Trick and Drolma followed Lotus-Born back to his temple. Drolma walked with her limping gait. They sat down in the ornate shrine room. The writhing wall carvings danced in the candlelight, and the sound of many fountains bubbled from the courtyard.

From the folds of his glowing robe, Lotus-Born took a triangular dagger. "You must both return to Dza, and kill Lang," he said. "This dagger will help you. It's special. It always finds its mark—if you can get close enough."

Lotus-Born gave the dagger to Monkey-Trick, who put it carefully inside his robe. His hands were trembling with eagerness to kill Lang—and fear of another journey over the mountains.

"After Lang is dead, his soldiers might pursue you. You must hide, and wait. You are young. You can wait for a long time. Swallow these—they will help you wait." He handed two small beads that looked like lapis lazuli to Drolma. She placed them carefully in a small pouch at her belt.

"That'll take care of the black one, for a while—until the wheel comes around again. The servants will bring provisions, and warm clothing for Drolma, so she can withstand your treacherous climate." The glowing old man clapped his hands, and servants brought woolens and furs, and bags of dried food.

"Now I shall give you one more demonstration of the nature of mind—and save you a tedious and dangerous journey." Lotus-Born moved his hands in an elaborate swirling motion. "Good luck," he called.

With a great whooshing sound, Monkey-Trick and Drolma saw the room grow into an immense cavern. Then it began to fragment into its component, atomic parts. The room vanished and they floated in a void, surrounded by an infinite swirl and whirl of energy and light.

With another great whoosh, their own bodies merged into the flaming atomic swirl, and moved rapidly through space.

Lotus-Born's voice came to them dimly: "Form is empty illusion. Illusion is empty form."

Then the glowing, swirling fragments reformed into their own bodies. The whirling energy solidified into a vast, mountainous landscape.

Monkey-Trick and Drolma were back in Dza. They were standing in the grassy foothills, above the center of the valley.

Monkey-Trick's head was spinning, from all the sudden changes. His teeth were chattering, and he felt breathless in the cold, thin air of Dza. Yet he was lighthearted and full of joy. Drolma was with him again—the friend he had always remembered and craved.

"I missed you so much," he said. "I only have some vague memories—from the last turn of the wheel of time, as Lotus-Born would say. Yet I remember you so well, and I missed you terribly."

"I missed you too," she said. "This time I wasn't embodied in the human world at all. I was born into the realm of the *dakinis,* the female spirits. Life was a pleasant blur of gardens, music, feasting and dancing. I had no thoughts about the world of people—yet I remembered you, and longed for you constantly. I was so happy that Lotus-Born drew me back into the human world. Though it isn't such a pleasant place." She shivered. "It has icy winds, hunger and disease, and black ones who must be killed. But I'm willing to face the dangers—with you."

They sat on the grassy hillside, talking quietly and rediscovering the pleasure of being together. The afternoon shadows grew long, and the sun dropped behind the snowy peaks. They camped there for the night.

A nearly full moon illuminated the stark landscape of their campsite with a pearly glow. Huddled together inside the sleeping furs, they were unable to sleep. They continued to explore and rediscover each other, with growing passion. Their bodies merged, and they became lovers as well as friends. Monkey-Trick never had felt happier in his life. All the fragmented parts and memories were joined together. He felt whole and complete, now that Drolma was with him again.

They finally dozed, and awoke to find a bright morning

sun. They quickly breakfasted and made themselves ready. There was important work to be done.

They walked rapidly into the center of Dza Valley, trying to elude Lang's mounted soldiers, and flying, spying crows. Drolma's face grew very sad when she saw the charred rubble and ruins of the Great Temple, now inhabited by unhappy ghosts, demonic spirits and wandering sorcerers.

It grew late. Monkey-Trick decided to return to the Garpa mansion, to see his family again. His beautiful mother, brothers and sisters, several fathers, uncles and aunts, grandparents, and servants and family retainers cried out with joy when they saw him.

But they became silent and tense when he introduced Drolma. How could a deformed musician—*of the untouchable caste*—be a proper Garpa daughter-in-law? Monkey-Trick and Drolma were given the finest food, and comfortable beds—in separate rooms.

During the moonlit night, the men of the Garpa clan visited Monkey-Trick's room and lectured him sternly on family responsibility. They urged him to get rid of the girl.

"She was a fine plaything, during your youthful travels in Hind, but you're back, and you're grown up now. We can *never* welcome her into the Garpa clan—except as a servant," said his eldest father. "Times are troubled in Dza, and we're glad you've returned. It's time to take your place in the family. Get rid of the girl, at once."

"No!" cried Monkey-Trick.

"Then we'll disown you. You'll never be welcome here again!" said his eldest father. "Get rid of her. She has you bewitched."

They both slept poorly that night, restless and unhappy at being separated. They rose early, and said hasty, subdued farewells. Hand in hand, they left the Garpa mansion, forever.

They went directly to the royal fortress, which was heavily guarded by Lang's black-robed men. Flocks of huge crows screamed and wheeled overhead.

"We have a gift for the king," Monkey-Trick told the guard at the gate. "We'd like to have audience with him."

"Give *me* the gift, Garpa," sneered the guard. "*I* will deliver it to King Lang. He's too busy for idle visitors."

"No, no," said Monkey-Trick. "This gift must be delivered personally."

"Suit yourself, Garpa," said the guard. "Either I deliver the gift, or you can throw it in the river. The king has no time for you."

Just then, there was a great burst of noise and excitement from inside the fortress. The crows screamed loudly. They heard a whinny of many horses, and the sound of pawing hooves.

A large royal hunting party rode out of the fortress gate. The men were all dressed in black chuba robes, riding on large black horses whose manes and tails were plaited with black ribbons.

In the center, wearing a large-brimmed black hat, was King Lang. Monkey-Trick and Drolma stared at him in surprise. He had changed. He was no longer a sullen and resentful courtier. He radiated power and evil energy. His black brocade robe was decorated with ornaments of human bone. His sallow skin had a phosphorescent sheen. His eyes glittered with malice.

His retainers sang an eerie chant of the old *shen*, in thick, drunken voices. They surrounded Lang, so that there was no way for Monkey-Trick and Drolma to get near him.

Yet Monkey-Trick could feel Lotus-Born's dagger tugging under his robe, with a life of its own. The dagger sensed its victim nearby, and it wanted to be free.

The king and his men rode off toward the foothills. The dagger shivered violently, wanting to fly.

"Throw the dagger," Drolma urged him. *"Now,* before they ride over the hills."

"Are we close enough?" Monkey-Trick asked.

"We'll never be any closer. Throw it now!"

Monkey-Trick drew the dagger out of his robe. The gleaming triangular knife flew out of his hand, nearly cutting his skin. It shot toward Lang, who was riding off into the distance.

A crow caught sight of the shining object. With a loud cry, the big bird swooped down and caught the knife in its beak. The dagger paused for a moment, then it burst through the body of the crow, its blade covered with black feathers and dark blood. The body of the crow fell to the earth, like a torn black rag. The other birds screeched with rage and flew after the speeding dagger, which raced toward the king.

Hearing the commotion, Lang and his retainers wheeled their horses around. They saw the dagger speeding toward them. They spurred their horses and raced away. But the dagger followed, faster than the horses, gradually drawing nearer to Lang.

In the distance, Monkey-Trick and Drolma saw King Lang make a sweeping gesture with his arms. The great flock of crows swooped down like black lightning, and whisked him off his horse—up, up into the sky. The dagger followed, inexorably.

The crows, carrying the black-robed figure, flew quickly over the hills, toward the sun. The gleaming dagger followed.

In the blinding sunlight, no one really saw what happened as the black blob that was Lang and his crows flew over the snowy mountain peaks, closely followed by the tiny, gleaming speck that was the dagger. Up, up they all flew. Up, up, until Lang and the dagger disappeared into the distant, sunlit sky.

"Did we get him?" asked Drolma, worried.

"I don't know, it's so hard to see," said Monkey-Trick.

There was no more time to wonder. Lang's men watched their leader soar into the sky, eluding the dagger—but soon they would be searching for the attackers.

"We should run and hide," cried Drolma. "But where?"

"There's an old fox's den nearby. I used to play there when I was a child," said Monkey-Trick. "Come on, hurry."

Hand in hand, they raced away from the fortress, into the tangle of woody underbrush on the lower foothills. They could see the guards at the gate, summoning Lang's men. Soon the troops would be after them. Could they get away and hide before they were found?

There! There was the abandoned fox's nest, a narrow burrow, hidden beneath some nettle bushes on the hillside. Quickly they squeezed inside. The thorny bushes scratched at them. They were safe—for now. But how long could they stay in this tiny den, and where could they go from here?

They were no longer welcome at the Garpa mansion. The gate guard had recognized Monkey-Trick's face, and knew he was the attacker. Soon all of Lang's men would be hunting for them. Where could they go? What could they do?

Monkey-Trick and Drolma huddled inside the fox's den. "It's so tight in here I can hardly breathe," whispered Drolma.

"I know," said Monkey-Trick, "and we don't have much food or water, and it'll freeze in here at night."

"I wish we could go back to my magical *dakini* garden," sighed Drolma. "It was so lovely there. I could play music for you, and we could eat sweet fruits in the warm, scented night."

"Do you regret coming with me?" asked Monkey-Trick, sadly. "Are you sorry I made Lotus-Born drag you into the human realm?"

"I'm content to be with you," she said, "even in this damp, thorny den. But we can't wait here forever."

"What about those bits of lapis lazuli that Lotus-Born gave us, to put in your belt?" asked Monkey Trick. "He said they'd help us wait."

"We might as well try them," she shrugged. "Though they won't fill our stomachs."

She fished in her belt and drew out the two tiny droplets of deep blue. They had nothing to do but wait—so they swallowed the blue bits, and they waited. Then they began to notice that everything around them was infused with deep-blue tones.

The deep lapis blue of the stones gradually filled the burrow, filled their eyes. Filled their minds. They were wrapped and shrouded in deep lapis blue. They were aware of nothing but deep, deep blue. Timeless, endless blue. Blue so deep, blue so calm that nothing and no one could penetrate the blue. Sunk in blue, they waited. They waited in the timeless blue.

Time passed, timeless time. They waited in the blue. Thorn bushes grew over the mouth of the burrow. Creepers and nettles covered them. Time passed. Years passed. Winter icicles hung in their matted hair. They waited in the timeless blue. They didn't age, they hardly breathed. Springtime birds and insects nested in their rotting clothes. Summer spiders spun webs between them. Autumn moths hung silk from their bodies. Winter frost shrouded them.

182

They waited in the timeless blue. Years passed. No one knew they were there. They waited in the lapis blue.

Then suddenly, a vast army moved toward the burrow. The ground quaked from thousands of thundering hooves, and the clatter of jangling swords. Finally, they were jolted awake from the timeless blue.

They opened their eyes, startled, and tore their way out of the burrow. Terrified, they looked across the foothills and saw an army stretching far as the horizon, galloping toward them.

Had Lang's troops grown so powerful—and found them at last?

XIII

Monkey-Trick and Drolma stood at the entrance to the fox's den dazed and confused, and blinking in the sunlight. How long had they waited in the burrow? What was this vast and terrifying army racing toward them, across the foothills? The clothing and weapons were strange, not like Lang's troops—not like men of Dza.

Then they spotted a shepherd higher up the slope. He was watching his goats browse on nettles and bushes, and peering at the advancing army with wide, frightened eyes.

Monkey-Trick and Drolma approached him. The youth looked at them, and his eyes grew wider. His mouth fell open, and he shrank back in terror, holding up his arms to shield himself.

"What's wrong, lad?" asked Monkey-Trick, in a voice hoarse from disuse. "Is that Lang's army, hunting the assassins of the Black King?"

The shepherd cried out, "Please, sir demon, or whatever you are, don't hurt me!"

"Sir demon?" asked Monkey-Trick. "Why do you call me that?"

"You're all strange and brambly, sir," stammered the boy.

Monkey-Trick looked down at himself, and realized it was true. His rotting robe was a mass of twining creepers and dusty cobwebs. His arms were emaciated sticks. His shiny black beard and hair were very long, and tangled with thorns and nettles. He looked at Drolma, and saw that her cheeks were sunken and hollow. Her robe and long black hair were tangled with twigs and mossy vegetation. *How long had they waited in the burrow?*

The shepherd tried to back away, into the bushes.

"Wait, lad," cried Monkey-Trick. "We're not demons. We're human folk like you. We've been waiting for a long

185

time—waiting and hiding. But I'm afraid we've finally been found."

"Were you hiding from your enemies?" asked the frightened shepherd.

"Yes," sighed Monkey-Trick. "We were hiding from Lang's troops. That huge army is coming—to capture us."

"Who is Lang?" asked the boy. "I've heard that name in stories and songs. He was the wicked king who destroyed the Great Temple, many generations ago. The legends say that he disappeared into the sky, pursued by a living dagger. But that was long, long ago, before my grandfather's time. I think you're both mad!"

"So long ago?" cried Drolma. "Then what is this huge army?"

"Haven't you heard?" cried the shepherd. "You're mad *and* simple. These are the raiding hordes of Golden Khan. No one can resist them. They ride on their horses, swift as lightning. They attack and raid, kill and burn. They've engulfed all the neighboring kingdoms. There's rumors that they've even taken Gyan. Everyone is terrified. They strike without warning, and slaughter people as if they were cattle. They're like vast packs of wolves, strong and cruel. There's no defense against them. Come, we must hide!"

"I've had enough hiding," grumbled Monkey-Trick. "Why isn't the militia defending the *la* pass? Who is king now, in the fortress?"

"King in the fortress?" cried the boy. "You really are crazy! There's been no king since Lang flew away. There's nothing but chaos and warring factions. Every clique wants its own leader as king. New kings come and go like snowflakes. In the meantime, the fortress has fallen into ruins. There have been famines and epidemics in Dza. The great families make war on each other, and there's no real king to fight the invaders. They trample on our weakness. You can stand there like mindless fools—if you want to die. I'm hiding in the bushes!"

The shepherd scurried away. Monkey-Trick and Drolma watched the advancing army. There were thousands of horses, without braids or saddles. There were thousands of men, dressed in rough leather armor and crude headdresses. There were thousands of swords, spears, bows and arrows. The army moved swiftly, with none of the stately songs and trumpets of the troops of Dza. They had a grimy, savage look—halfway between man and rabid animal.

Frightened, Monkey-Trick and Drolma shrank back in the bushes, as the dusty hordes thundered toward them. But it was too late. The sharp-eyed marksmen had already spotted them. With a loud whooping sound, two soldiers jumped off their horses and dragged Monkey-Trick and Drolma into the grassy clearing.

The soldiers' narrow, slitted eyes glittered cruelly under their helmets. Their yellowish faces were covered with sweat and grime. The stench of their unwashed bodies was overpowering. One of the big soldiers laughed, and said something in an unintelligible language. The two men whipped out their short knives. They were obviously in a hurry, and wanted to finish the job quickly. Drolma screamed and twisted in the soldier's powerful hand.

Suddenly, a large stallion broke out of the formation and came toward them. The man on the stallion barked a loud order. The two soldiers lowered their knives, though they still kept a firm grip on Drolma and Monkey-Trick.

The man on the stallion was obviously someone very important—though he shared the griminess of his men. He was large and powerfully built. His leather armor was worked with elaborate designs, and he wore a short fur cloak over his shoulders, fastened with a large gold-and-emerald brooch. His helmet was also worked with gold and jewels. He carried a gleaming bronze lance. He stared at Drolma and Monkey-Trick with intelligent but puzzled eyes.

Next to him, on a stubby gray mare, rode a very small and frightened old man of Dza. The old man stuck his tongue out at them in greeting, and said in a high, cracked voice, "Bow down to Golden Khan!"

Monkey-Trick and Drolma squirmed out of the soldiers' grasp and hastily kowtowed.

Golden Khan slapped his thigh and laughed heartily from his seat on the stallion.

"Good," quavered the old man. "You know our language, and you know how to pay respect. I am the Great Khan's translator. The mighty Khan spotted you as we rode by. He stayed his soldiers' sharp knives in order to find out what manner of creatures you are—before you are

187

slaughtered. What strange beings live in this forest, covered with creepers and brambles?"

Monkey-Trick knew that he must speak and think fast to save their lives. "The Great Khan does well to wonder about us," said Monkey-Trick, "for we are rare and wonderful creatures that have never before been seen or captured by human folk. We know all manner of magic and mystery."

The old translator hastily repeated this to Golden Khan, who chuckled and spoke to the translator.

"The mighty Khan is pleased with your answer," said the old translator. "He craves some diversion in his tent tonight. You will ride and feast with us today. Tonight you will perform amusing tricks to pleasure the Great Khan—then tomorrow you will be slaughtered."

Monkey-Trick and Drolma bowed silently in acquiescence. The two soldiers hauled them up, onto their snorting, wild horses. The huge army moved on quickly, with Monkey-Trick and Drolma riding a short way behind Golden Khan and his translator.

The dust of the horses' hooves burned Monkey-Trick's throat and eyes. The noise, jostling and fear made his head throb. How could he possibly amuse Golden Khan, the conqueror of Dza, and all the surrounding kingdoms? How could he beguile this mighty warrior with magic? And how could he avoid being slaughtered? He felt so weary at the prospect of another cycle on the wheel of time. It was all hopeless. He wanted to stay alive, but how?

Just then, Monkey-Trick happened to glance at the wizened old translator on his little gray mare. The old man was trying frantically to keep pace with Golden Khan. Suddenly the dust and confusion caused Monkey-Trick's eyes and mind to blur.

At that moment, instead of the translator, he saw a *glowing old man, dressed in the robes of Hind*. As the hooves of the gray mare touched the ground, there bubbled fountains of pure spring water. Monkey-Trick stared in wonder. But in a moment, the illusion disappeared. There was nothing left but dust, noise and despair.

The huge army camped for the night on a large grassy plain, near the center of Dza Valley. The ill-cured horse-hide tents filled the meadow like a sinister field of mush-rooms.

The horses were tethered and allowed to graze, and the mares were milked. Skins of fermented, curdled mare's milk were ladled into rough bowls. Although they were terribly hungry, Monkey-Trick and Drolma could barely stomach this odorous food.

Then their guards hustled them into Golden Khan's tent. The mighty warrior sat on a dirty carpet, sipping a bowl of warm horse's blood, with obvious relish. The stench of un-washed bodies and badly cured leather filled the tent. Golden Khan wiped a stocky hand across his mouth, smear-ing blood across his face. He spoke to them, through the translator.

"Come on, you wood spirits, show me some magic!" Golden Khan coughed up a mouthful of spittle, and spat it onto the ground near them.

Monkey-Trick and Drolma looked at each other in dis-may. The translator made a strange little gesture with his hands, and suddenly Monkey-Trick knew what to do.

"I'll teach you about your own mind," said Monkey-Trick to Golden Khan.

"Yes, good," said the warrior. "No one ever did that before. Show me. I want to learn."

Monkey-Trick and Drolma waved their hands in elab-orate but random gestures. The translator moved his hands purposefully, a shrewd expression on his face.

Suddenly, they were no longer in the tent. Everything dissolved into a swirl of energy, and they found themselves at the very top of the snowy mountain peaks.

"Hey, how did we get here?" bellowed Golden Khan.

The mountaintop dissolved, and they plunged into freez-ing water. They were at the icy bottom of a deep-blue lake. Schools of small fish darted away in surprise. The invincible Khan thrashed in terror, unable to swim.

The lake dissolved, and they were in the lovely *dakini* garden, filled with scented flowers and trees hung with ripe fruit. Beautiful girls danced in filmy veils. Drolma looked wistfully at her former home. The old translator appeared in the glowing robes of Hind, standing beside the bubbling fountain. Golden Khan grabbed one of the girls and fondled her roughly.

The garden dissolved, and they were back inside Golden Khan's tent.

"Hey, that's pretty good magic!" laughed Golden Khan. "That lake really gave me a scare. I want them girls back! Tell me how you do those tricks—we must've moved pretty fast."

"No, *we didn't move at all*," said Monkey-Trick. "We were here in the tent, the whole time. See, your clothes aren't even wet. Your food is still warm. Only our minds moved."

"Mind?" asked Golden Khan. "I don't understand. I know riding. I know raiding. I know killing and fighting and burning. My men can take any kingdom, and everyone kowtows to me. But I don't know nothing about mind."

"I'm sure that's true," smiled Monkey-Trick.

"So you gotta tell me. If you can teach me about mind, I'll let you go! I ride through lots of kingdoms. I see all the fancy nobles with their fancy religions and fancy writings. They all bow down to me, because I'm strong and powerful. But their eyes say that I'm dirty and crude. That's how I always been, 'cause I never learned nothing else. But *now I want to learn*. I'll let you live, if you can teach me."

"I'd be honored to teach the great Khan," said Monkey-Trick, through the translator. "My wife and your translator also know about mind. All three of us can teach you, right here, tonight!"

The fabulous warrior sat with Monkey-Trick, Drolma and his little old translator, far into the night. They sipped fresh warm mare's milk, and discussed the nature of mind.

The translator interpreted their words with fluent eloquence. Golden Khan was like a huge sponge, absorbing information and ideas with the same tremendous energy that made him invincible in battle. The warrior chief didn't tire, all through that night, though Monkey-Trick's mouth grew dry from talking.

The powerful Khan's understanding grew and expanded. Soon he was asking questions of great intelligence and depth. It was obvious that his intellect had been starved, while his army swallowed up the world. In one night, he absorbed more than most men learn in a lifetime.

The pale light of dawn was showing on the eastern horizon. The intense discussion was finally beginning to slow. Golden Khan yawned loudly, and sipped thoughtfully on his warm milk.

"I'm glad I captured you alive, wood spirit," he said. "You've answered lots of questions that have always bothered me. You've really made me think, for the first time. Is there any name you give them teachings?"

"We call it *Chos*, sir," said Monkey Trick.

"Your *Chos* is very good," said Golden Khan. "I don't want to destroy it. *I'll spare you and your puny kingdom.* I'll reward you. Is there anything you want, wood spirit? I can give you gold, and a life of luxury and ease. You can ride with me, and see the whole world."

"I don't need luxury, sir!" cried Monkey-Trick. "The Great Temple of *Chos* was destroyed long ago, by an evil, false king of Dza. Please, sir, give me the power and protection to restore peace in this kingdom, and to rebuild the Great Temple of *Chos* in Dza!"

"I'll do that for you, wood spirit. I'll give you patronage and protection—and the title of *Dalai,* with powers vast as the ocean. You can restore your temple and your kingdom. But tell me, wood spirit, is there some way that you can look more presentable? People will laugh if they see me backing such a brambly creature as you."

"Oh yes, sir!" cried Monkey-Trick. "Give me a new robe, and allow me to take a bath—and I'll look quite human."

"*Bath?*" growled Golden Khan, looking very puzzled. "Is that another mysterious teaching? I know nothing about such things as *baths*. Instruct me, please."

XIV

Monkey-Trick and Drolma were freshly washed, and robed in gold brocade. Then they rode with Golden Khan and his translator, at the head of the vast army. They went to the center of Dza Valley, and made their camp in front of the ruins of the Great Temple.

The people were terrified. They hid in their houses, or under haystacks, and refused to come out. For they all had heard rumors of Golden Khan, and knew that he slaughtered without mercy.

Monkey-Trick, Drolma and the translator rode swiftly around the valley, calling out in loud voices, "Don't be afraid, Golden Khan is our friend and benefactor. He wants to restore peace in Dza, and rebuild the Great Temple."

But the people huddled in their hiding places and refused to believe them. "Who is this strange traitor?" they muttered. "With the outcast whore from Hind, and the senile old translator? Why should we believe *them?* They want us to line up like sheep at the butcher. Let them come in and drag us out—and face our sharp daggers!"

Monkey-Trick, Drolma and the translator rode to the Garpa mansion, hoping to convince the descendants of his family that this was no trick. Monkey-Trick was stunned by what he saw. The stately old mansion lay in ruins! In the midst of the debris was a small stone hut, made of rubble from the destroyed mansion.

Monkey-Trick barged into the hut. "I am Garpa Lobsang Wangchuck Sangay Jamyang Gyalten," he called in a loud voice. "Are any members of the mighty Garpa clan still alive?"

In the dim, smoky light of the hut, he saw a young man and a very old woman crouched in front of a tiny yakdung brazier.

"We are the remains of the Garpa clan," said the old

193

woman in a feeble, fearful voice. "Are you a ghost, come to destroy us?"

"No, certainly not," said Monkey-Trick. "Why do you ask such a strange question?"

"Because Garpa Lobsang Wangchuck Sangay Jamyang Gyalten is the name of the rebellious son who caused the destruction of the Garpa clan!" cried the old woman. "He lived long before my time, but I have heard stories of him. He was called Monkey-Trick, and he was very wicked. He ran away from the family, and took a foreign outcast girl as his wife! He sent a living dagger to pursue false King Lang. Then he disappeared, through some magic. Lang's soldiers were wild with rage. They attacked the Garpa mansion, and destroyed it. They knocked down the walls, burned all the furnishings, and killed like ravening beasts. Some members of the Garpa clan survived. But civil wars, hunger and plague have stalked the land, since Lang disappeared. One by one, the Garpas have died. Only two remain. You see us here—an old woman, and this boy, Garpa Tashi. Have you come to finish the job, ghost?"

"I'm no ghost, Granny," said Monkey-Trick, sadly. "I've been hiding for a long, long time. I had to destroy Lang. He was filled with evil and hate. I'm sorry that the Garpa clan has suffered so cruelly, but I'll try to make amends. I've come back to restore *Chos* in Dza. I'll also restore the Garpa clan. Believe me, Granny, and try to forgive me, please." Monkey-Trick had tears in his eyes.

The old woman sighed. "If only that were true. If only you could restore *Chos*. The people long for the legendary days of the Great Temple, when everything was peaceful and prosperous. Those times sound like a paradise realm. This lad, Garpa Tashi, was named in honor of the wise king of those wonderful days. His body carries the same mark as that kind and gentle king—an arrow-shaped scar, right over his heart. Show the ghost your scar, Tashi," ordered the old woman.

The young man nervously parted his chuba, to reveal the arrow-shaped scar. The old translator began to laugh, quietly.

"That's a wonderful omen, Granny!" cried Monkey-Trick. "The Garpa family will become great again. I promise you—then perhaps you can forgive me."

"I'm too old for anger or forgiveness," sighed the old woman. "You must look to yourself for forgiving."

"Come with us, Tashi," cried Drolma. "Come and help us persuade the people, and restore the Great Temple of *Chos!*"

Garpa Tashi stared at her for a moment, with large, serious eyes. "I will come with you," he said quietly. "But if you are trying to deceive the people, I'll do my best to kill you."

"Oh come on!" cried the old translator. "You can have your family squabbles later. We've got important work to do."

Accompanied by Garpa Tashi, they left the old woman in her hut, and rode away from the ruined Garpa mansion.

They rode around the valley again, trying to reassure the people, but no one would believe them. "If only it were true!" whispered the Dza folk, in their hiding places. "If only peace and plenty, and the Great Temple, would return to us. But we don't believe this stranger. He's trying to fool us."

"You need some proof," said Tashi. "Is there nothing you can offer as proof?"

"The tablets of *Chos!*" cried Monkey-Trick. "Perhaps I should show them the gold tablets."

"You know where to find the tablets?" asked the old translator, amazed.

"Yes, I hid them before I left Dza," said Monkey-Trick.

"That's marvelous!" cried the translator. "Let's get them, at once."

They rode into the snowy foothills, to the hidden cave, which was now buried within a forest of large rhododendron trees. Monkey-Trick was shocked. The growth of these shrubs made him fully realize how much time had passed.

They dug through some deep snowdrifts, and crawled inside the cave opening. The icy floor of the cave was littered with debris. Where were the tablets? Monkey-Trick and the others began to dig. They dug and dug, until their fingers were scratched and torn—but they found nothing.

Tashi looked at them suspiciously. Monkey-Trick began to worry. Had some intruder or bandit found this cave and uncovered the tablets?

"Here!" cried Drolma. "There's something hard, deep

195

under this mound of rotten leaves. Maybe it's only a rock, I don't know."

They all began to dig at that spot. There was something metallic, something shiny, but covered with dirt. *The tablets!* They worked them free, and cleaned them off. Tashi stared in wonder. He had only heard songs and stories of the magnificent tablets of *Chos.*

Proudly, they carried the twin tablets back to Golden Khan's camp, calling loudly to the people to come and see.

The news flew through the valley like wildfire. The people were hesitant and suspicious, but terribly curious.

"Maybe we should go look," said some. "I'd love to see the legendary tablets of *Chos.*"

"But Golden Khan's soldiers will kill us!" cried others.

"They could have dragged us out of our houses to kill us—if they wanted. Perhaps the stranger is telling the truth, and they really have come in peace. Let's go look!"

Gradually, the people crept out of their houses and haystacks. They gathered in silent awe in front of the ruins of the Great Temple. Monkey-Trick and the translator held the glittering golden tablets high, for all to see.

"All the world is illusion," they chanted, reading from the tablets, "a magic show created by mind."

The people listened in wonder, and Golden Khan watched with satisfaction. "Them tablets look real fancy," he said to Monkey-Trick. "Let's build the temple bigger than before, with lots of gold work and jewels, real nice. Don't worry, I got plenty of gold in my treasure chests, and I'll make sure there's no trouble around here. Where's your king? I gotta make him my proper vassal, so we can get started. Bring him to kowtow to me!"

"There's been no king in Dza, since the temple was destroyed," said the old translator.

"No king? How can you run a kingdom without a king? We gotta have a king here. My oracle will pick a good one."

The oracle and his attendants were summoned from their tent. Monkey-Trick and the people of Dza stared. The oracle was a strange being, neither completely man nor woman. A thin, trailing beard grew from the oracle's chin, yet his cheeks were soft, and his face was very feminine. His shoulders were broad and powerful, yet full breasts

196

were clearly visible under his dirty robe of rich brocade. The oracle wore an elaborate gold and feathered headdress, and carried a large feathered staff, and a small jeweled box. A shiny copper mirror hung from his neck by a thick gold chain.

His attendants carried large, elaborately painted drums. The oracle took his place near Golden Khan, and the drums began to boom, with a rapid, rhythmic beat. The oracle closed his eyes, swaying. He held out the jeweled box and opened it. There was a loud, whooshing sound, as if the box contained some imprisoned spirit. The drums boomed faster and louder.

The legs of the oracle began to tremble and shake. Soon the tremor spread through his entire body, as if he were seized by a tremendous current of energy. His body began to convulse violently, possessed by some unknown power. His face twisted into a terrible grimace, and spittle ran down his beard.

Suddenly he seemed to grow much larger, several times his normal size—and filled with terrible energy. His face assumed a demonic expression. He began to lash out with his feathered staff, striking at Golden Khan and his attendants, who dodged away with practiced agility. He shouted loudly and his shouts mingled with the beating drums. The crowd moved back, frightened.

Then he fell to the ground, thrashing his arms and legs. He began to mumble. And suddenly words formed inside the head of each person. Each man, woman and child in the crowd heard the oracle's mumble differently, giving important secrets about the future, or necessary advice. Some people began to weep, awed and moved by the experience. The big drums continued to beat.

Then the bulky figure rose to his feet and spun wildly around a few times. He came to a stop, and pointed his staff—directly at Garpa Tashi. The oracle spoke clearly, so that everyone heard: "The youth with the arrow-shaped scar on his heart is—and always was—the rightful king of Dza!"

Then the oracle shrank back to his normal size and shape, neither man nor woman. He fell to the ground in a comatose heap of dirty brocade, and was carried off by his attendants.

Monkey-Trick and Drolma embraced Tashi, who stood

197

looking dazed. "I knew you were our king, the moment I saw you," said Monkey-Trick.

"Well," beamed Golden Khan, "we got our king. Bow down to me, King Garpa Tashi. You are the vassal of Golden Khan, and I am your patron and protector. From now on there will be peace in Dza."

Tashi and the crowd kowtowed to Golden Khan.

"Now, king," said Golden Khan, "what will be your first command?"

Tashi looked around, confused. Then a look of strength and resolve crossed his face. "I am your king," he called in a loud voice, "and I order you to begin work, rebuilding the Great Temple, at once!"

"Did you hear the king?" Golden Khan bellowed to his soldiers. "Time to take a rest from fighting. Get to work building that temple—fast!"

The work of rebuilding went swiftly, and the new temple was more magnificent than ever. The rooftops and the spires of the stupas glistened with gold. The walls were hung with brocade and banners, worked with silver and gold threads. An altar, tall as three men, was inlaid with gold and jewels, to hold the tablets of *Chos.*

Golden Khan watched the work with great interest, and continued his discussions with Monkey-Trick and the translator. Then he grew restless and bored. The work was nearly done, and he'd learned all he could, for now. There were new lands to conquer. Without warning, he rode off with most of his huge army, leaving only a small battalion behind, to finish the detail work on the temple, and to keep the peace under the new king, Garpa Tashi.

The people of Dza sighed with relief. The valley was theirs again. King Tashi worked with relentless energy, overseeing the completion of the temple and the restoration of the king's fortress and the Garpa mansion. It was a time of great activity and renewal in Dza.

Gradually, the descendants of the original priests of *Chos,* who had kept the teachings secretly alive, began to reappear. They brought the frayed and worn texts of *Chos* out of their hiding places, where they had been carefully preserved and guarded. Monkey-Trick gratefully realized that the traditions of *Chos* hadn't died out among the people. *Chos* had gone underground, a precious secret, passed on from parents to children.

Now that it was safe, the new generation that preserved the secret could come out into the open. They were greeted with great waves of excitement, throughout the valley. The ancient texts were carefully recopied by the best scribes in the land.

Musical instruments were fashioned of silver and bone. Soon the sonorous chanting and the eerie wailing of the big horns sang across the valley. Messengers were sent to the deer park at Hind, inviting the descendants of the scholars of *Chos* to cross the sky-high mountains, and instruct the people of Dza, once again.

With the restoration of the temple came the restoration of peace and prosperity in the land. A great calm settled in Dza. The people were so tired of civil war, chaos and fighting. They needed a strong, energetic king from a venerable family line. Everyone supported King Garpa Tashi, and urged him to keep the peace, with the aid of Golden Khan's soldiers.

Soon, the most violent disputes in Dza were the inevitable family squabbles—and the interminable debates of the scholars of *Chos,* sitting in the *puja* hall of the Great Temple, discussing fine points of doctrine.

Once again, processions of red-robed priests were seen and heard throughout the valley. Once again, the great families of Dza could devote themselves to feasts and hunting parties—instead of intrigue and self-defense. Once again, a strong king lived in the big stone fortress, and guarded the *la* passes. Once again, the way of compassion came to rule under the deep-blue skies of Dza—instead of the way of the assassins' swords. Once again, there was peace and prosperity in the sunny highland valley, ringed by immense, snow-capped mountains.

For Monkey-Trick and Drolma, these middle years of their lives were filled with activity and contentment. With vigor and intelligence, they guided King Tashi in his task of rebuilding the kingdom.

Drolma resumed her study of medicinal herbs. Soon she was the most skilled doctor in the kingdom. She and Monkey-Trick found new depths of pleasure in each other.

Monkey-Trick became the king's chief counselor, advising him in all important matters. He spent long hours at the Great Temple, studying the doctrine of *Chos,* with Golden Khan's old translator as his tutor.

Monkey-Trick and the king tracked down the scattered remnants of the Garpa clan, and brought them to live in the newly restored mansion, to carry on that old family line. It was a creative, energetic time for everyone.

One summer day, Drolma walked with her limping gait into the foothills to collect rare tree fungus. The fungus would be dried and powdered, mixed with crushed precious stones and other materials. The mixture would be used to cure certain types of ailments, caused by subtle imbalances of the patient's internal energies. This was one of her greatest talents—the diagnosis of energy flow, within the body, as well as the diagnosis of physical symptoms.

She was in a calm, cheery mood. The weather was mild, the sunshine was warm and pleasant, and the air was crystal clear, so that she could see details at great distances. She chanted her favorite mantra under her breath, in order to stimulate her own positive energy flow, and to accumulate merit. She kept track of how many mantras she'd chanted by counting them on a string of rare sandalwood beads that were wrapped around her wrist. She was thoughtful and alert as she searched for the fungus. The chattering in her mind was stilled by the repetition of the mantras.

Suddenly, a large shadow swept overhead. She heard a long, piercing cry. Startled, she looked up, and her face turned pale. Flying in low circles above her was a tremendous black crow.

She stood there, staring in disbelief—the mantra, the beads, the fungus and the subtle energies all forgotten. The bird swooped down and landed on a large, upthrusting boulder. The crow stared at her malevolently, with sharp, beady eyes. It was much larger than any normal bird, and its talons and beak were curved and razor-sharp.

"You!" cried Drolma. "Have you come back to torment us?"

The bird cocked its head to one side, listening. It idly preened a feather with one long, sharp claw.

"It is you, I know it!" cried Drolma. "You're not just a bird. I can see the evil in your eyes. Why can't you leave us alone? What do you want from us? Look at you! You fall lower and lower with each rebirth. You can no longer enter a human body—yet still you pursue us! Go away, leave us alone. *Leave me alone!*" Drolma realized that she was screaming at the huge bird on the rock—screaming with rage and terror.

With a throaty croak, the crow slowly lifted its wings.

"No!" cried Drolma. She began to run through the thick underbrush. But there was no way she could escape the crow.

The bird landed on her back. The sharp talons pierced her robe and flesh. Drolma twisted and deliberately fell onto her back, flinging the bird into the thorny bushes. They both leaped up and faced each other.

Drolma drew a small, sharp dagger from her belt. They stared at each other for a moment. Then the crow shrieked and sprang toward her, talons and beak outstretched. Drolma hacked at the bird with her knife, making deep, bloody gashes in its breast. The crow slashed at her with its beak and claws. She screamed. Her body was torn and bleeding. Then the crow was on top of her—aiming for her throat. It lunged, and drove its beak into her soft neck.

At the same time, gathering her last strength, she plunged the knife into the crow's black eye. Dark blood sprang from the eye. The crow screamed.

Then both bodies, the crow and Drolma, lay still and quiet on the ground.

When Drolma didn't return for the evening meal, Monkey-Trick grew very worried.

"I *told* her not to stay out so late," he grumbled to the old translator. "There are all sorts of wild creatures in those hills." He paced back and forth nervously, in a side room of the Great Temple.

The old translator also looked concerned. "If she's not back by dawn, we'll gather a search party."

She wasn't back by dawn.

Monkey-Trick was frantic with worry. The king ordered all his men into the foothills to search for the missing woman.

A troop of Golden Khan's soldiers found the bodies at midday. They exclaimed with surprise when they saw the corpse of the tremendous crow. Fearfully, they gathered the remains and carried them back to the temple.

When Monkey-Trick saw the bodies, he cried out hoarsely and tried to stab himself with his own ceremonial knife. The soldiers had to pin him down. He writhed and sobbed.

"Time is a vicious circle," muttered the old translator. "It goes relentlessly round and round."

Drolma's body was placed in the courtyard of the Great Temple. The priests of *Chos* gathered to chant the funeral rites, which would last long enough to ensure a successful rebirth. An effigy of her body was burned, and the smoke drifted slowly into the sky. The huge drums boomed through the valley, with a slow, somber rhythm. The big horns cried out with mournful tones.

Monkey-Trick sat huddled in his robe, wrapped in sorrow. Two soldiers watched him carefully, so that he wouldn't try to harm himself again.

"Look!" cried a soldier, suddenly pointing at Drolma's small, shrouded body.

They all stared in wonder. Before their eyes, Drolma's body began to shrivel up and disappear. It grew tinier and tinier, until it was just barely visible. Finally it faded altogether.

Then a great arc of rainbow light sprang from the spot where her body had been. It arched over the valley, across the deep-blue sky. The dazzling rainbow finally disappeared into the highest peaks of the snow-capped mountain range.

"Was she ever real?" murmured the old translator.

"Monkey-Trick sat and stared, sad but calm. "She's gone," he said, "really gone—to the far shore, beyond our world. Will I ever see her again?"

XV

After Drolma's death, Monkey-Trick sank into a deep depression. He ate and spoke very little. He seemed weary and sunk in thought. Then, gradually, he recovered. He began to eat and talk, and sometimes smile again. However, he didn't resume his duties as King Tashi's chief adviser. The young king was guiding the land and the restoration of *Chos* quite skillfully, without him.

Monkey-Trick began to show signs of rapid aging. His hair turned gray, and his skin grew wrinkled and leathery. His joints ached on frosty mornings. He was older and slower now, and ready to retire from active life.

"I'm so tired, going around and around on the wheel of time," he confided to King Tashi. "I must find a way to stop the spinning. I need to rest. You must continue on without me. You're young and strong, and your judgment is sound. You'll rule Dza wisely and compassionately, counseled by the priests of *Chos*. I'm going to spend my final years in retreat, in the Great Temple. I must find my way to the calm, unchanging center, within the wheel of time."

King Tashi nodded in assent—it was obvious that the old man was no longer interested in politics.

Monkey-Trick retired to a rear room of the Great Temple, whose doorway framed sweeping views of the vast, snowy mountain range. He spent the long hours, days and months in silent meditation, or in deep discussions with the ancient translator—exploring the nature of mind.

Gradually, under the rigorous mental discipline, the dark spot which had always troubled him passed away like a storm cloud. For the first time, his mind was open and clear.

One day, Monkey-Trick sat in profound meditation. The weather was clear and sunny, and the snow peaks were etched sharply against the dark blue sky. He'd chanted a long series of mantras to empty and focus his mind. Now he sat in deep peace. His eyes rested on the glacial dome of the tallest mountain peak. His mind was alert and content, enjoying the crisp autumn air. He felt suspended in time and space beyond all thought.

Suddenly, a strange vision came to him. He saw a large Monkey-God, with only a stump of a tail, locked in passionate embrace with a small demoness, with large bulging eyes. They were inside a cozy cave, in the valley of Dza—near this very spot! They gazed upon the same mountain peaks, with their eternal glacial caps. But there were no people in Dza. There was no one except the monkey-*lha*, and the large-eyed demoness, locked together, and lost in their own bliss.

Then all at once, *Monkey-Trick remembered*. He remembered the great mountain in the center of the universe, whose peak can never be seen. He remembered the mighty tree, filled with sweet, lifegiving fruit. He remembered his original quest for the secret of *Chos*, to clear the dark spot in his mind—and restore his tail. He laughed to himself when he recalled *that*. And he realized that his quest had finally been successful, here in the Great Temple, under the tutelage of the glowing old translator.

Then he remembered his first meeting with the howling little demoness—throwing her fruit, across the narrow channel, to satisfy her hunger. He remembered the first stirrings of longing for that large-eyed creature—longing that never disappeared. He remembered taking birth in the human realm. Startled, he realized that he and Drolma were the parents of all the people of Dza—and everyone in the valley were their children and descendants, needing their guidance and protection. Clear as the snowy peaks came the visions and the memories.

He remembered being born as a prince in the king's fortress, and searching for the Secret, among the old *shen*. He shuddered when he remembered his first meeting with Black Shen, in his fearsome cave on the western slopes. He remembered the joy of finding Drolma, once again, and escaping the terrible fire with her, through the cool gray mountain.

He remembered living among the kindly nomads, on the vast barren plateau. He remembered Drolma, radiant and pregnant with their beautiful son, Tashi. With tears in his eyes, he remembered shooting his arrows into the flank of the large-eyed doe, and the heart of the trembling fawn. He remembered his horror when they resumed their human shapes.

He remembered his first meeting with glowing Lotus-Born, and beautiful Yeshe, in the wild magnolia grove, and the huge battle with Black Shen. He smiled ironically when he remembered Lotus-Born's final words to him, as he lay dying in the snow—*"Mind itself is part of the illusion."*

He remembered being reborn as a farm boy, and becoming the singing abbot of the Great Temple of *Chos*. He remembered joyously running away from the temple with Drolma, and fighting the terrible *Rolang* in their cozy cave. He remembered the endless duel with the Black Emperor, and the grueling journey to Gyan. He laughed when he remembered Nor, and the little pellet of dung, that made him the size of a flea. He remembered fighting the cruel court physician of Gyan, and floating in the timeless *naga* realm.

He remembered Yeshe, looking like an ancient ivory figurine, warning him about Lang, and disappearing in an arc of rainbow light. How fortunate she was to leave the wearisome wheel of time!

Monkey-Trick remembered it all. He felt a sudden urge to return to the mountain in the center of the universe, whose peak can never be seen, and to taste the sweet, life-giving fruit of the mighty tree.

Then the vision of the past faded, and was replaced by a vision of the future. He saw that his children, the people of Dza, would continue to live in peace and prosperity, for many generations, under the guidance of *Chos*.

He realized that he could rest in the timeless peace of the Secret for a long, long time.

But eventually, sometime in the far, far future, the evil black one would reappear. He would grow strong again—in Gyan. His armies would be vast as a meadow of summer grasses. And the black one would learn the ultimate evil power of harnessing the energy of the sun, itself, to threaten the people of Dza. He saw that in the far future, the black one would try again to devour Dza. The people would flee in terror, and be scattered in exile.

He saw that he could dwell in the timeless peace of

Chos, until then. But in the far, far future, he must return to Dza, to lead his people—his children—over the impassable mountain passes.

Monkey-Trick decided that he would return to the mountain in the center of the universe. He would wait there, in peace, until he was called again, to the restless, chaotic human world.

The visions faded. Monkey-Trick sat clear and empty—and rather stunned. Then he sent a servant to summon the ancient translator.

The venerable old teacher came quickly. Now Monkey-Trick saw clearly that the old translator's skin had a diamond sheen. He wore the glowing robes of a man of Hind —and where his feet stepped, there gushed fountains of clear spring water. The two men embraced.

"I had a vision," said Monkey-Trick, breathlessly. "A vision of the past, and a vision of the future. *I remembered the mountain!*" Monkey-Trick poured out everything that he saw and remembered. The old translator smiled and nodded slowly.

"I want to return—to the central mountain—until I'm needed here again," said Monkey-Trick. "I want you to help me, as you've done so many times in the past."

The old translator laughed, in the high, thin voice of the very, very old. "You don't need me anymore," he said. "Don't you realize that? You have your own wisdom now. You know enough about the nature of mind to get back there yourself."

Monkey-Trick looked at him, puzzled. Then a look of understanding crossed his face, and he began to laugh. Their eyes met, and the two old men shared the sublime joke.

Monkey-Trick left his meditation seat, and went outside. The sun was just setting, and the snowy peaks had a violet glow, against a deep purple sky. He bowed to the old translator, and faced the mountain range for a few moments, allowing his mind to become completely clear.

Then summoning all his strength, he gave a mighty monkey's leap—jumping up—up—high—high as he could.

The glowing old translator stood in the doorway, watching and laughing. He saw Monkey-Trick jump, high, high into the sky. Up and up he went, growing smaller and smaller in the distance. Then Monkey-Trick's body faded away, and was transformed into a great arc of rainbow light that spanned across the entire sky.

All through the valley, the people looked up in wonder. "Do you see the beautiful rainbow, arching against the sunset?" they asked each other. "I think it's a good omen for Dza."

They all paused in their evening chores, to watch the marvelous sight. Until the light finally faded, and the rainbow could no longer be seen.

Monkey-Trick's leap carried him high into the sky, across the Valley of Dza, across the sky-high mountains, to the very edge of the southern continent called Earth. He flew across the channel of water, and the ring of granite mountains, where the little Demoness had nearly starved. He leaped across the next ring of water, and the ring of copper mountains. He leaped across seven rings of water and mountain, until he finally reached the great mountain in the center of the universe—whose peak can never be seen.

He felt himself change. He was both man and monkey, both human and *lha*. Then he was totally monkey, and totally *lha*.

The Monkey-God landed on the mountain, among upthrusting boulders of lapis and jade. He was safely back, among the animal-shaped *lha*. He quickly plucked handfuls of ripe, creamy fruit from the branches of the great tree, and ate them hungrily. The sweet nectar filled him with tingly feelings of vigor and life.

A troop of monkey-*lha* came frolicking along the branches of the great tree, wrestling and playing. They stopped when they saw him, and stared. Their nostrils twitched with curiosity. Then they recognized him. With glad cries, they leaped toward him, chattering with joyous welcome.

They jumped on him and wrestled playfully for a while. Then they stopped and pointed at his large purple buttocks, chattering and laughing in surprise. The Monkey-God felt his own behind, and discovered that all the other monkey-*lha* had long, strong tails. While he still wore a short, scarred stump.

The other monkey-*lha* chattered and teased, because his journey hadn't been successful. But the Monkey-God laughed and returned their cheerful banter, because he knew they were wrong.

Suddenly something thudded, and hit him on the side. It was a large piece of overripe fruit. Someone had thrown it down at him. He looked up, and saw a small creature perched on an upper branch—a little female creature that resembled the monkey-*lha*, but *with large, bulging eyes*.

With a joyous whoop, the Monkey-God leaped up to the high branch, and chased after the large-eyed creature. She raced away from him, chattering gleefully, and looking back at him with her big eyes.

He scampered after her, laughing and turning somersaults, through the branches of the tree. He was much larger, and could catch her easily—but there was so much fun in the chase! From time to time, she paused to throw a big, ripe fruit at him. Soon the tawny fur of his face and chest were covered with sticky, creamy nectar.

The other monkey-*lha* were always glad for some new games. They tumbled after them, whooping and chattering happily, and throwing fruit at each other.

So they raced and played through the long *lha* days. The Monkey-God played with them, peaceful and carefree—though he always remembered that he would be called back, someday.

All the beings on the great mountain in the center of the universe welcomed him warmly. They were delighted to see the lively Monkey-God, and his large-eyed playmate, tumbling through the branches of the tree. They were all glad that he'd returned home so quickly—from his brief visit to the remote southern continent, beyond the seven rings of water and mountain.